DRAWING
BLOOD

ALSO BY DEIRDRE VERNE

Drawing Conclustions (Midnight Ink 2015)

DRAWING BLOOD

A SKETCH IN CRIME MYSTERY

DEIRDRE VERNE

MIDNIGHT INK
WOODBURY, MINNESOTA

FIRST EDITION
First Printing, 2016

Book format by Teresa Pojar
Cover design by Kevin R. Brown
Cover Illustration by Bill Bruning/Deborah Wolfe Ltd.
Editing by Nicole Nugent

Midnight Ink, an imprint of Llewellyn Worldwide Ltd.

Library of Congress Cataloging-in-Publication Data (pending)
ISBN 9780738742281

Midnight Ink
Llewellyn Worldwide Ltd.
2143 Wooddale Drive
Woodbury, MN 55125-2989
www.midnightinkbooks.com
Printed in the United States of America

DEDICATION

For Christoph

ACKNOWLEDGMENTS

Until I wrote this book, I assumed the contents of my recycling bin landed in an enormous heap in a town far, far away. Not so. The wonderful folks at the Daniel P. Thomas Recovery Facility in Yonkers, New York, were nice enough to give me a behind-the-scenes tour of my local recycling center, where I learned all about the travels of a discarded metal can. Their expertise was instrumental in developing the plot.

As always, a big thanks to the Midnight Ink family—my editors Terri Bischoff and Nicole Nugent, and publicist Katie Mickschl. Of course, my books would never have found a home at Midnight Ink without the support of my agent, Victoria Skurnick. And to Bill Bruning, thank you for capturing the essence of my books through your wonderful cover designs.

A special thanks to Marta Tanrikulu, who read my first draft. Marta played a key role in getting this book into shape.

Finally, a special thanks to my family—Chris, Peter, and Mats. What would a family dinner be without a few plot pitches?

ONE

FRIDAY, APRIL 18

THE GREMLIN GRUNTED. NOT exactly a death rattle, but pretty close. I gave the car about two weeks or two miles, whichever came first. At this point, I'd be thrilled if it made it across the grass field to a parking spot at Cold Spring Harbor's Earth Day celebration, a three-day environmental extravaganza. It would be hard to say goodbye to the thirty-year-old clunker, but Big Bob, the king of the town dump, assured me last week that he had a guy willing to part with a 1982 Chevy Nova for less than $500. I recalled the conversation from my regular run to the dump as I rolled the Gremlin into an empty space.

"Can you get him down to $75?" I'd wheedled.

Bob's chuckle had started below his ears and reverberated south, settling in his third chin. His Dumpster-diving cronies coined it "the pinball tilt," because once Bob got to laughing, he was a goner. It appeared my low bid had pushed him over the edge.

I'd ignored Bob's convulsing and handed over a bag of dismembered doll parts I'd been collecting from the non-recyclable plastics bin for the past year.

"Holy cow." Bob's laughter ground to a halt as he withdrew a severed head. "A Dawn doll? I haven't seen one of these in years."

I swung a miniature torso no more than five inches in length in front of Bob's face. His eyes, mere slits at his current peak weight of three hundred pounds, lit up like torches.

"Two-fifty for the car. It's my final offer," I'd said as I handed over the matching body.

Bob reassembled the doll and pushed it deep into his pant pocket for safe keeping. "This baby is not going anywhere," he said as he patted his hip.

"Talk to your car guy. For now, Dawn's on loan. If you can't cut me a deal, I'm selling her on eBay."

Big Bob will come through, I thought. *My life literally depends on it*, I thought, as I jammed a rock behind the Gremlin's rear wheel in place of the broken emergency brake. The doll parts were a great find for an avid collector like Bob. If I was lucky, and Bob worked his magic, I'd be tooling around in a different automotive relic within days. I manually released the hatchback and loaded trays of jelly jars onto a Radio Flyer red wagon.

"Don't move," a shrill voice called from across the parking lot. An overly-sunbaked woman with impossibly blond hair signaled me from an SUV window. "Are those Kat's Kans jellies? I have to have a jar." The woman pulled up behind the Gremlin in a car built like a tank. She climbed out and produced a purse that exceeded the airport weight limit for carry-ons.

"Ten dollars a jar." I smiled, doubling the price. Katrina, my housemate, best friend, and business partner, would be pleased. It was Friday, the first day of the Earth Day festival, and at this rate, we might sell out of our inventory before Sunday. "Fifteen percent off if you buy a case," I added.

"A case? That's a lot of jelly."

"I dig that sticker on the window." I pointed to the cartoonish cut-out of a family with three kids affixed to her rear window. "Home-made jellies make great teacher gifts."

"Oh, you are so right," the woman agreed eagerly as she popped her trunk. "Don't you just love Earth Day?"

"I just do," I responded. I deposited a tray of jelly in the rear of the SUV, a hunk of metal and plastic named after a group of Native Americans that hadn't roamed North America in over three centuries. "You ever take this off road?"

"Off road? Why would I do that?" the woman replied as she climbed back into the driver's seat.

I simply smiled and waved her off, then stuck the cash in my jeans pocket and headed over to the park entrance, wondering if SUV really stood for Suburban Useless Vehicle. I put the thought aside and tried to remember how much I really did love Earth Day. The venue for the three-day weekend festival, the Cold Spring Harbor State Park, was a forty-acre spread tumbling precariously down to the shores of Long Island Sound. I took in the field of colored tents sprinkled across the open green. Swarms of visitors had dug deep in their closets to re-cover their one tie-dyed shirt reserved for the holiday when we could all be hippies.

"Thar she blows," I said, spotting my own home across the bay. Harbor House, a rambling nineteenth-century building, had been in my family for generations, and I had spent the last ten years renovating the property. Today it was a self-sustaining organic farm managed by me and my housemates—Katrina, her boyfriend Jonathan, and Charlie.

My great-great-great grandfather was Cold Spring Harbor's first harbor master, and I had inherited the home as part of my trust fund. For a century our Prentice family lineage was as pure as the waters the early settlers fished. Now, of course, the sound was a polluted waterway with glowing sea animals weaned on toxic sludge. And, sadly, the Prentice family name too was no better than mud, thanks to my father. Close to my house was another sad sight: the world-renowned Sound View Laboratories. My brother, Dr. Theodore Prentice, was murdered there just twelve months ago. My father, had he the ability to scale down his own ego, could have prevented it.

I shook off the memory of Teddy's death with a shimmy of my shoulders and a shake of my butt.

"Hey, hot stuff!"

"Charlie," I said, steering the wagon his way, "take these to the booth. Katrina is probably running low."

"That's it? I call you hot and you give me a job to do?"

I leaned in and pecked Charlie. "Sorry, I left my sketchbook in the car."

Charlie knew better than to step between me and my sketchbook. Some people are addicted to their cell phones, but my vice was a pad with sheets of empty paper. Portraits, my specialty, supplemented my subsistence living, and thankfully there was still the occasional wealthy patron who insisted on a mantel show piece. Or the occasional police matter that hinged on an accurate likeness. A year ago, I'd never have guessed my talent would be the deciding factor in a criminal investigation. I was just as surprised as the police when my sketches had provided crucial evidence in my brother's murder case.

"Go on," Charlie said as he led the wagon toward the entrance.

TWO

On my return from the car, I made my way to our booth, taking careful note of competing vendors. There were a good number of people selling canned goods, but when I came across our stand, I felt that Kat's Kans offered something special. It helped that Katrina looked like she had swallowed a watermelon sideways. Her condition drew the sympathy traffic.

"Don't hide your stomach. You're doing the Martha Stewart thing," I said as I lined up the jelly jars on our authentic farm table. Each jar was unique, culled from various recycling bins in the neighborhood. The finished effect was charming in its unevenness. The bright red *Kat's Kans* label, designed by yours truly, pulled it all together.

"What's the Martha Stewart thing?" Katrina asked.

"You've got the jars strategically blocking your stomach. Martha Stewart never takes a photo without a picture frame or an industrial mixer covering her midsection. Unlike Martha's midsection, your belly is a crowd-pleaser. Show it off."

"I'm a house," Kat moaned as she popped open a jar and stuck in a spoon. "I'm not going to last another two weeks."

"If only it were your decision," I replied. "What's up with Jonathan? Is he going to make it back in time or am I filling in at the old birthin' table?"

"He's trying to move his rounds." Katrina offered me a sinfully delicious dollop of raspberry jam. Damn, we had gotten good at this jelly-making venture.

"*Doula, doula, doula, do you love me?*" I sang.

"*Doula, doula, doula, do you care?*" Katrina sang back.

I wiped my mouth and reached for *my* baby, my sketchbook. "Jonathan is two years away from finishing medical school. I'd put my money on him as your doula or labor coach or whatever the baby brigade is calling it now."

"As long as they're not calling it Charlie," Charlie said, juggling a hacky sack with his feet. "Sign me up for cigars."

I blew on the end of my pencil and showed my friends my latest sketch of an adorable young boy who had just dashed away after tasting our jellies.

Katrina scrutinized the boy's picture. "Not him."

"Nope," Charlie added.

I tore the sheet from the pad, signed it *An uncanny likeness, compliments of Kat's Kans*, and handed it to the boy's mother, who promptly bought three jars of our peach jam.

I scanned the crowd. My new drawing obsession was any child under the age of seventeen. I had trained myself to eliminate Asians, Hispanics, and biracial children. Nothing personal, just not my kid. In a crowd the size of Earth Day's—maybe a few thousand at any one point in time—I could knock off fifty images in a few hours. Since Teddy's death, only one child had seriously caught my attention. A boy of about five at the public library. He had the telltale wispy white hair and piercing blue eyes like my own. Unfortunately, his white-haired, blue-eyed mother was not particularly pleased with my sudden interest in her son.

I have a way with people. Sometimes it's just not the right way.

My eyes narrowed in on a subject. I drew quickly. This one came easily. A mop of dark curly hair, purposeful gait, and movement in the jaw. I shifted in the lawn chair as my target approached. Not bad. Not bad at all.

Detective Frank DeRosa made his way over to the Kat's Kans booth, a package under his arm.

I closed my book. "I'm finding it hard to believe my ultra-conservative boyfriend found something to purchase at Earth Day."

Frank peeled back a thin layer of tissue paper. "It's a present."

"For me?"

Frank nodded. "I need your help down at the station," he said as he handed me a brand-new recycled sketchbook.

"Now?" I asked.

"Now would be better than later," Frank said as he gave Katrina an apologetic look.

Katrina huffed. "Oh, Charlie and I will be fine. Just go."

THREE

"LET ME GET THIS straight," I said, pulling up a chair in Frank's office at the Cold Spring Harbor stationhouse. "You've got two warehouses full of garbage."

"Technically, its tech equipment," he replied, pleased with his alliteration. "Used computers, phones, fax machines. Anything with a cord." Frank opened a picture on his iPad to reveal a football field–sized warehouse crammed floor to ceiling with equipment. "This photo was taken at one of the storage units at the industrial park near the railroad tracks."

The office door swung open and Officers Cheski and Lamendola, both of whom were instrumental in solving my brother's murder, joined us.

"How about that picture, CeCe?" Cheski said, taking a seat. "It was so dense in the warehouse, we needed our cellphones to keep track of each other," he added, pointing eagerly at his rookie partner, Lamendola. I was happy to see that Cheski, who was near retirement, had not lost his vigor for the job.

"Looks like a great place for a paintball party," I commented.

"See? You always got me," Cheski said as he patted my back. "I'm so glad to see you," he added, and then turned to Frank. "Here are the files you wanted."

He opened a folder. "The warehouses are in separate industrial parks, owned by different companies."

"Did the owners call the police?" I asked.

"No," Cheski said. He slid another manila folder, marked EPA HAZARDOUS CONTAMINANT REPORT in red block letters, across the table. "There's a local environmental group called GroundSweep."

"Sure," I confirmed. "I know them. It's a national organization with local chapters. Group members plan weekly hikes in high-risk areas to measure air and ground quality. I'm guessing they step up their efforts as Earth Day approaches."

"Yeah, well apparently, one of the hiker's meters went berserk on their tour of these two industrial parks." Cheski tapped his phone and retrieved an app. "Can you believe this? There's an app for metal meter readings. Anyone cruising their neighborhood can get a quick count just like the GroundSweep volunteers."

The arrow on Cheski's phone wobbled unevenly to the right. His face flinched. I led his hand away from the metal topped desk, and the arrow repositioned itself to zero.

"I think we'll live," I said, and turned to Frank. "I'm assuming GroundSweep uses something more reliable than a phone app meter?"

"They do," Frank replied. "Their local leader reported their findings to the Environmental Conservation Board where it made its way up to the EPA." He narrowed his eyes, picking key facts from the report. "Their chapter leader, a woman named Janice Bates, called it in and that's when it got ugly. The EPA slapped the storage unit owners with fines upwards of fifty thousand, and Ms. Bates now claims she is being harassed by the owners for filing the complaint."

"Those EPA guys," Lamendola added, "it's like they fine by the pound."

"I'm confused," I said. "How are the Cold Spring Harbor police involved?"

"The warehouses are within town lines," Frank explained. "As it turns out, the storage unit owners may have been scammed. The lessee, a company called United Eco-Systems, rented space at both warehouses, paid five years in advance, and disappeared, leaving tons of electronic waste. And, Ms. Bates, also a resident of Cold Spring Harbor, is requesting police protection." He rolled his eyes. "The last part is probably a public relations play on the part of GroundSweep."

I flipped through the EPA report. It read like the first broadcasts from Chernobyl. I had visions of office workers fleeing the industrial park tearing at their eyes. I blinked reflexively.

"I'm sufficiently freaked out," I admitted. The surroundings didn't help. The last time I'd been in this room I had sketched the woman ultimately responsible for my brother's death. Talk about a pencil-gnawing situation. I could have gone through a box of number twos faster than a team of beavers that day. The Cold Spring Harbor police station wasn't a feel-good place for me.

"What do you want from me?" I asked as I held up the new sketchbook. "Drawing garbage is not my forte."

"But you do have a certain familiarity with garbage," Cheski said, referring to my Dumpster diving.

"I just need information at his point," Frank cleared his throat. "Four days ago, I took the liberty of introducing myself to your friend Bob at the town dump. I called him, told him I knew you, and he said he'd be happy to help."

"Was he helpful?" I asked.

"I expected he would be, but he never called back," Frank said.

That's not like Bob, I thought. "Did you get anything from him?"

Frank deconstructed the only phone conversation he had had with Bob.

"He asked me if I wanted to trash-talk," Frank said, and then added, "He's quite the jokester. Am I right about that?"

"Bob's a pun machine."

"I told him I just needed to understand the players in the recycling business, and he said he'd be happy to give me the lay of the landfill." Frank smirked.

"That's Bob."

"I mentioned my interest was e-waste," Frank said, "and that's where I felt like I'd lost him."

"The garbage business can be messy," I said, enjoying my own pun.

"So I'm learning," Frank replied. "Anyway, he said to give him a day or two. I've left a few messages, but no response."

Now that was a disconnect I couldn't let pass. "Bob is always at the recycling center. He's a permanent fixture, like a hunk of non-compostable plastic."

Lamendola grunted at the comparison.

"No, I mean it. He and his wife Barbara live about a quarter mile from the entrance."

Frank perked up at my input. He signaled to Lamendola and Cheski. "Check it out," he directed as they filed out.

Frank swung his chair next to me. He ran his fingers along the length of my forearms. I knew what he was thinking. My wrists were slender, my arms toned. I could have been any twenty-something addicted to yoga and herbal cleanses, but my look is deceptive. My strength and skin tone are honed from working Harbor House's farm, jumping in and out of Dumpsters, and lugging cans of paint to my attic studio. Frank traced my fingers with his. It's what he

11

loved most, my hands. He knew my mind unfolded in the accuracy of my sketches.

"Hey," he started, "I screwed up. I didn't expect a ton of e-waste to snowball."

"Into a missing persons case?"

"Let's not get ahead of ourselves."

I weaved my hands into his. "You get that my Dumpster diving is a ridiculously tiny piece of the larger world of garbage?"

"I do."

"Reusing old furniture, digging up old car parts to fix the Gremlin, diving for an occasional meal."

Frank winced at the mention of eating food from a Dumpster. It was a lingering piece of my lifestyle he couldn't quite digest.

"That's child's play." I retracted my hand. "Me, Bob, Charlie, Katrina, Jonathan—we're simple Freegans."

"Garbage for the greater good." Frank confirmed his twelve-month indoctrination into my wacky world of Dumpster diving and Freegan living. "I'm aware."

"You also know that some really bad people deal in garbage, exchanging a lot of dirty cash. The kind of people that carry weapons and have names that sound an awful lot like DeRosa."

I thought about the last time I had seen Bob. We had discussed the lead on my "previously driven" new car last Friday, exactly a week ago. Plenty of time for Bob to get back to me. Although I now realized I hadn't heard from Bob, either.

"So you talked to Bob on Monday?" I asked.

Frank nodded.

If something were wrong and bad people were involved, Bob had nothing more in his pocket for protection than the five-inch plastic doll I had given him a week ago. Not much of a weapon. Too bad I didn't offer Bob a GI Joe with Kung Fu grip.

"I'm with you," Frank replied, "and I'm equally concerned about Bob's whereabouts."

"How concerned?"

Frank stood up to pace. *If I had a penny for every foot this guy trod*, I thought. I watched as he circled the conference room at the Cold Spring Harbor station. He settled at the windows, staring at the Long Island Sound lapping against the bay beaches.

"It's mesmerizing," I said, coming up behind him. "I could look at it all day."

"But *you* don't." He nodded at my sketchbook, my daily distraction.

I placed the back of my fingers at the exact point where his beard line met his cheekbone. His masculinity was palpable. I skimmed the bristle running along his jawline. "Are we going to have this conversation?" I said, referencing an issue we'd been avoiding for as long as our courtship.

"We need to find Bob," Frank said.

"And then you'll help me?"

"We'll talk about it later," he said.

Later? This could get old, I thought. Not to mention boring, frustrating, and downright maddening. Frank had been the detective on my brother's case, and although the murderer was ultimately found, Frank had made a more gruesome discovery: My father, a DNA expert and the founder of the world renowned Sound View Laboratories, had used his own children as subjects in a long-term DNA study. When Teddy had figured out that he and I had been involved, it set off a chain reaction that subsequently led to his death. My brother and I, unbeknownst to us, were not actually related, a blow I still couldn't process. In fact, my brother had a genetically related sibling; it just wasn't me. My father had adopted Teddy as a twin and then separated the boys as infants. Teddy was raised with all the privileges that come to the child of a wealthy doctor. My father placed the other twin with a family of poor, uneducated immigrants. Then the good doctor waited to see if these two boys with nearly identical DNA would become products of their surroundings or their genetics.

Of course, my father, being an important and impatient man, couldn't wait the years it would take for his multigenerational study to unfold. When Teddy hit puberty, he took a sample of Teddy's sperm in hopes of speeding up a study of subsequent generations. At that point, he needed an egg, but human ova are tough to come by. Unless, of course, you have a daughter.

While my father was busy mixing and matching our DNA, he was also regularly observing Teddy's twin, who was living a decent life a few towns away from the Prentice's palatial spread on the Gold Coast of Long Island. He hoped that little boy would repeat the pattern of poverty his parents exhibited. Nurture over nature, the ability to override the genes you're born with. But despite a challenging environment, that boy had grown up to become a damn good cop. It must have driven my father nuts.

Frank, as it turned out, was Teddy's brother.

Frank's face was familiar although not an exact replica of my brother. Looking at him always left me with a sense of déjà vu. It was the same feeling I got when I thought about my father's experiment. In truth, I wasn't even sure the product of my egg and my brother's sperm had resulted in a baby. There was no evidence to support it, yet I couldn't shake the idea that something familiar was close by. My father, who admitted to the experiment, insisted he had lost track of my egg and my brother's sperm—but how could I believe the man who had concocted the bizarre experiment in the first place? I couldn't. I was only a tween when my egg was taken. Now, at the ripe old age of twenty-eight, I could have a baby out there or even a teenager.

"I don't want to talk about it later," I said as I challenged Frank's patent response.

"I don't want to talk about it now," he replied.

I'd never been to couples therapy, but I was pretty sure this wasn't how good communication worked. Again, we were at a standstill.

FOUR

THE UPSIDE TO BUILDING a dump in a high-end town like Cold Spring Harbor is that town leaders will go to extraordinary lengths to mask the fact that the townspeople actually produce garbage. The creation and disposal of refuse was apparently a habit practiced in lesser zip codes. Cold Spring Harbor was a town that had banned unsightly garbage pails at curbs. Residents had willingly ponied up additional tax dollars to ensure their garbage men, recently renamed "recycling engineers," would stroll unobserved to the back of their stately homes, retrieve the hidden pails, and return them to their rightful place—out of sight.

The state-of-the-art recycling facility had been built under careful supervision by the town's Architectural Review Board. Normally assigned to critiquing, in excruciating detail, the exterior molding on renovated Victorians, the board spent three years arguing about appropriate street signage at the entrance to the dump. The final conclusion: no sign.

"Where the hell do I turn?" Frank barked.

I reached across the steering wheel and yanked right. "Here, between those two pine trees."

The Gremlin took the road ruts like a trooper, bounding in and out of grooves like a Jeep on an African safari. Who knew? Maybe I'd get three more weeks out of the clunker.

"Left," I said, motioning. "Bob's house is down this road."

"*Road?*" Frank questioned. "That's a bit generous. This is a footpath."

I looked in the rearview mirror and spotted Cheski and Lamendola in their black and white. So much for a police-grade GPS. We'd beat them by two minutes. "Tell them to back off. Barbara will freak out if she sees cops."

Frank waved them off, and we approached the house alone.

"You've got to be kidding me," Frank mumbled under his breath as he took in the circular yurt listing precariously on one side of a small clearing. Bob and Barbara's living quarters were nothing more than a puzzle-shaped octagon fashioned out of corrugated metal and strips of repurposed construction materials.

I shrugged, unwilling to apologize for my fellow Freegans. Curb appeal zero; mortgage zero. How was this equation not attractive to Frank?

Barbara was around back tending to a small garden near one of the outer buildings.

"Barbara," I called softly.

Barbara stood up slowly and rested a hand on her lower back. I'd put her age at about sixty-five. The lines on her face curved gently upward. She was a smiler. "Bob likes to laugh," I had mentioned to Frank on the car ride over. "Barbara is his biggest fan."

She placed the gardening shovel down and walked toward me. We embraced like the friends we were, and then she shook Frank's hand. She was aware that Frank and I were dating, and she didn't appear to be concerned about our visit.

"Bob told me about the Dawn doll," she said. "I had to pull it out of his pocket to wash his pants, and then he insisted on sticking it right back in. Are you here to drop off more?"

"I'm fresh out, but I had hoped to show Frank around."

"If you find Bob, let me know. It appears we've been on opposite schedules. I was at a friend's house on the North Fork, and I just got back."

I shot Frank a look. Barbara didn't know where Bob was, or at least she assumed he was at work.

Barbara motioned to a small shed, one of a few shacks dotting the property. Frank looked at me uneasily, and I'm sure he was thinking *hoarders*. Every police officer, at least once in his life, will respond to a call that alters his view of basic humanity. Frank had told me about his first such call, ten years earlier. He responded to what he thought was a routine domestic violence complaint. As it had turned out, the call had been made by a man so fed up with his wife's excessive hoarding that he had barricaded himself in a room filled with rotting garbage, refusing to leave until his wife received psychiatric treatment. It took a Hazmat-clad cleaning crew a week to dismantle and detox the house, but Frank had been scarred for years.

Barbara flicked the shed light on.

"Holy shit," Frank blurted out.

The room was, in fact, filled with garbage, but it had been transformed into a gallery of sorts.

"What *is* this?"

"It's called Outsider Art," I responded. "Bob's an artist. That's how we met."

Barbara proceeded to give Frank a tour of Bob's work—an intricate series of dioramas, each telling a story painstakingly rendered in pieces of discarded junk. A bent fork rejiggered into a park bench, vintage buttons for hubcaps adhered to miniature cars built from tin boxes. Barbara positioned Frank at various vantage points. From a distance, the scenes were fluid, almost fanciful. As the viewer neared the display, each carefully selected piece materialized into its true form. The art, up close, was raw and primitive.

"This is amazing," Frank said, bending over a scene from Cold Spring Harbor's whaling history. Score one for the Freegans.

Bob had created a choppy ocean of water using recycled blue plastic bags, the kind that get tossed two seconds after the newspaper is removed. Bob didn't bother to cut around the black print, which created a sense of depth and danger in the water. "I feel like it's an impossible task," Frank commented.

"Harpooning a whale?" I asked.

"Yes," Frank replied.

"It's perspective," Barbara offered. "The whale's tail is unnaturally large relative to the whaling boat, as is the size of the waves. He's trying to convey a sense of futility."

"But whales *were* captured," Frank said. "Without a successful whaling industry, these towns would have perished."

Barbara nodded, passing the baton to me.

"It's hope. Bob also allows you to feel the potential."

Barbara took Frank's arm and pointed to the figure of the man holding the harpoon. "The sea and the whale are unnervingly large versus the size of the crew and their boat. But look at the harpoon."

Frank took in the details of Bob's artistry. "It's too big for the man."

"Now look closely at his face."

Frank leaned into the diorama. Bob had reformed the doll's mouth.

"Oversized and grinning." Frank closed his eyes and reopened them staring straight into the whaler's hopeful face. Big Bob wasn't a man who just didn't come home. I knew that, and now Frank did too.

He stood up and faced Barbara. "We need to talk."

FIVE

"ARE YOU HERE ABOUT Bob?" Barbara finally asked. Frank chose his words carefully and explained that Bob hadn't been available to close the recycling center yesterday.

"The recycling center is a dangerous place," Frank said. "The town can't afford to have it unmanned. We sent a car over when we got word there was no one there." Of course, the police department hadn't been notified, but Barbara seemed to buy the white lie. Maybe we'd never have to tell Barbara the truth—that Bob may have had a tip for Frank that led to his disappearance.

"So Bob was at work yesterday morning?" Barbara asked.

"As far as we know."

"We had breakfast together at seven thirty, and then we went our separate ways. I offered to drive him to work, but he likes to walk." Barbara glanced at their metal yurt. "He's not here, and you're telling me that he's not at work now. Is that right?"

I nodded and added, "I'm guessing Jimmy is covering for Bob." I turned to Frank. "Jimmy is Bob's second-in-command."

Barbara appeared calm, but her hands were restless. She puttered around Bob's workspace reorganizing his piles of art supplies. "It's never been easy being married to Bob," she said. "I've learned to appreciate an artist's temperament, because I know at the end I'll be rewarded with these wonderful creations. You can't box him in. His mind is constantly moving, so I've learned to be flexible and give him the space he needs."

"Does Bob spend the night out often?"

Silence.

"Barbara?"

"Years ago"—she paused—"when we first met, in our twenties, Bob was a bit of a drinker."

"Drugs?"

Barbara tilted her head from side to side. A noncommittal motion. "Everyone did drugs back then. Bob wasn't called up, but his friends were coming home with limbs shot off and their brains blown out. Drugs seemed to be a solution."

"So a few weekend benders as a young man?"

"You could say that." Barbara's shoulders released as tears rolled down her face. "Maybe a few times when we got older, but really not in years. Lately, it seemed he was distracted by his art. His mind seemed to always be somewhere except here." She was worried but not panicked. Of course, she didn't know about the warehouses stocked with leaking toxic tech equipment. She didn't know Frank had called Bob before he went missing.

Almost a day had passed, and Bob's wife deserved an answer. We all wanted an answer. This was a woman who thought maybe her husband had slipped up—a handful of pills, some beers, and a night on someone's couch or an artistic excursion that kept him away from home. It wasn't completely out of character, given Bob's previous behaviors.

Here's hoping she's right, I thought.

SIX

"Jimmy," I yelled from the unloading dock.

Jimmy gave me the thumbs-up, and I grabbed at a pile of yellow hard hats stacked on a shelf at the entrance, passing them out to Frank, Lamendola, and Cheski. The *snap, crackle, pop* of crushing cans and glass was partially muffled by the deafening roar of grinding machinery. I tugged the construction helmet down over my ears, demonstrating for my recycling-center neophytes.

Lamendola placed his hands on my shoulders. "I feel like everything is moving."

"It is," I said. Using hand signals, I directed our group through the airplane-sized hangar.

The routine was relatively simple. Trucks drove directly into the facility and deposited heaps of paper-related items in one half of the hangar. The other half was reserved for plastics and glass. Non-recyclables got deposited in containers outside the facility. Recycled materials were sorted, flattened, and tied in bales the size of a single wide trailer. The bales were sold based on the fluctuating market for reusable materials. As we made our way up a grooved metal ramp, men and woman in orange suits nodded.

"Pickers," I shouted at Frank. "They sort items the mechanical sorters miss." Conveyer belts lining the perimeter moved bits and pieces in a never-ending stream of refuse toward a monstrous machine. One second faster and Lucille Ball would have been cramming the garbage down her shirt. Without missing a beat, one of the orange-suited women handed me a Bloomingdale's bag. It was a treasure trove of interestingly shaped glass jars—*with* matching tops.

I held up an eye-catching green plaid screw top and mouthed my thanks to the woman. Then I led the crew to the second-level catwalk with its enclosed observation booth towering about two stories above the facility. Jimmy held the door, his hard hat clipped the top of the doorframe. Easily over six-two, Jimmy's industrial cover-all hung loosely, like it was still on a metal hanger. With his wiry hand on the doorknob, his sleeve had risen halfway up to his forearm. Jimmy smiled until Frank flashed his badge.

"Okay if my guys walk around?"

Jimmy pointed to the yellow line running down the middle of the catwalk. "Stay in the marked areas," he instructed Cheski and Lamendola. He shut the door, effectively cutting the decibels in half. Frank scanned the scene, which seemed suddenly still. He shook his head. "What just happened? Are the pickers on break?" Nothing got by Detective Frank DeRosa.

Jimmy looked directly at me and raised his eyebrows.

"Seriously? You think I brought INS with me?" I said.

Jimmy shrugged and nodded to a worker below, who signaled to his coworkers. Orange-suited pickers repopulated the floor.

"Where's Bob?" I asked.

Jimmy removed his hard hat and offered Frank and myself a chair. He folded his long limbs under the table and leaned in. "I got a call last night from one of our regular truckers with a full load of corrugated cardboard. The loading dock was open, but Bob wasn't here." Jimmy looked confused. "Is Bob sick?"

"What time?" Frank interrupted. "What time did the trucker call?"

"About five o'clock. Bob's usually here until around six thirty."

"Who else is here at five?"

"Myself or Bob, depending on the schedule. The pickers and machinists start at seven a.m. and wind down about three."

Frank looked out the observation room window again. Eight hours sorting garbage. I knew what Frank was thinking. He'd powered through twice that time on stakeouts, but at least there was a chance for a car chase or a shoot-out. For Frank, picking probably seemed like stabbing a darting guppy with a pin.

"Picking is tough work," Jimmy confirmed.

"How did the trucker reach you?" I asked.

Jimmy searched inside his jumpsuit, retrieved his phone, and opened his recent calls. "We have an emergency number that rolls over to our cell phones."

I leaned in to see Jimmy's phone. "That's Bob's number." I tapped Jimmy's phone. "There, at four thirty yesterday. He called you?"

"Yeah," Jimmy said. "Bob called me about a half hour before the trucker, but he didn't leave a message. I thought maybe he wasn't feeling well, so I drove over, supervised the load, and locked up." He shrugged. "I figured I'd see Bob today."

"How well do you know Bob?" Frank asked.

"Well, we didn't talk too much." Jimmy opened the door, and the roar of recycling garbage enveloped the room. "Not much chance for conversation here," Jimmy shouted, his lanky frame filling the doorway. "But I know Bob."

"He walks home from work?" Frank yelled.

"Every day."

Frank ran his finger along the time line he had created on his iPad and pointed to the gap between Bob's phone call to Jimmy and the trucker's arrival. I could see what he was suggesting. It was possible Bob left work and walked home. Enough time, even at Bob's ambling pace. Any longer, and the trucker or Jimmy would have passed Bob walking away from the recycling center toward his house. I wondered if Bob, given his size, had had a heart attack on his walk, but then again, he would have been spotted lying in the road. Yet neither the trucker or Jimmy, or us for that matter, had seen Bob's body in the road.

Frank pointed toward a door that led away from the facility's entrance. "What if Bob left on foot in another direction?" he yelled.

I knew the recycling center was strategically placed in the center of a ten-acre wooded area. The trees created a natural sound and smell barrier between the center and the outlying suburban neighborhoods.

Lots of places to get lost, I thought.

Frank jotted down some notes about a foot search of the woods when I caught a glimpse of Cheski on the catwalk on all fours.

As Cheski bent over, his helmet popped off, rocking side to side like a stranded turtle. Cheski ignored the helmet and poked at a crossbar in the catwalk railing. I watched as it gave easily, swinging freely toward the open floor below. Cheski may not have been able to use a meter-reading app correctly, but he was quick to spot the broken railing. I watched as Cheski leaned toward the damaged railing for a closer inspection. He wasn't as steady as I hoped. I checked Jimmy in the shoulder and bolted toward Cheski, who attempted to rise to a kneeling position.

"Stop," I screeched, reaching Cheski just before he lost his balance. I looked down. The garbage below us was piled twenty feet high. I rolled back on my heels and grasped for a hunk of Cheski's blue collar, forcing us both backward.

The catwalk swayed as my insides lurched in the opposite direction. I rolled over onto my stomach and gripped my fingers through the metal grating. I fixed my eyes on the garbage below and prayed it would stop moving.

Then something caught my attention. A lock of polyester red hair no longer than my thumb stood out amongst the garbage. I followed the strands with my eyes a few centimeters and spotted a stripe of sky blue, an eye shadow color favored by young girls in the 1970s.

Dawn. Dawn was in Bob's pocket. Bob…

With one hand free, I stretched down toward the pile, but it was useless. Even at its highest peak, the garbage was four feet below the catwalk. I stood up, pushed the broken railing aside and jumped.

I lifted my head from the pile and watched as a worker slammed a red button the size of a Frisbee. An emergency siren blew through the premises like a tornado. The relentless motion of the recycling center came to a screeching halt. No crunching, no grinding, no sound.

It was there, the doll's head. The one I had given Bob. I tore at the garbage as pieces of plastic and glass sunk and resurfaced like a waterlogged sand castle. *New strategy,* I thought as I pinched my fingers together like tweezers, reached down, and squeezed.

"Gotcha." I held up the doll's head like I'd won the Tour de France. A worker nearby gasped. Bob's vintage doll collection was well known.

Jimmy tossed down a pail on a rope, and I placed the doll's head in the bucket.

I watched as the pail flew up to the catwalk.

Jimmy stuck the doll's head on the end of a pencil. Even from a distance, I could see his hands shaking. He pointed the instrument down and flipped the red hair over, studying the seam along the nape.

I knelt back down in the garbage. "What are you waiting for?" I yelled. "Dig."

The sound picked up, but this time it was generated by manual labor. Hands, dozens of them, started searching through the refuse. Cheski and Lamendola climbed on to the mound wearing rubberized gloves. Orange-suited pickers, an army of them, attacked a typically monotonous task with newfound fervor. Overhead, a worker maneuvered an excavator truck, skimming its toothed bucket within an inch of the mound as pickers placed fistful after fistful inside.

"Ouch," I cried, snatching my hand back to my chest. I watched a speck of blood drip down my shirt, then grabbed a broken wine bottle in my other hand and hurled it into an empty dumpster.

"Damn it. I'm going to bleed everywhere," I said as I scrambled off the pile of garbage, making way for workers to continue the search.

SEVEN

I HUSTLED AFTER FRANK, who hustled after Jimmy, who sprinted toward a plastic-framed container the size of a washing machine. The plastic box was suspended from the ceiling and attached to a conveyer belt on both ends. An industrial-size hose entered from the left side. Jimmy flicked the machine on and air swirled through the box, lifting pieces of garbage up like a popcorn maker.

Jimmy studied the doll's head and punched numbers into an electronic pad mounted on the back of the machine.

"What are you doing?" Frank asked.

"It's an optical sorter. The machine can identify recyclables based on their composition of the polymers," Jimmy said. An infrared beam shot across the interior and Jimmy entered a few more numbers. "Dolls from this decade have a particular resin combination that is relatively unique and easy to match. Bob uses the machine for that sometimes." Jimmy stepped back and watched as electromagnetic flames whipped through the items. A hunk of molten plastic shot out the bottom like a gumball dispenser. "People throw out garbage in batches. It's possible someone discarded a box full of doll parts and

Bob spotted them in the …" Jimmy's voice cracked as he continued his thought. "I'm not saying Bob would risk his life for one doll part, but a box of parts? Who knows? *If* Bob fell trying to get the parts off the pile, the machine will pick up the loose pieces. They're lightweight, more likely to stay on the surface. But if Bob struggled in the pile while he was searching…"

Frank hadn't met Big Bob, but I'm sure he realized that, given the man's nickname, Bob's size would act as an anchor and draw him farther into the pile. If he had struggled, as Jimmy suggested, it would have been like swimming in quicksand. Doll parts on the surface of the pile might indicate Bob below.

"How quickly does the garbage move from this pile to the sorter?" Frank asked Jimmy.

"The machines don't run at night. Its noon now and we've been at it since about eight a.m. We'll go through half the pile today," Jimmy said, and then stopped. "He's not in the sorter, if that's what you're thinking. The sorter is designed to move smaller items."

I let my breath out slowly. *Small favors for a big man*, I thought.

"But you think Bob might have fallen off the catwalk looking for doll parts?" Frank asked.

Jimmy shrugged, helpless. "You got another theory?"

I sucked on my finger to stanch the flow of blood.

Frank frowned and pulled me to the side. "Don't say anything," he whispered. "Understood?"

I nodded. It was smart of Jimmy to check if the doll was vintage, but I knew Bob wasn't looking for doll parts; he already had the doll parts I had given him. They were in his pocket when he fell and most likely spilled out after. Bob hadn't climbed onto or into the pile looking for anything. Yes, he was a crazy collector of junk, a builder of outrageously bizarre art pieces, and a champion of the Freegan lifestyle, but Bob wasn't nuts enough to tackle a garbage mound to score a tiny doll part. Unlike me, who had just free-fallen into a mound of garbage, Bob was a civil servant who took his job and the safety regulations seriously. If Bob was under this pile, it wasn't on purpose.

The problem was that if he was in the pile, he'd been there overnight.

I was trying to erase that thought from my mind when I noticed the door to the women's bathroom was open an inch. An orange-suited picker waved to me through the crack. It was Marissa, the same woman who had collected the bag of glass jars for me. She frequented the farmers' markets around town, and I had bumped into her once or twice at the Salvation Army sifting through the children's clothing. She must have seen me cut my finger. *Maybe she's got a Band-Aid*, I thought as I made my way to the bathroom.

"Hey, Marissa, thanks for the jars," I said. "Do you have a Band-Aid for me?"

"I see Bob yesterday," Marissa said quietly. Her lips were dry but coated with a fresh skim of lipstick. In fact, her whole face was meticulously made up. The lowered zipper on her orange suit revealed a colorful silk blouse underneath. The contradiction struck me, in a good way. Work was important to Marissa, even if the work was sorting garbage.

"Okay," I said. I stepped into the bathroom and closed the door behind us. I instinctively peered under the stalls and then nodded to Marissa.

"I see Mr. Bob after my shift yesterday."

"As you were leaving?"

"No, I forget my pocketbook. I come back."

I sensed a tinge of anxiety from Marissa. "Are you not allowed back after a shift?"

"Safety regulations." She wagged her finger. "No one come in after hours."

"But you came in, and you saw Bob?"

"Yes, he talking to a man." Marissa scrunched her brow. "Mad."

I suspected as much. We weren't digging through garbage for nothing.

"I leave quick and run down the driveway," Marissa said. She licked her stained lips. "I see a woman too. She running."

A woman? Marissa's information caught me off-guard. There were trails in the surrounding woods, but it would be an odd choice for a jog considering the recycling center attracted rats. "Was she wearing running clothes?"

"No, she wear jeans." Marissa leaned over and gripped her calves. "Tight, here."

A phone trilled, echoing off the ceramic walls. I jumped. It was my phone.

"Katrina's in labor," Charlie's voice burst out. "We're heading to the hospital.""

"What?" My reality shifted 180 degrees. "Is there a complication?"

"Yeah, the complication is I'm the only one home." Charlie wasn't pleased. "Kat's midwife, Vicky, is delivering another baby."

"Call Dr. Grovit," I said. Dr. Grovit was pushing eighty, but he'd been my family doctor since the beginning of time. Even in semi-retirement, Dr. Grovit always seemed happy to help the Prentice clan, which now included my uninsured housemates. "Tell Katrina to hold tight."

I hung up and searched Marissa's face. This woman was scared. I took Marissa by the elbow and opened the bathroom door. "It's all good. I need you to tell Detective DeRosa what you told me."

"I no tell," Marissa said.

Be nice. Be calm, I thought. I loosened my grip on Marissa and ran through some options in my head. I couldn't shake the image of the bulging mountain of garbage. The thought caused my brain to hopscotch back to Katrina's impending delivery.

"Tell Detective DeRosa you came back for your phone, but then you found it in your bag. Tell him you never entered the plant." I forced a smile. "Can you do that? For Bob?

"I do that."

We walked, arms linked like young girls, toward the catwalk. Frank had cordoned off the damaged section.

"Frank," I said, "this is Marissa. She thought she left her phone here yesterday."

"When I come back," Marissa said, tag teaming my lie, "I still standing outside, and I see Mr. Bob."

I took a half step back, literally handing Marissa off to Frank. "My sketchbook is in the car."

I ran at full stride back to the parking lot. Memory is fleeting. The faster I got back to Marissa, the better the sketches would be. She mentioned two unidentified people: an angry man and a running woman. I felt the details slipping away as the seconds passed. I dug into my pants' pockets for my keys when a man's voice cried out, followed by shouting in Spanish. Another alarm blared, but it wasn't the signal for danger I'd heard earlier when I dove into the garbage. This was faster, more frenetic, with an urgency that felt like a punching bag. Ignoring the alarm, I continued to my car.

My phone rang again.

Charlie, I don't have time for a baby, I thought. *Please figure this out yourself.* The phone continued to trill while the alarm blared. Dismissing both sounds, I focused my attention on retrieving the sketchbook. I pulled it from the side pocket of the car door and jogged back into the warehouse just as four straining men pulled a body from the heap.

Oh Bob.

I kept my distance, but still, I could see the damage the garbage had inflicted. Bob's clothes were torn and his exposed flesh, like my finger, was covered in sharp nicks. I noticed one particularly deep gash in his neck before turning away.

The alarm died as suddenly as it had started. In the new silence, I stepped quietly to the side and dialed Charlie back as I walked a circuitous route around the pile to find Marissa and Frank.

"Hey," I said, wearily, hoping Charlie had made a proactive decision concerning Katrina.

"We're almost there," Charlie said, referring to the hospital. "Grovit will see Katrina in his office."

I sighed in relief. Even if Katrina was truly in labor, it wasn't as if I was delivering the baby. She'd be in good hands with Dr. Grovit, and my hands would be more useful transferring Marissa's visuals to lead on paper.

I heard an approaching ambulance, but from the look of Bob, a hearse seemed more appropriate.

"Gimme an hour," I said to Charlie. I was a fast sketch, and I sensed, given Marissa's attention to detail, that her information would come quickly. "I'll check in with Dr. Grovit when I get to the hospital," I said and then hung up.

EIGHT

Dr. Grovit's office at Huntington Hospital was jam-packed with medical journals. Stacks of files, stuffed with papers so ancient they appeared yellowed at the edges, littered surfaces. This was a world where the term "carbon copy" still had meaning and the faint smell of bluish inky mimeographed paper refused to dissipate. It looked nothing like my father's office, which would have served as an ideal location for an Anal Retentives Anonymous meeting. I sunk back into Dr. Grovit's nubby couch. My sketchbook, half filled with pictures of my maybe-baby and now sprinkled with Marissa's recollections of Bob's conversation with an unknown man, lay on my lap.

"I'm sorry about your friend Bob," Dr. Grovit said. He came out from his desk and handed me a box of tissues. "Tragic, actually." Dr. Grovit shook. He'd been around a long time, but I assumed being crushed to death by garbage was a first even for him.

I blew my nose hard.

"It's not a consolation," Dr. Grovit sympathized, "but Katrina is fine. False labor. You can bring her home within the hour. She's got a good two weeks ahead of her."

"Thanks for seeing her," I said, and then added, "I know she's not your patient." He wasn't even an obstetrician, just an old-school doctor who believed the Hippocratic Oath preempted health care protocol. The type of doctor who responded without hesitation when a stranger yelled, "Is there a doctor in the house?" Based on the account from Charlie, who seemed to be channeling Sissie from *Gone with the Wind*, Dr. Grovit still had a few tricks up his sleeve. Apparently he examined Katrina right on his office couch, bypassing any form of hospital registration.

Dr. Grovit reached for his prescription pad. "Of course, Charlie might require sedation," he said, smirking.

I honked through a laugh. "I think he's got that covered on his own." I tossed my soggy tissue in the basket.

"You two aren't still dating, are you?" Dr. Grovit asked.

"No, but nice recall." Dr. Grovit's memory impressed me. Charlie and I hadn't dated seriously since college … with a few hook-ups along the way. Most recently, after Teddy died. Charlie was a tough habit to break.

"I do remember when you were about sixteen and you asked me for birth control." Dr. Grovit raised an eyebrow. "We had a nice long talk."

"Now you're embarrassing me."

"Then I guess there's no harm in asking if there's someone new in the picture?"

Had someone else asked, I might have balked, but Dr. Grovit was like family. He had also been connected professionally to my brother and father, since they had all been employed by the Sound View Labs. Dr. Grovit took Teddy's death hard. He felt terribly responsible for the dysfunctional environment my father had created at the labs. Dr. Grovit and Teddy had worked together, peers and pawns in my father's twisted world of DNA manipulation.

I appreciated Dr. Grovit's concern for me and my family. I had been an especially difficult teenager, and it amazed me that after years of my antisocial antics, he remained surprisingly neutral toward me. Unfortunately, I'd tested every boundary as a teen, single-handedly driving my parents bananas. Once I had mastered the standard teen fare—staying out past curfew, skipping school, and drinking—I cranked it up a notch. My adherence to Freeganism, a philosophy that elevates garbage to God status, seemed insane at the time, but Dr. Grovit never failed to interpret my actions with an eye to the big picture.

"She's got character," Dr. Grovit reminded my parents after they'd considered the possibility of an Outward Bound program that required more vaccinations than I had available skin on my arms. "Let her express herself."

"I am seeing someone," I admitted. A bit of blood surfaced on my injured finger. I reached for another tissue. "It's a little complicated."

"Try me."

Without hesitation, I fessed up. "I'm dating Detective Frank DeRosa."

Dr. Grovit's mouth remained open until I spoke again.

"I don't disappoint, do I?"

Dr. Grovit's face struggled between disappointment and mild amusement. It's the look a parent gives a child when the child curses inappropriately at exactly the right moment. "Mommy said you left the fucking sprinkler on all night."

"You realize that if we play out your father's original intent seventeen years ago, you may actually have a child out there." Dr. Grovit leaned across his cluttered desk, clearing a narrow path. He tilted his nose forward to peer through smudged glasses.

Bring it on Doc, I thought. *And while you're at it, take my sketchbook filled with children's faces and burn it.*

"Tell me about it. I still can't sleep," I confirmed. "It's killing me."

Dr. Grovit lowered his head. "It's my greatest professional regret. I was there. I should have asked more questions."

"It's not your fault. No one could have stopped my father."

"Just to be clear," Dr. Grovit said, "Frank does understand that your father removed your egg and Teddy's sperm against your will, and that the result of that procedure is unknown?" Dr. Grovit removed his glasses. "We have no proof, but given your father's objective to conduct a long-term DNA study, there is a possibility that your egg was fertilized with your brother's sperm. If that, in fact happened, Frank would be the child's uncle."

The only saving grace in this insane scenario was that Teddy and I were not actually related. If there were a child, at the least I was comforted by the fact it wouldn't have two heads.

"Does Frank understand this?" Dr. Grovit repeated.

"Only in the context of a story. It's not real for him." I swallowed hard. Specks of blood were staining my tissue. "He never met Teddy. At this point, he can't grasp that Teddy was his brother. I feel like he has to come to terms with his own story before I try to change the ending by throwing a kid into the mix."

"How would you categorize your relationship?"

Before I could stop myself I said, "Tense."

"That doesn't sound like much fun."

"Scratch that," I corrected. "I think we jumped in too fast." It was true. We both fell hard and without thinking twice, Frank transferred from a county police position to the Cold Spring Harbor local force. Suddenly, he was around all the time. "We realized there was baggage, it started to get in the way, and now we've stepped back." I stopped speaking. I wasn't sure how much I wanted to tell Dr. Grovit.

"You'll feel better when you finish your sentence."

"I really love Frank and he loves me, but we were intimate too quickly."

"Then I think stepping back was a very mature decision."

"We're trying."

Dr. Grovit wobbled his head like a turkey until he caught my evasive eye. "It's devastating to lose a sibling," he counseled. "For many people, it's more damaging than losing a parent, because a parent's death is expected. However, discovering after his death that you were not genetically related to your sibling might break some people."

Oh, I'm pretty sure I'm broken, I thought. And now that Bob was dead, my mobility was also in question.

"Constance."

I looked away.

"I know you're thinking of witty comebacks, but I need to ask you something: is it possible your attraction to Frank is a case of transference?"

Nothing like having your psyche called out on the carpet. Dr. Grovit's suggestion was more than possible. The idea that I inadvertently transferred the love for my brother to Frank was entirely credible. In fact, when I wasn't bogged down by thoughts of potentially having a child I'd never met, I was hitting my mental rewind, dissecting the night I'd met Detective Frank DeRosa. It was unforgettable, being the same night I learned of my brother's death. Frank came to Harbor House in his capacity as a police officer to deliver the tragic news.

Like the scene from *The Wizard of Oz* when Dorothy's house is tossed into the air, Harbor House had exploded into chaos. Charlie, my brother's best friend, had passed out upon hearing the tragic news. Katrina and Jonathan were hysterical. My father appeared to have a sudden onset of Asperger's. My mother was soused and not even in attendance. The only two people forming coherent sentences had been me and Frank. My feelings toward him were instantaneous. I hated him, this cold, logical bearer of bad news. Come to find out, love and hate hold the same intensity for me, just at opposite ends of the spectrum. Maybe cupid was posing as the devil that night a year ago.

I offered Dr. Grovit my full face. He deserved it. "All I can tell you is that I had strong feelings for Frank before I knew he was related to my brother."

"You've had a long day, CeCe," Dr. Grovit said. "Get some sleep."

It had been a long day. One moment I was selling jelly in a parking lot, and the next I was hurdling into a mound of garbage in search of a body. Dr. Grovit was right. I needed sleep.

NINE
SATURDAY, APRIL 19

"On this day last year, Teddy was still alive," I announced.

Frank and I sat on the front porch of the Harbor House. Despite a solid eight hours of sleep, the events of the previous day had worn me out. I was cranky and looking for a fight. Mentioning Teddy was mean and unnecessary, yet for some reason I desperately needed Frank to talk about Teddy.

Pots of herbs baked in the sun. Frank ignored me, and my mind drifted to Bob. I grabbed a watering can and tried to drown some innocent basil sprouts.

"I went by Barbara's last night," Frank said. "Maybe you could stop by later."

"Some life you got there, Detective," I said. "Show up at people's doors to tell them they've lost a loved one."

"I'll never get used to it."

"Have you considered a new and improved version? Like ringing a doorbell to tell a family you've found their long-lost loved one?"

Frank got up from his chair to check out the herbs. He squatted and pinched back the leggy basil stems. He squeezed a little too hard, and a wad of dirt landed on the porch. Now I'd pissed him off.

"Frank," I apologized, "I'm sorry." It sounded more like, *Frank, you jerk, I'm kidding.*

Frank turned his back and reached for his iPad, a form of electronic avoidance. I guessed this was the part where he stuck his head in work-related nonsense until I did something sweet. I kicked the ball of dirt away. It was a start.

"Here," he said and pointed to his screen. An article from *The New York Times* about fertility centers filled the screen. I skimmed the page quickly until a date caught my attention.

"This is from the mid-nineties," I commented.

Frank highlighted the fifth clinic on the list, a facility called Lifely. He dropped the company name in the search box.

I slid the rocking chair next to Frank. "Is this you helping me?"

"This is me helping us."

"I like that," I said. I held firm on his gaze. He knew I was secreting away every last detail of his facial features. If you truly want to capture a face, the subtleties paint the picture. DaVinci was good, but he certainly didn't capture Mona's smirk in one sitting. My guess is he analyzed dozens, maybe hundreds of women's faces, stockpiling expressions like logs of seasoned firewood.

Frank gave me my time, and I overdosed on each and every pore on his face. His expression was, well, frank, and I loved him for it. He could be ornery, curt, doubting, short-tempered, and cynical, but when Frank DeRosa was on your side, he was 100 percent yours. An online dating site couldn't have done a better job with their fancy dating algorithms; Frank was it for me.

"Are you thinking there's a connection between this fertility clinic and my father?"

Frank Googled the clinic name again, this time with an ampersand, followed by *Dr. William Prentice*. The results linked to a newsletter dated 1995 and an article exploring advanced procedures offered at the clinic.

"Your father is quoted in the article," Frank said, "on the topic of fertility enhancements."

"He's been quoted in every medical journal and translated into hundreds of languages," I pointed out. "This quote could have been reprinted from another article."

"That occurred to me too." Frank scrolled down. A list of benefactors appeared and sure enough, the Ps included a name I recognized.

"So, he gave money."

"He did, but here's the interesting part." Frank rotated his jaw. I loved when he did that because it meant he was problem solving. "It was a personal donation. Normally, your father donated money in the name of the Sound View labs."

"How did you find that out?"

"I visited Norma," Frank said. Norma, my mother's housekeeper, managed the Prentice mansion while my mother was in rehab. "I made up a story about needing healthcare paperwork for your mother's stay. She let me into your father's office. She even brought me a cup of coffee."

"I love Norma."

"She's great. She helped me sort through your father's files. He had a folder on Lifely going back to the 1980s."

"Plenty of time to establish a relationship with the clinic before my egg was ready to be hatched." I tilted the rocking chair and stared at the chipped boards on the porch ceiling. *Bastard*, I thought. "What else?"

"Are you sure you want to date a cop?"

"I'm not afraid of what you found." I released the chair and swung forward toward Frank. "Is that what you're asking?"

Frank smiled. "What I found is that I make one thirty-third of your father's salary. The guy is loaded."

"Then it appears my Freeganism is a perfect match for your salary," I said. I took over the iPad and scrolled through the references on Lifely. Words like *fraud* and *scam* appeared.

I shifted uncomfortably in my porch chair. "You're still protecting me, aren't you?"

Frank nodded. "I think I'm protecting both of us." He took a full minute to compose himself before he spoke. "Lifely provided fertility and surrogacy services for substandard candidates."

"*Substandard?*" I could feel my legs start to shake. "Like people not tall enough for the big roller coaster?"

"Not quite," Frank said. "We're talking partners or individuals turned down by legitimate fertility centers. People willing to pay twice the price for Lifely to look the other way."

"Former drug addicts?"

Frank nodded and added, "People with a history of abuse or psychological problems."

"Of course," I exclaimed as my anger rose. "The kind of people who adopt a dog from a shelter and leave it tied to a fence." I had actually convinced myself that somewhere, I had a perfect kid being raised by a perfect family. That it was just a matter of time before we reunited. Dr. William Prentice strikes again.

"CeCe, we don't know if your egg was even fertilized. We're not even sure it ended up at this clinic."

"But if it was and it did, there's a very good chance my child is being raised by ..." I laughed at the irony. "Who am I kidding? I eat from a Dumpster." Frank interrupted before I could roll out a diatribe of self-deprecating jabs.

"You're amazing."

I let Frank's compliment sink in. "I'm okay," I said. I closed the article on the iPad and handed it back to Frank. "But my kid isn't."

"I've got some feelers out," he said. "We'll get there."

"What do you want in return?"

"Sketches," he said. "The Cold Spring Harbor police department is officially offering you work as a sketch artist on Bob's case."

I took a deep breath as I considered the paid offer.

"Bob was my friend. You realize I would have done it anyway." Frank knew, of course, that I had already started sketching what Marissa had seen.

"Same goes for me," he said, referring to the case of my missing genetic material.

With our agreement finalized, I opened my sketchbook to show him the progress I had already made.

"Legs?" Frank asked, looking at my drawings. He titled the pad away from the sun to lower the glare.

"Calves," I said. "I'll get to that in a second. I want to focus on the man Marissa saw first."

My drawing wasn't so much a portrait as a scene. From the floor of the recycling center, it had been difficult for Marissa to see distinct facial features. However, she did get a full body view of the man Bob had spoken to, which provided clues for sketching.

"Check out the clothes."

"Hmm," Frank said. "He's not a suit."

"No, but he's wearing khakis with a button down, tucked in with a belt."

"Middle management?"

"Maybe." I pointed to the man's chest.

Frank raised an eyebrow. "An ID card. Good catch."

"Marissa remembered that he had some type of tag on his shirt."

"Like an emblem?"

"No, I quizzed her on that. It wasn't a logo sewn into the shirt. She said it clipped on near the shirt pocket."

"Now, that's interesting."

Here we go, I thought. Frank DeRosa's brain kicked into high gear. He rubbed his jaw and ground away. I'd be surprised if he had any molars left in a few years.

"Small companies don't need IDs. Everyone knows each other," he thought out loud. "Large companies have lots of employees with regular turnover. Big buildings have multiple entrances requiring doors and rooms that lock. The ID tag is the access key."

"Why do the doors need to lock?"

"So a competitor can't enter," Frank offered.

"Or, maybe the company was working on something secret," I added. "The identification tag implies some type of clearance."

Frank nodded. "That's a possibility." He stared at the picture and frowned. "Oh man, I hope he's not government."

"Like who? What department?"

"I don't know. Someone from the county? An inspector? You give a guy a plastic badge, and he thinks he's FBI."

I thought about Bob's personality. His priority was the productivity level of the recycling center, and I was sure he followed prescribed safety codes. However, Bob, like me, tended to live just outside the margin. He had a way of making his own rules. "I don't see Bob getting along with a paper pusher wearing a fancy badge," I said.

"That issue may have been the root of the argument with this man." Frank pointed at my drawing and then took a closer look. "The man you drew is soft."

Odd. I didn't remember Marissa describing the man as soft, yet the man I drew was slightly doughy. "That's a good point. Marissa must have said something about his shape." I thought about our disjointed conversation, which alternated between Spanish and English. Unfortunately, I only spoke one of the two languages. We made do with hand gestures at times when Marissa didn't know the English words she needed, which is how I figured out the man wore an ID.

"I remember," I said. "She showed me his chest heaving. I think I envisioned him running up the stairs to the catwalk. A healthy man wouldn't be out of breath."

"And Marissa saw the finished sketch?"

"Sure. She seemed fine with it."

"I'll bet this guy sits at a desk all day." Frank tapped his finger on the man's tag. "I'll get Cheski and Lamendola to create a list of mid to large companies in the surrounding area that use employee ID cards, as well as any municipal agencies."

"Frank, we're thirty miles from Manhattan and thousands of companies. This guy could have driven out from the city."

"True, but we've got to start somewhere. The warehouses and the recycling center are within the vicinity, so for now we'll confine the list to local organizations."

I flipped the pages of my sketchbook back to the woman's legs. "Let's talk about the legs."

TEN

"D
ID SOMEONE SAY LEGS?" Charlie joined us on the porch. "I'm a leg man, myself."

We were an odd group, the three of us. I had dated Charlie, and now I dated Frank. Charlie had been so close to Teddy they'd considered themselves brothers, yet Frank was Teddy's actual brother. It's a miracle we hadn't self-combusted into a fiery ball of jealousy. Although this was all new, we seemed to have gravitated toward each other in the past year, and I expected we could work quite well together going forward. And Charlie was right. He knew women's legs.

I flipped to the page of the mystery woman.

"Here's what caught my ear." I ran my pencil along the woman's calf. "Marissa said the pants were snug at the bottom."

"Stand up, Ce," Charlie instructed. I rose, and he pointed to my bootleg Levi's. "Those are out."

I looked down. As if Levi's could ever be out of style. "Seriously?"

"When you get your clothes from a Dumpster, there's a good chance it's not hot off the rack," Charlie said.

Frank laughed.

"So tight is in?"

"They're called skinny jeans," Charlie said. "All the girls wear them."

"*Girls?*" Frank said.

Charlie smiled. "You're good, Frank." He leaned into the sketch. "Let's just say, this chick's not forty."

"What do forty-year-old woman wear?" I asked wondering what I'd be wearing at fifty since, according to Charlie, my fashion sense was a decade behind.

"Yoga pants," Charlie said. "Why don't I buy you a pair now, and we'll put them away for a few years before you can wear them. I'll even take the tags off and wash them a few times so you don't feel like you're cheating by wearing something new."

"Very funny," I said as I sat back down and crossed my dated legs.

"So are we ready for our road trip?" Charlie asked.

"Where are we going?"

Charlie tossed Frank the Gremlin's keys.

"I want Charlie to see the warehouses," Frank said. That made sense. Charlie, an MIT dropout, had two specialties—debugging computers and bugging women. Hopefully, Frank's interest stopped at Charlie's computer expertise.

Katrina's stomach made an appearance on the front porch three seconds ahead of her body. She was at the point in her pregnancy where the front of her skirt hem was shorter than the back. A temporary condition, I had assured her.

"I'm coming with," she said and produced a plate full of jelly sandwiches. "Dr. Grovit just called for you." She handed me a sandwich. "Go call him back while we're eating. We'll wait."

———

Dr. Grovit picked up on the first ring. I heard papers shuffling in the background, the beginnings of an avalanche.

"It's CeCe," I said through a mouthful of strawberry jelly.

"I have an idea," he replied, bypassing chitchat. "Why don't we look up your father's lab assistants from the late 1990s? That's when your procedure took place. Your father was very particular about his assistants. I have to assume a few were familiar with the comings and goings in the lab."

"By *goings*, you mean where my eggs ended up?"

"I do."

I filled Dr. Grovit in on Lifely. There was silence at the other end of the line.

"I remember the Lifely scandal," Dr. Grovit admitted. "I didn't realize your father was involved with the fertility center. On the bright side," he rationalized, "the lab assistants might be able to debunk your suspicion. I'll do some digging on my end and see who I can locate. At least now we've got a name, Lifely, to float to the assistants."

A scab had formed on my finger. I picked at it until I felt a pinch.

"Okay, see what you can find."

ELEVEN

"WE SHOULD DRIVE THROUGH town," Katrina said. "I'm getting that nesting feeling. This might be my last outing."

Frank honored Katrina's request and hooked a left on Main Street. Traffic, a thin line of tourists enjoying Cold Spring Harbor's Colonial setting, was minimal. The town's shopping strip was short but packed with candle shops, gift shops, antique stores, and expensive women's boutiques. Even off-season, store owners crammed their windows with useless dust collectors like angel statues and fairy chimes. I loved the overall feel but considered the retail fare worthless garbage.

I liked garbage that serves a purpose. The town's gourmet food shop, for example, discarded day-old baguettes every day at four p.m. I typically dropped off a case of Kat's Kans jellies once a week, right about that time. I looked instinctively at my watch as we drove by. It was only one.

We headed north on 25A past the Cold Spring Harbor Fish Hatcheries. Charlie nodded to me as if to say, *Remember?* When we were kids, we pinched some fish from the growing pools. The fire department caught us in the woods later that day trying to grill our catch on an out-of-control camp fire. I smiled. I had considered leaving Cold Spring Harbor after Teddy died, but there were just too many memories worth being close to, like getting nabbed by the police for a baby trout barbeque.

Frank pulled into the first of the two industrial parks. This one was located near the train station. One hundred yards to the left and we'd be in the next town—literally, the other side of the tracks. Cold Spring Harbor officials were masters of architectural obscurity, burying their working class necessities as close to the neighbors as possible.

We cruised a maze of interconnected streets lined with low slung, nondescript buildings with odd names like Semhauzer Industries or MediLaw Inc.

"I don't get these places," I said. "They're always empty, like no one actually goes to work."

"*You* don't actually go to work," Charlie said, commenting on our Freeganism. He was right—we rarely left Harbor House for traditional work. Katrina and I had estimated a windfall of $10,000 from our canning business this year, and I had a spotty income painting portraits. Charlie, on the other hand, got by just fine selling a myriad of tech apps he had designed. We pooled our money to run the farm and the house—an incredibly efficient and low-cost venture. I wasn't sure how well our system would work when Katrina's baby arrived. Jonathan, our absent housemate and Katrina's baby daddy, would also be returning from medical school in a few weeks. And then there was Frank. I wondered if our relationship would ever mature to the point where he might consider moving into our friendly commune.

Frank steered the car into a choice spot right under a sign that read, HG SPACE SAVERS, $99 A MONTH. The entire lot was empty save for one car.

We piled out, and I extended a helping hand to Katrina, who struggled to extricate herself from the back seat.

"The owner is meeting us here," Frank said, as a sturdy man of about fifty in a well-tailored suit opened the office door.

"Harry Goldberg," the man greeted us with a firm handshake.

Frank introduced Charlie as a computer consultant and me as a sketch artist. Harry raised an eyebrow when he got to Katrina. She handed him a jelly sandwich and mumbled something about catering.

Our covers seemed to suffice, and we were invited into the front office.

"About the threatening phone calls to the Groundsweep coordinator, Ms. Bates," Harry Goldberg said, referring to the local organizer who initially identified the toxic seepage. "I believe the night manager at the other storage facility was afraid to lose his job." He cleared his throat. "I wasn't involved, but I've asked my lawyer to call Ms. Bates and smooth things over."

"I'll follow up with her," Frank said, scrolling through his iPad notes. "When I spoke to the owner of the other facility, DG Self Storage—" Frank paused and looked at Harry. "Are you two related?"

"David Goldberg is my cousin." Harry rolled his eyes as if we could relate. *Nice try, Harry, but there was no way the Goldbergs could top the insanity of my family*, I thought.

"My grandfather owned two storage facilities," Harry explained. "I got the one in Queens and David got the other, the one he currently owns." Harry pointed to a series of ribbon-cutting photos behind the front desk. "Unlike my cousin, I decided to make a real go of it." He adjusted his tie as if he was about to pose for another publicity shot. "I now have five facilities on Long Island and the original place in Queens." He paused before adding, "David wasn't happy when I bought this place a few miles from his."

"Are you direct competitors?" Frank asked.

"David likes to think so, but he's not in my league. Neither of us has the cash to compete with the major storage chains, but my goal is to get big enough to get bought out by a chain."

I threw Harry some rope. "Maybe you could buy out your cousin?"

Harry smirked, and I wondered who really made the threatening phone calls. It seemed a little too convenient that Harry had offered up his lawyer when it wasn't his employee that threatened Ms. Bates. I studied Harry Goldberg's features. I noticed when he responded to a question, he looked over your shoulder, as if a more believable answer might materialize out of thin air. I made a quick decision: I didn't like Harry Goldberg. Frank must have had the same feeling, because he jotted down something on his iPad. I hoped it read, *Don't trust the guy in the suit.*

"So, can we see the warehouse?" Charlie asked.

"Sure thing," Harry Goldberg replied.

We convinced Katrina to stay in the car on the outside chance the computer waste was as toxic as GroundSweep's meters had indicated. Then we headed through the office to the back door. A jumble of mismatched furniture, including a fully made bed, screamed *storage unit leftovers.* The handful of rooms I saw were unkempt and cramped, but nothing I hadn't expected. Harry led us out the back. Rows of metal storage units, about half the size of a single car garage, covered about an acre of the property.

"We rent these units to individuals with too much junk." Harry seemed amused. "It's a crazy business. There's probably nothing worth saving in any of these units, yet people fork over a hundred bucks a month for stuff they haven't seen in years." The man was probably multiplying the number of units by the monthly fee, by his six facilities, as we spoke.

I drew in a frustrated breath as Harry's disdain for junk got under my skin. Frank glared at me. He knew what I was thinking. Useless junk? Sure, these units probably had their fair share of dust covered angels and hanging fairies, but the potential for reusable garbage titillated me. Harry swung a ring of keys by his side, and it took all my strength not to snag it. Who knows what treasures I'd find in these units?

"What's the profile of the individual renter?" Frank asked.

Harry counted down on his fingers. "The sentimental types can't part with grandma's smoke-stained doilies. People in transition, like divorce, think they'll eventually need their old stuff in their new life. I've got a half mil in rentals says they're wrong. Then you've got the obsessives, who collect everything from old magazines to ..."

"Dolls?" I said, thinking of Bob.

"That too." Harry had barely taken a breath. "And, finally you got your day trippers."

Day trippers? Now there was a reference to junk I hadn't heard before.

"Day trippers come a few times a week and actually use the space. I've got a lady here who plays the tuba in her unit." We all laughed at the image of a woman playing a tuba in a storage unit.

At the end of the last row of storage units stood a large warehouse with enormous garage doors. Charlie walked up, peered through a crack, and then poked around the side of the warehouse.

"Any thoughts, Charlie?" Frank asked.

"It's bigger than I expected. You could store truckloads of equipment in here."

"Easily," Frank said, and then added, "I don't understand who would have that much equipment."

"Maybe the question is, who was trying to get rid of that much equipment?" Charlie amended Frank's statement. "I think we've got our first case of green washing in Cold Spring Harbor."

Green washing, or the act of not being green but misleading others to think you are, was a common complaint among true conservationists. In the past few years, giant corporations had recognized the sales potential in "going green." In most cases, this effort amounted to nothing more than green-colored packaging or labeling. I wasn't an expert on the topic, but I assumed Charlie knew the ins and outs of green washing in the tech world.

"Explain," Frank said.

Charlie shoved his hands into his pockets and rolled back on his checkered Van sneakers. "A few years back there was a strong market for recycled tube glass. That's the glass in a television or computer monitor. It can easily be recycled and reused for the same purpose. The problem is the newer flat screens no longer use tube glass. The market for recycled tech glass fell apart about three years ago. From what I've read, recyclers have been telling officials they've disposed of the equipment properly but, in fact, they've just moved it to a new location."

"A shell game," Frank said.

"Yup, until the recycler finally gives up and abandons it," Charlie said. "Worse, when the prices were high, municipalities ran 'take-back programs' to encourage residents to get rid of their old equipment. The market was flooded. Recyclers must have collected tons of this stuff in a short time frame, and now they can't unload it."

Frank took some notes. "So our local recycling center incentivized residents to bring in equipment?"

"Sure," Charlie said. "We unloaded a bunch of crap from Harbor House about two years ago."

I nodded. Charlie was right.

"When did the lease start on this warehouse?" Frank turned to Harry.

"A year ago," Harry replied. "I think David cut his deal at the same time." I could see beads of sweat surfacing along Harry's hairline. "Man, I can't get stuck with this e-waste," he moaned. "The warehouse sat empty for years, and I was happy to sign this lease. The last rental I had turned out to be a front for those rave parties, about ten years ago. I didn't find out until we had a couple of hundred kids crawling all over the place."

Charlie did a double take. "Hey," he started to say as he recognized the surroundings.

I quickly redirected the conversation and asked, "What information do we have about the recycling company who rented the unit?"

"Bogus," Frank replied. "Cheski checked into it. There's no record of incorporation for United Eco-Systems."

I watched as Harry lost a few more ounces of fluid along his hair line. Clearly, he had not vetted his tenant.

Frank motioned to Harry's keys.

The metal doors, coated in rust, had seen better days. When you lived a half mile from a body of seawater, you got used to salt decay. Unfortunately, the salt had probably accelerated the tech equipment's rate of decomposition. Charlie and Harry each took a handle and forced the doors open. Sunshine flooded the floor.

The warehouse was completely empty.

Harry ran inside. "Fabulous," he said, his voice booming across the vacant space. He took a victory lap around the warehouse and exclaimed, "The equipment, it's all gone!"

Frank looked at Charlie. Charlie shrugged. Frank gave Harry Goldberg a few minutes to bask in the warehouse's emptiness.

"Do me a favor, Harry," Frank asked when Harry slowed to a walking pace. "Call your cousin and have him check on his warehouse. We're going to look around."

Charlie, Frank, and I entered HG Space Savers's now empty warehouse. Despite Harry Goldberg's burst of excitement, the setting was eerie. Except for the front doors, there was only a small shaft of light from an interior office at the far end of the unit. The warehouse was damp, with pieces of broken computers scattered across the floor. I tiptoed over oozing blobs of corrosive liquid and then skidded my feet along the cement floor just in case the goop ate through the soles of my shoes. An acidic aroma lingered, leaving a metallic taste in my mouth. Charlie picked up a stray piece of wire and chucked it across the room as we made our way to the back office.

The office was wedged into the farthest corner of the warehouse. It had no windows and covered about one hundred square feet.

I looked at Frank. "Any chance there's a body in there?"

Before Frank considered the possibility, Charlie reached for the doorknob. "And behind curtain one ..." The door opened with a rusty creak.

The room was stacked, floor to ceiling with old computers. A coiled cord sprung out aimlessly from the top of the pile. Apparently whoever emptied the warehouse had forgotten about the office.

Charlie turned to Frank. "Can we get this emptied?" He motioned to the open floor of the warehouse. "If we could place the items in rows by equipment type and model, I'll go through it."

"What do you think you'll find?" I asked.

Charlie frowned. "Don't know."

"I'm game," Frank said as he texted instructions to Cheski and Lamendola.

Harry Goldberg strolled back into his warehouse as we were leaving. He did a bit of a jig before he announced that David's warehouse was also empty. *How convenient,* I thought.

"Case closed," Harry said, wiping his hands of the e-waste mess.

"Not just yet, Mr. Goldberg," Frank said. "We've got another issue that might be related to this missing equipment. Until I've ruled out a connection between your warehouse and another case I'm working on, you're not going to be able to rent the warehouse." He then proceeded to rattle off a to-do list that would prevent HG from re-renting its warehouse for the next thirty to sixty days. The list included access to the unit to study the remaining computers, interviews with HG employees, and a report on account activity for United Eco-Systems.

Harry Goldberg quickly lost the spring in his step as Frank's directions sunk in. "I'm not comfortable with this," he said.

Frank ignored Harry's comment and continued, "Do your employees wear clip tags?"

"No."

Frank's smile dropped, and he added, "I'll need a copy of your security footage. Last forty-eight hours."

"We don't have cameras," Harry said.

Charlie pointed to a mounted camera on a pole facing the warehouse.

"Like I said, we're not one of the big guys. No name tags, no uniforms and, as for the cameras, I can't afford to turn them on."

Not without cutting into your margin, I wanted to add.

So much for HG Space Savers's glossy brochures promising twenty-four-hour security. No surprise that psychedelic rave parties went on undetected. I wondered what other shenanigans took place at the isolated storage facility. As I pondered the possibilities, I saw a pregnant woman running toward us, arms flailing.

Is that the universal sign for labor?

"Trina?" I yelled running toward her. "Stop running, we'll get you to the hospital."

Frank threw the keys to Charlie. "Get the car." Charlie took off. Frank made it to Katrina steps ahead of me.

"I'm not in labor." She bent over but was unable to stretch her palms to her knees. She leaned back, instead using her hands as support on her hips. Harry found a folding chair and dragged it out from the warehouse.

"Phew," she exhaled and took a seat. "Wow. I didn't know I could still run."

Katrina's hair was matted, and her cheeks were bright red. Her stomach was undulating in waves as if a baby's foot might break through her belly button at any second.

"Why were you running?"

"I took a catnap," Katrina wheezed. "When I woke up, I saw someone forcing the door on the main office, but I think I scared them off."

"David," Harry spat. We all looked at Harry. Why did he think his cousin would break into his office?

"A woman," Katrina corrected. "I saw the back of a woman."

My eyes were still on Harry. He turned his shoulder to me.

"Were her pants tight?" I asked.

Katrina was flummoxed. "Who are you? Charlie?" she asked.

I was about to explain the significance of tight pants when I saw Frank's jaw start to move. He took a few steps forward and raised his finger at Harry Goldberg. "I want information on those tuba people you talked about."

"Excuse me?" Harry snapped, as his true personality surfaced. "Do I work for you?" he asked Frank. "You've been demanding things from me, but you haven't even explained how my empty warehouse is part of your problem. Why do I have to do anything for you?"

That was mighty defensive, I thought.

"You're correct. You don't work for me," Frank said. He took a giant step into Harry's personal space, pushing his finger into the storage king's chest. "As a public servant I work for you, and if you want me to figure out who attempted to break into your office, you'll get me what I need to ensure another crime does not take place on these premises."

Harry hesitated. You didn't need to be a shrewd business person to see where Frank was going, but just in case Harry overlooked the obvious, Frank elaborated.

"Let me put it another way," Frank said, moving an uncomfortable half inch forward. "HG Space Savers's liability will increase if it ignores crimes that impact the safety of its tenants and their belongings. You've already got a toxic complaint. I don't think your insurance company would like to see additional infractions. And since you've asked, there's been a death at the recycling center that might be connected to the e-waste in your warehouse. I'd say it's going to be hard to drum up new tenants while a murder investigation remains open." Frank pointed to the empty warehouse. "I'm assuming you want to rent this eventually?"

Harry scraped his polished wing-tipped shoe along the cement a few times while he evaluated Frank's assessment. "Who died?" he asked.

Frank raised his eyebrows in my direction. He wanted me to look closely at Goldberg's face when he revealed Bob's name.

"Do you know Bob Rooney?" Frank asked Goldberg. The second before Frank mentioned Bob's name, Harry Goldberg shoved his hands in his pockets and closed his eyes. It was an extraordinarily sly move on Harry's part. In the time it took Frank to say Bob's name,

Goldberg had a chance to take a deep breath before opening his eyes. His face, as a result, appeared completely relaxed when he answered, "No. Do you want just the tuba player's name?"

"I'll need a list of your day trippers with contact information by tonight."

Harry Goldberg's shoulders rolled forward in defeat. "Fine," he said as he headed back to his office. "I'll see what I can do."

It was a small victory for Frank. With no cameras, you need eyes, just like Katrina's. If one of the day trippers was playing tuba or shooting pool or taking a dunk in a storage unit hot tub, they might have seen something. Something like ten trucks unloading a warehouse of toxic computer equipment or a woman in tight pants.

I waited until Harry was out of earshot.

"That was weird, the way he closed his eyes," I said. "He also didn't seem to care that someone tried to break in to his office."

"I think he hoped Frank would let it all go," Katrina added. "He's just happy his warehouse is empty."

Frank strolled around Katrina's chair, one hand shoved deep in a pocket and the other clutching his iPad.

"Maybe," he finally said as he came to a stop.

TWELVE
SUNDAY, APRIL 20

"Seems like old times," Cheski reminisced. He cleared the work table to make space for Katrina's homemade chips and dip. "It doesn't even seem that bad coming in on a Sunday."

Lamendola grabbed a handful of chips.

"No double-dipping this time around," Cheski ordered his partner. Then he wheeled in a filing cabinet. "Same place as before, CeCe?"

"Sure, by the window." I pointed. "But don't block the view. We need to see the water." I pulled back a set of threadbare curtains circa Betsy Ross.

Frank and I had emptied one of the extra bedrooms in Harbor House earlier in the day. It was the same room we had used for Teddy's investigation. The last time the police had descended upon Harbor House, the arrangement had made sense; my life had been threatened by Teddy's killer, and the police had been on-site for my protection. This was different.

"This is completely unorthodox," I'd said, fingering the ancient curtains. Frank nodded his agreement. "Then why are we doing it?"

"It feels right," he'd said, and shrugged. "Plus, I think I'm going to need regular access to both you and Charlie. It seemed to work out for us the last time."

I was skeptical. Charlie was a computer whiz, but my contributions at this point in Bob's case were some rough drawings of a doughy man and a pair of calves. Helpful, but not crucial.

Frank crawled under a computer desk and fiddled with loose cords. "Maybe we could talk about Dr. Grovit's next steps when we're done here," he called from the floor.

Well, I certainly didn't expect that comment from Frank. I stared at his feet wondering if the rest of him would make an appearance so I could evaluate his expression. *May we talk about Dr. Grovit's next steps? Do you even need to ask?* I took a quick inventory of the newly converted room. Hmm. Was it possible Frank's secondary office had nothing to do with Bob's case? A seed of an idea was planted. Was Bob's case just a cover to be closer to me?

Frank came out from the under the desk. "Will you have time later?"

"Of course," I said. I worked hard to soften my face to hide my surprise. It was a ridiculous question—I had nothing but time. I didn't have a regular job, and my only responsibility was self-sustainment. My mind, in response to Frank's questions, spit out sarcastic zingers, but I held back.

I wondered if Frank was practicing his own form of transference. If he treated the whereabouts of my potential child like a real case, he could work on it like a cop and remove himself emotionally. I realized he had been doing this since we originally learned about my missing genetic material. He always referred to the whereabouts of my eggs as "your child" as opposed to "my niece or nephew." In reality, I suspected the theft of my eggs and Teddy's sperm was highly emotional for him. It might explain why he had moved his office to Harbor House. He needed me for support, because if he discovered I had a child and that child was the product of my eggs and Teddy's sperm, then he'd be meeting his niece or nephew. Since Frank was adopted and learned about Teddy only after his death, he'd never had blood family around him. If it were me, I'd want to be holding someone's hand when I made the discovery.

Fine, I thought. *Let's do it your way. We'll pretend you're here for Bob. In the end, Bob's case will probably benefit.* I wanted to kiss Frank, but then he'd know that I knew his true motivation for setting up a secondary office in Harbor House. I turned my head back to the window and allowed myself a gotcha smirk.

THIRTEEN

"FRANK, SHOULD I START?" Cheski asked. Charlie, Frank, Lamendola, and I were seated at the conference table. Bits of tortilla chip dust covered our workspace. The guacamole bowl looked like someone had licked it clean.

I handed Cheski a cloth napkin. The general public thinks nothing of overusing paper goods, as if rolls of toilet paper were dropping out of the sky by the truckload. I blame the warehouse-style box stores for selling paper goods at cut-rate prices and advertisers for training people to use a full sheet to mop up a teaspoon of water. Cloth—a rewashable, reusable alternative—is the way to go if you have a conscience with more depth than a single-ply square of bathroom tissue. Cloth napkins make the food taste better too.

"I love eating here," Cheski admitted. "I'm getting really good at ignoring the source of your food. Whatever Katrina does in that kitchen works for me." Frank's face pinched up. "You'll get there," Cheski encouraged him, as he wiped a blob of green goo off his lip. He looked at the monogrammed S on the napkin, meaningless since none of our family names started with an S.

I shrugged at Cheski. Who knows where I picked up half of the stuff we reused?

"Let's start with badges," Frank said, ignoring Cheski's food fest. "You've made a list of large companies in the area?"

Cheski nodded to Lamendola, who ran through a group of local name-tag toting organizations. He paused awkwardly and looked at me. "The labs are on the list. After your brother's death, they started to require electronic badges."

"I guess that was the right thing to do," I said, wondering if a simple name tag could have prevented Teddy's death. "Go on."

"There's a midsized software company about ten miles east of here. They employ seventy-five people and produce software that manages employee efficiency."

"Totally Big Brother," Charlie said, shaking his head. "I know a few guys that work there. The software monitors the activity on your work computer and spits out efficiency scores to weed out the slackers."

"Oh god, we'd last a day," I laughed.

Lamendola smiled and then continued. "The local hospital requires badges. The county court house in Riverhead requires badges."

"Nothing I didn't expect," Frank said. "Keep going."

"All the banks in the area," Lamendola continued. "Even those with just an ATM and small back office require badges. And we've got one insurance claims center, a satellite office with headquarters in Albany."

"Ha, a satellite office," Charlie said, stabbing his finger in the air. "You know those guys are racking up hours a day on Facebook."

"What about the software company?" I asked. "If they can monitor efficiency, then they must know what employees are doing when they're not doing the job. You know, like plotting a murder?"

"Charlie," Frank said, "can you feel out your contacts there, see who their clients are?"

"Sure thing."

"CeCe, did you get anything out of Katrina?"

"Nothing, really. She got a quick glimpse of the woman's back and then a brief profile view as she took off."

"Hair color?"

"Scarf with some dark hair underneath." As I said it, it sounded weird. Who wears a scarf these days? "And Jackie O sunglasses," I added.

Cheski laughed. "How about a fake nose and mustache?"

"I know," I said. "It's like this woman picked the most obvious undercover outfit of all time."

"Amateur," Frank commented. He was probably right. "Age and weight?"

"Eighteen to fifty, 120 to 140 pounds." I raised my palms. "Basically, everyone who's not a male."

The group fell quiet as we mulled over the first batch of information.

Charlie raised his hand. "I'm going to just say it, because I know we're all thinking the same thing: Is it possible Bob was involved in a green-washing scam?"

And just like that the flood gates opened. If fact, dozens of variations on the same theme spilled forth, none favorable.

Lamendola took a shot at it. "What if Bob had skimmed tech equipment off the recycling centers' haul and sold it directly to a trash trader?"

"Maybe the equipment in the warehouse was his," Cheski added. "Maybe Bob tried to cut out the middleman and got stuck when the market fell."

"Could be," Charlie said as he rubbed his face. "We should check the volume of tech waste processed through the recycling center. I wonder if we'd see big swings in the past couple of years."

"I'm on it," Lamendola said, eagerly turning to his partner, Cheski. "Let's hit up the recycling center today and chat with Jimmy."

The color in Cheski's beefy face rose as the possibilities swirled. "Then we'll swing by the storage place and find out if the Goldberg cousin knew Bob," he added.

Charlie leaned back and ran his fingers through his healthy head of blond curls. "Shit. What if they all knew each other? I got a bad vibe from Goldberg. That dude had something to hide."

With my sketchpad open, I listened to the crucifixion of my friend Bob by well-intentioned but seriously misguided assumptions. As the accusations escalated, my drawing pace picked up. Finally, I slid my sketchpad into the middle of the table. In the few minutes it took my crime-stopping team members to lambast Bob, I had sketched every roll on Bob's chins in exquisite detail. I captured his grin, his kindness, and his mirth.

"This is an honest face," I said, tapping my pencil on the page.

Frank's head was in his iPad.

"Frank?" I implored. "Say something nice about Bob."

He looked up. His face was pale. "The EMT found faint needle marks on Bob's arm."

Dead air wafted through the room.

"Maybe something in the garbage punctured his arm?" I winced.

"A syringe, maybe," Frank mumbled, "but not likely from the garbage."

Cheski and Lamendola darted their eyes in every direction but mine. Charlie excused himself and left the room. The mention of drugs always sent Charlie running for an alibi. *I can't do this,* I thought. *I can't keep defending my world alone.* I'd chosen an alternative path, and I was drawn to others who lived outside the lines, like Bob. By definition, you can't cross lines without ignoring a few rules. Now, some people might refer to rules as laws, but I liked to think of them as hurdles. Whatever Bob's actions, I certainly wouldn't let Bob's memory be disgraced.

"So?" I snorted.

"We're cops," Frank said as he nodded to Cheski and Lamendola. "Evidence of track marks is important to us. If Bob had a drug problem, it will change the nature of this investigation."

"Sure, now it's an investigation," I shot back lamely. What had I just said? I wasn't even making sense. I had drowned in my inability to defend Bob. Of course, this was an investigation. I knew that, but I was angry and embarrassed. I had no idea whether or not Bob had a drug problem. I considered Bob's dioramas for a second—intense, emotional, deep. An artistic lay person might add *bizarre, psychedelic, scary, drug-induced.*

"His art," I said and smiled.

"It impressed me too," Frank agreed, and then added, "It also got me thinking."

"About what?"

Frank's voice was low and careful. "About Bob, the human being."

I drew a massive, loopy heart around Bob's head. "He was a good person," I said.

"Then let's start with that. Up until this point, we've only received positive feedback about Bob."

"Thank you," I said.

Frank turned to Cheski and Lamendola. "See if you can find manufacturers that supply name tags to companies in the area. Then take Charlie to the warehouse and help him organize the tech equipment in whatever way makes sense to him." Charlie poked his head in the door and gave a thumbs-up. Frank rose from the table and reached out for my hand. "You and I will go talk to Jimmy, find out how the tech equipment gets to the recycling center and where it goes after. Then we'll stop by Barbara's."

"Okay," I nodded.

"We start tomorrow," Frank said as he packed up his papers. "Bright and early."

FOURTEEN

I RETREATED TO MY attic studio and stretched out on my unmade futon. I tried to close my eyes for a bit, but it was useless. I rolled over and stared at my collection of sketches. The walls of the attic were impossibly slanted. To make the space more usable, I had hung old ladders from the rafters to display my work. Charlie had hinged the ladders to a pulley mechanism originally designed for formal drapes. This allowed me to slide the ladders from left to right. Then Charlie and I ran picture hanger wire across the rungs and I tacked my sketches to the wire with clothespins. Sometimes I'd leave a drawing up for months until the edges curled just enough to drive me crazy. At that point, I'd transfer a drawing to an ever-growing pile shoved into the corner.

The doughy man had been hanging for a few days now. His facial detail was particularly frustrating because Marissa's eyewitness account occurred from a distance. I had to be careful here, because without an accurate description, I might fill in the blanks with my imagination. Case in point, my postman and I have had an ongoing feud for the last few years, and his face seems to crop up in my sketches every time I'm in a nasty mood. I, incorrectly, have blamed my postman for junk mail. I do understand the postal service is an innocent distributor of third-class mail, but my damn postman is so smug when he drops a pound of rubber-banded circulars on my front porch. As much as I have grown to dislike our daily exchange—me chasing him down the driveway to take the mail back—I realize it would also be in bad taste to implicate the postman in a crime just because I associated his face with all things bad. Until I had a second sighting of the doughy man, his face would have to remain vague.

I gave the woman's calves the once-over. Based on Charlie's description, I had started to pay more attention to current clothing styles. I had even dragged Katrina to the mall where we sat for hours watching people come and go. Charlie was right. The yoga pants craze is a real thing and young women do, in fact, wear skinny jeans.

I heard the lower door to the attic creak open followed by footsteps on the stairs. Was it possible Frank had considered staying the night? I sat up quickly and messed with my hair. Then I positioned myself in front of my easel and appeared to be deep in thought.

"Hey, Ce," Charlie said.

"Oh," I sighed.

"Disappointed?"

I tossed my pencil aside and resumed my splayed position on the bed. "Of course not," I said, patting my bed. "What's up?"

"Something about the track marks on Bob's arm seemed wrong."

"I know. It's just not Bob."

Charlie sunk back into my bed. "Maybe I'm being too optimistic, but even heavy dabblers get it together at some point. You can't keep up the hard stuff that long. You're either dead or out of recovery by the time you're Bob's age."

My heart kicked up a beat. The topic of drugs made me think about the unqualified parents that Lifely had serviced. What if my egg had been co-opted by a drug-addled couple? What if these crazy pill-popping parents checked out on their commitment and abandoned the product of my genes? I had visions of a baby in dirty diapers toddling around a crack house with a crusted spoon in its fist. I needed to talk to Dr. Grovit and fast. I was heartbroken over Bob, but the fate of my viable egg remained a real and present concern.

"You're breathing heavy," Charlie said, raising an eyebrow.

"I'm upset about Bob," I lied, placing my hand over my chest. "But you're right. Maybe the marks are old."

"Wouldn't Barbara know if her husband had an ongoing addiction?" Charlie asked.

I thought back to the day Frank and I saw Barbara. There was nothing about her demeanor that was false or even awkward. "I don't think Barbara hid anything. She seemed as surprised as we were that Bob hadn't shown up for work."

We lay next to each other staring at the ceiling. Lacy strands of dust clung to the beams. For years, I had wondered if dust balls could be converted into something usable, but I'd come up dry every time.

"Are you dating anyone?" I asked.

"I met a web designer at a tech conference recently."

"Wow," I said, truly surprised. "A web designer. That's perfect for you. A web designer is like an artsy engineer."

Charlie nodded. "How about you and Frank?" He turned on his side propping his head up on his well-defined arm. Charlie wore t-shirts no matter what the weather. Tempting. It was almost cruel on his part.

"It's good," I said, keeping my eyes on the rafters.

"Good?" Charlie repeated.

"Sure," I said, a little too quickly. "It's good."

Charlie lifted himself up and hung his head over mine. Our noses were so close I could see the hair in Charlie's nostrils wiggle when I exhaled in his direction.

"You haven't slept with him yet. Have you?"

I swallowed hard. "None of your business," I said, pushing him away.

He bounced up and clunked his head on the slanted wall. "Shit," he yelled, and then rolled over to muffle a laugh. "No offense, Ms. Prentice, but you're pretty easy. This is totally out of character."

"Shut up." I punched hard this time, but Charlie's stomach didn't give. "Don't you worry. I've slept with him."

"Liar."

"Fine," I admitted. "We've only done it a few times."

"What?" Charlie asked in only the way a guy who gets it anytime he wants could ask. He was utterly dumbfounded.

I sat up and folded my arms across my chest. "I really like Frank."

Charlie poked me in the ribs.

"Fine. Maybe I love him." That was hard to admit to Charlie. We had been on and off for so many years, I wasn't sure how he'd take my confession.

He hugged me gently and then whispered in my ear. "Why just a few?"

I blew air slowly out my mouth as I considered my dilemma. "It was weird, especially the first time. Too soon, maybe. So we've decided to slow it down."

"I think the term is a 'born-again virgin.'"

"Sounds like a great blog topic."

"We'll call it 'Virtual Virgins.'"

I smiled at Charlie. "Can we still do this?"

"What? The witty banter?" he said, becoming serious. "Don't think you're taking that away from me."

I sat up. "Look, I never would have met Frank had Teddy lived. That's very difficult for me to accept. The same goes for Frank."

"I get that," Charlie said. "But you're thinking of it as a penalty. Maybe Teddy's karma is what brought you to Frank."

I titled my head and stared at Charlie, who only on the rarest occasions showed his emotions. "How spiritual of you."

"I have a soft side." Charlie blushed and then switched gears. "For real, just a few times?"

"That's right."

Charlie rose from the bed and rubbed his head. "Call if you need me." He winked and sauntered off. I threw a pillow, missing Charlie but connecting with my easel. The doughy man's picture slid to the floor. I climbed off the futon and stood above the unnamed man. I had drawn him with long sleeves. Now, I wondered what was under those sleeves. I really needed to call Dr. Grovit, but it would have to wait. First thing tomorrow, Frank and I were headed back to the recycling center to talk to Jimmy, Bob's right-hand man.

FIFTEEN
MONDAY, APRIL 21

It took a full five minutes for the conveyor belts to grind to a halt and the employees to congregate on the ground floor of the recycling center.

"This is Detective DeRosa," Jimmy announced. "And most of you know CeCe."

Marissa waved to me. Her hair and make-up were impeccable, as always.

"They're here to ask questions about Bob," Jimmy said as he hung his head. The plant workers responded in kind with an impromptu moment of silence. "Please do your best to be helpful." The sea of orange suits dissolved as workers made their way back to their stations. Jimmy handed Frank a plastic Ziploc.

"It's Bob's tool kit and his receipt pad. We found it in the pile. It must have fallen out of his pants pocket."

Frank glanced at me, and I nodded. I recognized the small leather case that held Bob's tool kit as well as his spiral notepad. Now that

Jimmy mentioned it, Bob did always have the pad on him. Periodically, he'd pull it out and jot down notes.

"I don't think it will help," Jimmy said. "I paged through it already, just receipts."

"I'll take a look at it," Frank said, accepting the plastic baggie. "We need to talk about the e-waste that comes into the facility."

"Sure," Jimmy said as he led us outside to a row of ten Dumpsters lined neatly under a metal overhang. Jimmy unlocked a gate too high to scale, which effectively rendered the containers unreachable by the public. I placed my foot on the bottom rim of the first container and hoisted myself up. It was about half full of electronic products—televisions, phones, screens, computers.

"How does the stuff end up in here?" Frank asked.

"A few ways," Jimmy said. "A resident can curb it and then call in for a special pick-up on items they can't lift, like a television. We charge a small fee for scheduled pick-up. Some residents, the cheap ones, drive right up and dump their garbage at no charge. Then we get calls from businesses who are overhauling their equipment. We recommend an independent mover who picks up large loads and drops off here."

"I'll need names of the independent haulers," Frank said.

Jimmy nodded and then continued. "Last, we run a free residential program once a year where we'll pick up any type of e-waste at your curb."

"I thought it was more frequent than yearly?" I asked, distinctly remembering carting stuff to the curb with Charlie.

"We used to do it quarterly," Jimmy responded, "but the scavengers were eating away at our profits."

Frank dropped his arms and looked up at the sky. I knew exactly what he was thinking. Freegans, Dumpster divers, pickers, day trippers, and now scavengers. Garbage had its own language, and Frank was a non-native speaker.

"I guess I need to ask," Frank said. "What is a scavenger?"

Jimmy smiled and pointed to a discarded bench. We sat down and listened as Jimmy explained the inner workings of the trash business. "Most garbage can be repurposed, but in the United States, only twenty percent actually gets recycled. It's a shame, because when you do it right, garbage is a profitable and environmentally sound venture." Jimmy straightened his back and swept his gangly arms across the recycling center. "I wish we had more of it. When we started twenty years ago, this place was half the size and costing taxpayers a couple of hundred thousand bucks a year. Now, we're netting over a million dollars a year through properly sorting, packaging, and redistributing materials."

"Who did what?" Frank asked.

"Bob watched the market and cut the deals, and I handled the day-to-day."

Frank folded the cover on his iPad and leaned forward. "Give me an example."

"Water bottles," Jimmy responded quickly. "Bob found a manufacturer in Minnesota who turns plastic bottles into polyester fabric. Plastic bottles can be ground down to a flake-like consistency. Those flakes can then be melted into a spaghetti-thin filament."

I nodded eagerly. "Like thread," I said. I had heard of this recent innovation in water bottle recycling, and I was happy to discover that Bob and Jimmy were on top of it.

"Exactly," Jimmy confirmed. "Thread that can be woven into polyester material. Anyway, Bob was a master at staying on top of the next greatest green trend. I worked on my end to streamline the sorting and baling."

"So what's a scavenger?"

"Scavengers also watch the market, and they attempt to get to the hot items before the legitimate dealers. They're low-level middlemen who add another layer of distribution to the system. Our problem was the curbside pickup. Scavengers keep track of municipality recycling schedules. They study the calendars looking for the special pickups—like the quarterly collection of tech items. In the middle of the night, they comb the streets and strip the computers clean. By the time we picked up in the morning there was nothing left to sell." Jimmy took a deep breath. "It drove Bob crazy. We'd be left with a computer shell."

"A true non-recyclable," Frank said.

"Yeah, useless garbage—how's that for redundant? So now we run the program once a year, and we don't print the date. We use an automated robo-call two days before pickup. Our yield is lower because residents are caught off-guard, but scavengers also have less time to mobilize."

"Who do the scavengers sell to?" I asked.

"That's a bit of a gray area. We're a public facility. Bob dealt with reputable, large-scale recyclers. Have you ever seen a town purchasing order?"

"Twenty people have to sign to place a three-dollar order for paper clips," Frank laughed. "But it doesn't mean that your legitimate recyclers didn't buy from the scavengers. The town recycling center may have constraints, but the other players don't."

"True," Jimmy said, and then added, "Our red tape creates a window of opportunity for scavengers. Regulations slow us down. Scavengers will work through the night, sell to anyone, no paperwork, all cash."

"The garbage black market," Frank said. "As long as there's a monetary spread and two parties willing to trade, you'll find a match."

Jimmy stood and rubbed his hollow cheeks. The rims of his eyes were rheumy with memories. "Bob loved this business. He thought every piece of garbage had a story, and he was happy to listen to people as they unloaded their junk." Jimmy was silent for a moment, and I could see he wrestled to put Bob's philosophy into words.

I started to hum a familiar song, quietly at first, but as the tune came back to me, I broke out in a string of la la's.

Jimmy's eyes widened as if he'd seen a ghost. "That's Bob's song," he said, pointing at me. "He used to whistle that song."

"Actually, the song belongs to Oscar the Grouch." I started to sing again, filling in with the words until Jimmy couldn't help but join me in the chorus of "I Love Trash."

"Had you heard Bob whistle it?" Jimmy said.

"I did," I answered. "Bob loved trash because he knew he could give meaning back to people's items by transforming them into something else." The inspiration for his dioramas.

Frank stood up and began to pace. I nodded to Jimmy and said, "Give him two minutes. He's thinking."

Frank stopped and crossed his arms over his chest, then he tossed his head as if to say *I'm not ready.* Instead, he shook Jimmy's hand, signaling the wrap-up. We were preparing to leave when Frank stopped again.

"These containers," Frank said finally, pointing to the row of e-waste Dumpsters. "How long can you hold what's in there?"

"As long as you want."

"Jimmy," I asked as I looked at the plastic bag Frank held, "did Bob give people a receipt when they dumped their e-waste?"

"Yes. The last three containers are donations that might be useful to nonprofits like churches and preschools. They'll pick through the stuff and see what they can use. Not everyone needs the latest version.

The donations are a write-off for the resident, and Bob gave them a receipt for their efforts."

Frank looked at the bag and then looked at me. Bob's notebook wouldn't get tossed anytime soon.

Before we left, Frank and I toured the recycling center to inquire about the doughy man. We circulated photocopies of my sketch, leaving extra copies in the lunch area. Not a single bite.

"Do you think the workers are afraid?" I asked Frank.

"Hard to say. We're not even sure the doughy man is involved," he said. "He may have nothing to do with Bob's death." I stared at Frank. Neither of us believed that.

"Now what?" I asked as we made our way to the parking lot with not much more information than when we arrived.

"I keep coming back to Bob's dioramas," Frank said. "His art was so …" He trailed off.

"Connected?"

"Yes, and I get the sense Bob knew people. He had to be connected to someone who knows something, and I'm guessing his wife is the best place to start."

We decided to travel in Bob's footsteps to see Barbara, walking the same path he took to and from work. After we put a few hundred yards between us and the recycling center, the sound died down, and the woods enveloped us as we strolled. It was surprisingly quiet and not unpleasant. We walked in silence until I could see the turnoff for Bob's driveway.

Frank reached for my hand and slowed to a stop. "Who would have thought the grounds of a recycling center could be so romantic?"

I tensed up.

"Is it me?" Frank asked. "Or the smell of garbage?"

"You're perfect, and you smell delicious," I said. I gave Frank a perfunctory kiss. "I'm just a little spooked. We do agree that someone pushed Bob?"

"I think that's what happened on the catwalk." Frank squeezed my hand and then released it. "We're fine out here, but maybe it would be better for Barbara if we weren't hanging all over each other."

We turned into Bob and Barbara's driveway, a narrow dirt path lined with bursting lilacs. I wondered if the couple's plantings had been designed to diffuse the odorous output of their closest neighbor.

From about halfway up the drive, we had a clear shot of the hodge-podge home, which appeared permanently askew. One thing, however, stood out today: the metal front door was wide open.

Frank shoved me to the side and mouthed *stay here*. He rose up on his toes and trod silently down the driveway toward the side of the house. A lump formed in my throat as I watched Frank feel around his back. I detested guns, but in this instance, it felt appropriate.

I took one giant step sideways and plastered myself to a pine tree. With my nose against the bark, the sap stunk like overmedicated menthol. *You can do this*, I thought, breathing in and out of my mouth.

A twig snapped behind me. *Sounds of the forest*, I screamed in my head. Like the cliché, "If a tree falls in the forest and no one is there, does it make a sound?" Well, since I was there, I took my own word for it, because I'd heard it. I tried to find comfort in the fact that I hadn't lost my hearing. Of course, if you happen to be in the middle of a murder investigation and you're hiding behind a tree while your boyfriend has his gun drawn, random sounds in the woods will scare the pants off you. As I thought about my pants flying off, I sensed something brush across my leg. I lowered my eyes without moving my head. Not as easy as it sounds.

Bob's cat had wrapped itself around my leg.

"Good kitty," I croaked. I tried to blow slowly through pursed lips, like Katrina practicing her birthing exercises. I reached down for the cat, who curled into my arms.

"You scared me," I said, nuzzling the nape of his neck. The cat's purring did miracles for my nerves. I peered around the tree and saw Frank waving to me that the coast was clear. I turned to put the cat down and stepped directly into the path of a woman.

My vocal abilities, undiscovered until this moment, lit up the woods like a horror movie soundtrack, sending the cat into a full frenzy of icicle sharp claws. I spun around like a Zumba dancer on speed while the cat did laps up and down my body. In the split second it took to peel the cat off my chest, the woman disappeared.

At a distance, all Frank could see was me as I grasped frantically at my chest. He charged toward me, his gun out.

"Don't shoot," I screeched again. The poor cat scrambled back up my body like a scratch post.

"A cat?" Frank's face registered disbelief. "You're screaming about a cat?"

I sunk to the ground with the cat shivering in my arms. "No." My chest heaved uncontrollably. I had to tell Katrina her controlled breathing birth method probably wouldn't work. I looked up at Frank. "I saw someone."

Frank knelt on the pine-carpeted ground and placed his steady hands on my shoulders. "Take a deep breath."

Been there, I thought. I shook my head yes, but my mouth was closed. Maybe that had been my problem.

"Try opening your mouth."

I stretched my jaw wide and let my lungs fill with air.

"I'm fine," I whispered faintly as I put the stunned cat down. He whipped his tail and scampered away. *Get out while you can*, I thought.

"Who did you see?"

I shook my head. "I have no idea."

"I realize that, but can you describe the person?"

I looked up at the blue sky peeking through the bows of arching pine branches. A patch of cottony clouds drifted swiftly by, each one unique, but somehow indistinguishable.

"I can't see her," I said slowly. I looked hopelessly at Frank. "I'm drawing a blank."

"No, you're not."

"I am."

"You just said 'her.' You saw a woman."

True. It was a woman, but as I explained to Frank again, I couldn't visualize her face.

"Was her face obscured?"

"No"

"Were you focused on something else?"

I shrugged. "Maybe the cat?"

"Come on, Ce. This doesn't make sense," Frank countered. "This is what you do. You memorize people's faces. If you weren't looking at her face, what were you looking at?"

I put my hands on my knees and bent over. My stomach rolled, and I thought I might throw up. My rock, my stability, my core—the root of my person was dependent on my ability to truly see faces. I had always had the ability to capture the exact expression that made an individual's face their own. Yet suddenly, I felt blinded. Just at the moment the woman's face formed in my mind, it dissolved like an overexposed photograph.

"I can't see her," I repeated.

"Why? Did she scare you? Threaten you?"

The one thing I could see was Frank's face. His brow crumpled and his bottom lip jutted forward. He had lost patience. Sometimes I forgot that solving crimes wasn't a sideline for him. It was his bread and butter, and now I was just another slow-witted eyewitness.

I didn't want to disappoint Frank, but my mind was vacant, and I couldn't even fake a description.

I blinked hard like an old-fashioned slide carousel moving my memory backward with each click of my lids. The cat had been at my feet. I had picked her up, and then I saw Frank signaling me. I remembered a feeling of relief when Frank gave me the thumbs-up. I had taken a step away from the tree and turned toward the road. The woman had been standing about twenty feet away from me, but there was something wrong about the encounter. "Think," I said as I squeezed my eyes shut. I remembered the cat's claws digging into me. I must have clutched the cat too hard. But why? I opened my eyes.

The woman had leaned toward me, and as she tilted her head the bright sun over her shoulder filled my visual frame.

Frank shook my shoulders. "Why can't you see her?"

As my body jerked under Frank's grasp, I replayed the woman taking a step in my direction, her neck stretched forward, my eyes squinting toward the sky.

"CeCe," Frank implored. "Why can't you see her?'

"The sun," I said. "It was in my eyes."

"Are you sure?"

I wasn't sure, but I nodded anyway. There was something about the way the woman had tilted her head, as if she wanted to ask me a question, that struck me.

"I don't know," I said as I shook my head. "I'm so used to looking at people, and it seemed as if *she* was looking at *me*. It was," I confessed, "confusing."

Frank loosened his grip on my shoulders. "Listen carefully before you answer. Did you look away because of the sun or was it something about her face?"

I searched for an answer.

Frank scratched his noontime beard. "You need a break, CeCe."

"No, I don't." I raised my voice with each syllable.

"Look, you're not a trained officer. I think I'm pushing you too hard." Frank stood up and began a useless pace around the woods, as if the woman would suddenly materialize from behind a tree with all the information we needed to solve the crime. "It's a shock, and it's not uncommon when a witness experiences fear." Frank sighed. "Did you get a chance to see her pants?"

At first I thought Frank was joking, and then a vision popped into my head. "Actually"—I grimaced—"I think she was wearing skinny jeans."

"Let's leave it at that," Frank said. "I want you to step back from the case for a few days, maybe a week."

"A week?" I moaned.

He rubbed my head as if I had a boo-boo. "Take a break, relax, and give your memory a chance to surface."

"What am I going to do for a whole week?"

Frank laughed. He knew I didn't do a whole lot of anything. "You can help Katrina get ready for the baby."

SIXTEEN
THURSDAY, APRIL 24

MY WEEK OF FORCED furlough so far included two tasks: I watched Katrina not give birth and I assisted her in the kitchen. In her last few weeks of freedom, Katrina had decided to cook, freeze, and can anything within arm's reach, and I had become her gofer. My KP duties, although mind-numbing, freed me at the same time. With every jar I boiled and bowl I washed, I sensed a breakthrough building until it fizzled like soap down the drain. I genuinely could not conjure up a single detail related to the mystery woman's face, despite the fact that I'd had a full-on, unobstructed view of the stranger. In one particularly low moment, I tried to tempt Frank with a few poorly executed sketches of the unidentified woman, but he immediately saw through my ruse.

"Isn't that the baker from the gourmet shop where you get the day-old bread?"

Boy, he had some memory. It wasn't easy dating a detective.

My plan B involved using Cheski's stomach and Katrina's pre-natal cooking frenzy to win back my spot on the team.

"Homemade pie," I yelled upstairs where Frank, Cheski, Lamendola, and Charlie had been holed up for the last two hours. "Katrina and I are setting the table on the front porch." And then I added, "Fresh whipped cream."

"Only two days past the expiration date," Katrina added with a laugh.

As I expected, the steaming pie lured the group to the front porch of Harbor House.

"Nothing wrong with a break," I said as I passed out plates of peach pie. Cheski was in heaven and close to a food coma. Frank took a few polite bites, careful to never fill up on anything we offered lest its origin come into question.

I didn't have much of an appetite, as Bob's death had begun to weigh on me. Frank's connection to Bob was through me, and that one phone conversation seemed to have triggered the events that led to Bob's murder. I wanted nothing more than to undo the events of the past week. Worse, my visual block had rendered my talents useless, which made me as purposeful as a computer stripped by scavengers.

We had learned one thing since the sighting of the unidentified woman at Bob's house: Barbara had left Cold Spring Harbor. Frank found a note tacked to a box of dry cat food on the porch. *Please feed cat. Be back in a few months.*

"Do we even know she wrote it?" I asked as I plopped an extra spoonful of cream on my pie.

"It seems to check out," Frank offered, although I sensed he wasn't sold. "The refrigerator had been emptied, and her bedroom drawers appeared half full. I also checked with the utility companies, and she paid a handful of bills forward the day after Bob died. Her actions seem consistent with the note."

"What about the front door?" I asked. Barbara and Bob might have been a bit bohemian, but their lifestyle didn't justify leaving a door wide open. "If you're not planning on locking your front door, why leave the cat food on the porch?"

"I think we have to assume that the door was closed, and your unidentified woman had been in the house as we approached. It's possible she heard us coming."

As I hoped, my simple observation about the cat food started the ball rolling, and I used the opening to insert myself back into the investigation. Charlie, it turned out, had been busy cataloging the remaining equipment in the warehouse as well as going through the containers of e-waste at the recycling center. Despite the fact that I was under thirty years old, my technical literacy skills were a bit underdeveloped. While my peers had been riding the Internet boom, I had been renovating a 150-year-old house and nurturing a self-sustaining farm. My goal had been to plug into life by unplugging. As a result, I had no idea what Charlie had been looking for in a pile of used computers, but if a lead or a connection existed, Charlie was Frank's man.

"I need two more days with the equipment," Charlie said, and Frank nodded.

"Whatever you can give would be great."

Cheski and Lamendola had been tasked with dissecting HG Space Savers's business. This included analyzing the accounts in the hopes a renter's name would provide an elusive clue. They were also in the process of interviewing the day trippers on the outside chance a renter had seen something. Cheski and Lamendola were also eager to uncover the bad blood between Harry Goldberg and his cousin

David. Were the Goldberg cousins involved in a green-washing scam gone bad, or was it simple family rivalry, as Harry Goldberg had suggested? Moreover, was there any evidence, no matter how thin, that either Goldberg cousin knew Bob? It seemed a bit of a stretch since the Goldbergs made money storing junk, and the recycling center made money getting rid of junk. In my opinion, the purpose of these two organizations were diametrically opposed, thus reducing the chance for an overlap. I reminded everyone of their divergent goals.

"It's a fair point," Cheski said. "We got a keeper and a tosser. I can't think of any reason for Bob to connect with the Goldbergs."

"I had a storage unit once," Lamendola said thoughtfully as he scraped his plate. "After the police academy, I was living in a huge house in Queens with two other guys. When I got my own place, a 400-square-foot studio, I stored my stuff."

"I guess that's the routine," I said.

"Not exactly," Lamendola corrected. "I stopped paying rent after about a year. I couldn't even remember what I had in the unit. The storage place hit my credit card with a removal penalty. I have no idea what happened to my stuff after that."

Frank's ears perked up. "You're right. The Goldbergs must get stuck with defaulted units all the time," he said, and then asked, "Don't these storage places auction off the contents?"

"That sounds familiar," Cheski said. "Maybe there's a link there. I'll go back to Harry and ask him about default procedures."

"No," Frank said. "Find another storage facility and figure out the industry standard on defaulted units first. I don't trust Harry. If units are auctioned, find a local auctioneer and see if he's done business with the Goldbergs. If Harry is lying, we shouldn't use him as our go-to source on all things storage related."

Cheski and Lamendola agreed.

I was encouraged by this revelation, but the pile of unanswered questions grew faster than the answered. Frank had secured an account list from the largest manufacturer of laminated badges. He was in the process of visiting the local companies with badges under the pretense that there had been some break-ins in the area. There was also Bob's receipt book, which included at least twenty pages of recent tech drop-offs by local residents. The team planned on reviewing all the names in Bob's pad and cross-checking them with the renters at HG storage. Then there was the issue of Barbara. Frank had planned to contact her friends and family in hopes Barbara had sought refuge with someone close to her.

The painfully obvious hole in the investigation remained my visual recall. If I could get a sketch on paper, we'd have a tangible piece of evidence. As it stood, we had a jumble of loosely connected threads.

The one thing we agreed upon was that Bob had most likely been pushed to his death. Although there was no eyewitness to his fall, he had been observed in a heated conversation with a man at the recycling center after the center had closed. A few days before Bob's death, he had had a benign conversation with the police about e-waste. At that point, Frank and Bob had never met and only spoken over the phone. At the time, Bob's knowledge of e-waste appeared unrelated to the two storage warehouses packed with toxic waste. Bob's death, so soon after the conversation with Frank, now appeared to be connected. The fact that Bob and Barbara's house had been broken into fed the theory that Bob knew something about the warehouses.

The marks on Bob's arm were harder to understand as were the now-emptied warehouses. Possibly, the marks had nothing to do with his death. Possibly, the warehouse e-waste was simply en route to a legal recycling buyer. And, although three women had been spotted either right before or after Bob's death—one at the recycling center, one at the storage unit office, and one at Bob's house—there was no evidence they were the same person or that they were involved in Bob's murder.

The last tidbit, the unidentified women, bothered me to no end. My sketching talents had failed both me and Bob. I let a triangle of gooey peach rest on my tongue until the fruit's acidity overpowered the sugar. I swallowed the pie and laid my fork to rest.

"I need to unclog my head," I announced.

Charlie raised an eyebrow seductively, and I swatted his arm.

"Bowling works for me," Cheski said. "And Frank likes to pace."

"And grind his teeth," I added.

Frank's jaw dropped. Did he think we hadn't noticed the tread marks he had left in the floorboards and the gnawing sounds emanating from his mouth?

"Sorry," I said, "but you pace and grind. I have something else in mind to clear my head." In fact, I had started to think that my brain bank had been overloaded with images of children. The children's faces that filled my sketchbook. Dozens of them, maybe hundreds. To make room for the unidentified woman, I'd have to clean house. There was another woman I needed to see who I thought could help.

My mother.

SEVENTEEN

THE RECEPTIONIST AT HILLTOP Rehabilitation was friendly but guarded.

"Who did you say you were?"

"Constance Prentice," I replied. "I'm here to see my mother, Elizabeth Prentice."

The woman leafed through a leather-bound date book. Of course, there was no paperwork for my unannounced visit, but I waited with an air of impatience as if I had actually gone through the proper scheduling procedures. I stepped back from the desk and pretended to look around for someone senior to the receptionist.

The rehabilitation center was a bit unusual for Long Island. I had expected a Gold Coast mansion with soft hills and park benches. This facility, a little over an hour east of Cold Spring Harbor, well into the flatlands of Suffolk County, had a California open feel, lots of glass and polished wood beams. In the distance, perfectly coiled rows of grapevines highlighted the East End's growing wine industry. *What a strange view for recovering addicts,* I thought.

The interior of the building screamed *spa*. Meditation areas dotted the main floor as if at any moment a patient might care to sit and reflect on their train wreck of a life. The airiness and open public seating implied sharing. As much as I liked the redistribution of garbage, I wasn't much for sharing emotions. My mother and I were similar in that respect, and I wondered how she and her new housemates were getting along.

The initial stage of my mother's rehabilitation involved a long stay under well-supervised medical care. My brother's death, coupled with my father's disappearance and her chronic drinking, had triggered a nervous breakdown. The unraveling had scared me, and I had visited her at the hospital often. Hilltop Rehabilitation, where "new beginnings unfolded," was a new location for my mother as she had recently been promoted out of the hospital psych unit. It was my first visit to Hilltop.

"Have you been here before?" The desk lady asked.

"Yes," I lied.

"Well, this is highly unusual. We're very careful with visitation paperwork."

"One of the reasons my family chose Hilltop for my mother," I lied again, unfolding my arms in gratitude of Hilltop's airtight visitation policies. "The thing is, it's my birthday today, and it would mean a lot to both us if we could see each other briefly."

The woman's expression softened. My fib proved just enough for her to pick up the phone and start the approval process. While she worked her way through layers of security, I found my way to a meditation pod, but my mother's ears must have been burning.

"Constance," she said, swooping into the lobby her arms stretched open. She was dressed for an outing, even carrying her pocketbook, as if she had been awaiting my arrival. Her eyes were crystal clear and her skin translucent. It was an amazing transformation, and I could feel the renewed strength in her body as she folded me into a bear hug.

She whispered in my ear. "Get me out of here."

"A walk?" I said loudly. "You read my mind." I took her hand, and we dashed for the door.

EIGHTEEN

"WE'RE SUPPOSED TO STAY on the grounds," I said as we headed to the parking lot.

"Well, that's not happening."

"You're good with that?"

"I'm fine." She smiled. "In fact, I'm better than fine. I've moved from self-loathing to outright anger. It's a much better place to be."

"Good," I said. "Because you're going to need a little chutzpah today."

I filled my mother in on Bob's case and how my sketching had failed me. I was like a singer who had lost her voice, and I hoped my mother understood the stress it had caused. When you rely heavily on a single strength, it's unnerving to come up short. My mother, being an artist herself, understood this, but I could see she was distracted by my friendship with Bob.

"So you're friends with the man who runs the recycling center?"

"Yes, but he's an artist too. We actually met at a gallery showing on Outsider Art. His dioramas were showcased, and I was fascinated with his medium." I described the intricacies of Bob's work to my mother.

"Very elaborate?" my mother asked, and then added. "I actually remember seeing some of his work. It had a fantasy feel."

"Surreal, but relatable."

"That's probably how you felt growing up."

"A tortured history is required for an artist," I laughed. "My problem now is all I've got is history. I can't seem to move forward visually. I've got painter's block."

"Been there for about twenty years," my mother said, "and it's awful. But, let me get back to your friend Bob. Can't Frank do his job without you?"

"Of course, but I feel responsible because Bob was my friend, and his connection to Frank was through me. And now that I've seen this woman, I can't stop thinking about it."

"That's ridiculous, and you shouldn't feel guilty, but I won't argue. You've always tried to save the world. Charlie and I were just talking about it."

"Charlie?" I said, laughing. "Has he been here?"

"Sure," my mother said. "He was here a few days ago."

I couldn't help but grin. For all of Charlie's bravado, he loved my family, and since half the members of my family weren't related to who we thought they were, it was perfectly fine for Charlie to pretend he was one of us. Although lately, being a Prentice wasn't all that cool.

"You two always had a thing," I teased.

"It's those t-shirts he wears," my mother replied slyly as she rolled down the window and ran her fingers through the wind. A gust of warm air sent ripples up and down her silk blouse. "How can I help?" she said as I pulled into the driveway of a true Gold Coast mansion: the home I grew up in.

The circular driveway was empty, but I expected Norma, the housekeeper, was home. I put the car in park and turned to my mother.

"It's not Teddy's death that's held me back. It's what has come since."

It was faint, but my I could see the muscles in my mother's face droop. What had come since was a dangerous topic—the very last thing my mother and I spoke about before she slipped into a catatonic state. I had a suspicion, however, that until it was resolved, neither of us would truly heal.

"I can't stop thinking I might have a child."

"Funny," she said, reaching for my hand. "I can't stop thinking I might have a grandchild."

I held my mother's hand, and then I watched her face as she saw mine fall.

"What is it, Constance?"

"I sense this child isn't safe, and I think it's the root of my visual block." And with that, I explained the Lifely fertility center and my father's potential association. There was no reason to sugar coat the story at this point. My mother let out an audible gasp when I explained how Lifely serviced undesirable clients.

"I can't say I'm shocked, but I have to wonder, even with your father's horrible track record, whether he'd actually go so far as to place your eggs with an unfit parent. It would be child abuse."

"Look what he did to Frank."

My mother opened the car door, and we walked to the front door. "I'm not defending your father, but Frank's parents were actually good people. They were poor and had no command of the English language, but they weren't deficient."

"How do you know that?"

My mother led me to a stone bench in a side garden. "Immediately after Frank was removed from our home, I harassed your father regarding his whereabouts. Of course, he wouldn't say a thing, but your father's driver at the time was a very nice man. At one of my lower moments, the driver took pity on me. Apparently, he'd driven your father to Frank's new home. He gave me the address."

"Mom!" I screamed. "You knew where Frank was all this time."

"Calm down," she said. "It's not what you think. The family moved to another neighborhood shortly after, but not before I made at least one attempt to see Frank and, honestly, he was perfectly fine. It wasn't a *great* neighborhood, but I saw his adopted mother pushing him on a swing, and the outside of the house and yard were well kept."

"Why didn't you try to find them again?"

"Your father fired the driver after he found out the man had given me the address, and that was the end of it. Your father continued to insist it was a normal adoption. I know it's hard to see, but at the time, I didn't understand your father had split up the boys for a study. I actually thought this was a genuine adoption."

I frowned at my mother. "You owe me one."

"I owe you more than one, so why don't we start now."

We entered my childhood home and no matter how many times I'd walked through the front door, I was always amazed at the grandeur. The house didn't exude a homey feel, as most of the rooms were designed for large-scale entertaining, but the back of the house had a cozy atrium off the kitchen that my mother had added when I was young.

After plenty of hugs from Norma—my mother's housekeeper, companion, and confidante—we headed back to my favorite room and settled into the patio chairs surrounding a small indoor pond.

"Mom, here's where I need your help," I said as I gratefully accepted a glass of iced tea from Norma. "Dr. Grovit called me earlier. He's found one of Dad's former lab assistants, and he's willing to meet with us. Apparently, he's now a doctor, and he remained on at the labs to run the Plant Biology division."

My mother's breathing slowed. "Go on."

"You were there when my egg and Teddy's sperm were harvested."

She tried to interrupt, but there was no room or time to backpedal.

"No apologies," I said. "I know you couldn't stop it. Dad probably threw a bunch of medical mumbo jumbo around."

"He told me you had fibroids and, in fact, you had bad cramps. It seemed so logical, I didn't think twice. All I wanted was for you to feel better."

"See, you're remembering things that hadn't come up before."

"Still, I don't know how I can be of any help."

"If you could remember some of the people involved, it may lead us to something more valuable. Maybe meeting this doctor will spark your memory."

"It's possible," she said, glancing at her watch. "Now that I'm sober, I seem to be infinitely more productive. I can't get over how many hours are actually in a day." My mother rose from her lounge chair and kissed me. "Let me grab a change of clothes, and then we'll head over to the labs."

NINETEEN

DR. GROVIT WORE BROWN corduroys, a greenish wool sports jacket, and penny loafers. I had swapped out my Levi's for cargo shorts in deference to a late-April warm spell, but I imagined in my senior years, I too, would lose my sense of temperature. Body heat modulation issues probably get sandwiched somewhere *before* incontinence and *after* hearing loss. I knew, however, that Dr. Grovit's seasonally challenged attire had nothing to do with his mental acumen. My mother, of course, looked impossibly chic in a sleeveless silk shirt-waist dress and Ferragamo flats. If nothing else, a trip home had allowed her to raid her closets for new outfits.

I pulled up to the front entrance of the Sound View labs and rolled down the car window.

"Hey, Doc," I said.

"I'll get in, and you can drive us to the west campus," Dr. Grovit replied as he hopped in the car. As usual, Dr. Grovit bypassed pleasantries in favor of progress, although he did take a second to kiss my mother before settling into the back seat.

"You look wonderful, Elizabeth," Dr. Grovit complimented.

"Thank you for committing me," she said. "Apparently, I owe everyone in this car at least one return favor."

I spun the car around and drove past the main building, a barnlike structure with a modern aesthetic. With the water on our right, we had a panoramic view of the campus, which covered ten acres of highly desirable real estate on a protected cove of the North Shore of Long Island. The compound housed at least thirty buildings that included labs, auditoriums, recreational areas, and a pretty swank restaurant. The outdoor grounds were worthy of a glossy magazine shoot with indigenous plants lining crooked paths down to the water. Science, it seemed, paid off.

Harbor House sat on the opposite side of the bay facing the labs. For the last year, it had been hard to wake up to a full-on view of the place where my brother had died. On the other hand, this picturesque area of Long Island had been my family's stomping ground for decades. I had decided, after some random relocation attempts via Google search, that I couldn't run away from my home. The whole point of family is to celebrate and suffer the passage of life. No matter how bizarre, this was my family and the town we'd helped build. I'd have accomplished nothing if I had run away. I also felt that Teddy knew our mother and I were here, on his campus.

I glanced at Dr. Grovit in the rearview mirror. He leaned forward and squeezed my mother's shoulder.

"Where to?" I asked.

"Plant Biology," Dr. Grovit instructed. "One of the lab assistants, now Dr. Jack Wilson, stayed on and runs the division," Dr. Grovit said.

"What did you tell him?"

"The truth," Dr. Grovit said. "And believe me, it worked."

My mother laughed wryly. "Guilt is a wonderful motivator."

Dr. Wilson was in the lobby when we arrived. I pegged him for about forty, maybe a few years younger. Other than his full head of dark red hair, there was nothing outwardly memorable about Dr. Wilson. He wore the requisite lab coat covering up a bland button-down and nondescript pants. Given my estimate of his current age, he would have been no more than in his early twenties when my procedure took place. Not so young that an adult decision would have been beyond his reach but young enough still to trust an authority, like my father. I wondered if Dr. Wilson was a follower or a leader. Or a challenger, like me.

I looked at his shoes—worn-out running sneakers. A nonconformist. Maybe I liked this guy.

My mother gave Dr. Wilson the once-over and shook her head in a quick no to me. She didn't recognize him.

A conference room with a view of the lab's greenhouses was available for our meeting. Despite the short notice, Dr. Wilson had a thickly stuffed manila folder in front of him. I wondered if he felt this meeting would provide a form of absolution for him. Maybe he had nothing important to impart, but the act itself would probably prove cathartic for him if he'd been at all suspicious of my father's activities.

"I don't want to waste your time," Dr. Wilson said matter-of-factly.

That worked for me since I'd already been kept in the dark for more than a decade.

"Great," I said. "Let's get started."

"I'm going to be blunt. We were testing sperm mobility when I started my fellowship in this very lab. There was nothing unusual about it at the time, and I wouldn't have given it a second thought until Dr. Grovit called."

I looked around the room. The entrance to the building had seemed familiar. The hall lined with photographs of prominent staff scientists rang a bell, and I guessed this was where my egg extraction took place.

"Many of the doctors and medical students donated sperm for the studies," Dr. Wilson continued. "The natural progression was to test categories of sperm with categories of eggs. Medically, there was nothing wrong with our work. In fact, it was quite progressive." Dr. Wilson paused, deep in his own thoughts of scientific breakthroughs. His face took on a glow, and I was reminded of Teddy's passion for his medical studies. Within seconds, Dr. Wilson's eager expression dissolved. "When we began to fertilize the eggs . . ." Dr. Wilson said. "Well, I guess you could say, we were creating life in a petri dish."

I had a million questions, but Dr. Wilson's confession, it seemed, couldn't be contained. He continued before I could interject.

"I'm not sure what happened to the fertilized embryos," he admitted, looking absolutely lost. "It's the oversized elephant in the room."

"Did you donate?" my mother asked.

"I sure did," he replied. "And now, from what Dr. Grovit has told me about Lifely and what I could pull together in the last day"—he frowned at his bursting folder—"I may have hundreds of children out there."

Oh my, I thought. And I was worried about having one child. Was it possible I had more? This poor guy may have fathered a small country of redheads. Then I thought about Teddy. There could be dozens of mini-Teddys running around. Frank's Christmas list for his nieces and nephews could be miles long. My mouth felt dry, and

I reached into my bag for my water bottle. My mother's eyes started to glaze over, and I passed her the bottle. She waved it off, probably hoping for something stronger. Maybe I had overestimated my mother's resiliency. And Dr. Grovit? I turned my head to him. He had finally started to sweat under his winter garb.

"Do you think I have multiple children?" I asked Dr. Grovit.

"I don't. In fact, the chance of you having even one child is miniscule," Dr. Grovit said.

Dr. Wilson nodded and then addressed my mother and me. "Do you remember getting a series of shots before the extraction?"

We both shook our heads no. "Would I have needed shots?"

"In a typical IVF case, the woman wants to increase her odds of pregnancy, so hormones are used to stimulate an overproduction of eggs. The more eggs, the better the odds. If you *didn't* have shots, which would be highly unusual before an extraction, then you could only provide one egg."

"Which lowers the chance that this single egg even made it to a womb and survived," I said as I thought about it. I turned to my mother. "I don't remember shots."

"I don't either," she said, and then turned to Dr. Grovit. "So we're talking one egg. The odds were so slim. Why would William even make an attempt?"

"He thought he was God," Dr. Grovit said as he shook his head. "As much as I hate to admit it, he had a knack for making scientific miracles happen. At the least, I think we can agree that if there is a baby, there is just one." Dr. Grovit addressed Dr. Wilson, "What happened to the test vials of sperm?"

Dr. Wilson let out a groan. "We were under the assumption the vials were being discarded, but now I'm not so sure. I think we have to assume that some of these samples made it to Lifely." His nose twitched as if he'd smelt something offensive. "Clearly, your father was interested in long-term DNA studies, and if there was one sample worth studying, despite the low odds, it was yours and your brother's."

I drained the last of my water. "Isn't it possible my egg is sitting in a freezer somewhere?"

"No," Dr. Wilson said. "Sperm sits in a freezer. Science is just now figuring out how to successfully freeze, unfreeze, and fertilize eggs. At that time, eggs had one purpose—fertilization followed by immediate insemination, typically within forty-eight hours."

"Shit," I said, and I meant it. "I don't know why, but all this time I've been thinking this kid would be a toddler or small child. But if what you're saying is true and my egg had to be used immediately, I may be the mother of a teenager."

"Sixteen years old to be exact," my mother chimed in. "Is there anyone else we can talk to? There had to be a lab assistant that facilitated the transfers to Lifely. My husband never touched administrative work."

"I thought about that," Dr. Wilson said as he opened his folder. "The lab turned over about every twelve months depending on who was headed to a fellowship or medical school. I wrote down everyone I could remember and researched the names online." He passed over a sheet of paper with contact information.

Dr. Grovit's glasses slid to the tip of his nose while he ran his finger down the list. It was faint, but his finger shook slightly. "Why is there a question mark by Liz James?"

"I didn't try to locate her, because I don't think she'd be of any help. She wasn't a medical student." Dr. Wilson smirked, seeming somewhat amused at the memory of Ms. James. "Lizzy was a bit loose and not much of a typist. She had a few flings with some of the younger guys. She was supposed to be managing medical supplies, but let's just say not all the medications found their way to an assigned shelf or bottle."

"I don't remember her," Dr. Grovit said.

"She didn't last long," Dr. Wilson replied. "She left when she was about four months pregnant."

My mother's brain synapses fired a millisecond ahead of mine. "This woman left because she was pregnant?" she asked.

Dr. Wilson nodded.

My mother rose unsteadily. She smoothed the folds of her dress and readjusted the belt accentuating her narrow waist. "I haven't had a great run with doctors," she said, and then smiled at Dr. Grovit. "Present company excluded. However, I can confirm that my husband surrounded himself with very intelligent people. If his lab assistants knew how to make a baby in a petri dish, then I'm pretty sure they knew how to prevent conception the old-fashioned way. No one on this campus mistakenly impregnated Liz James. And, since I'm still receiving the exceedingly generous health benefits from this institution, I can't imagine why a single woman on the company health plan would leave four months into a pregnancy."

Hello, chutzpah. *Thanks, Mom*, I mouthed. Finally a lead—the name of a woman with a questionable background, working in close proximity to my father, in the same lab with my egg and my brother's sperm, and most probably pregnant seventeen years ago.

TWENTY

MY MOTHER AND I returned to Hilltop with ten minutes to spare before curfew. We pulled into the lot just as the service-challenged receptionist left for the day.

My mother wiggled her fingers politely in a halfhearted wave. "That one hates me," she said, flashing her most disingenuous smile.

"Happy birthday to your daughter," the receptionist replied.

I matched my mother's smile and said, "Thanks for remembering." Then I turned to my mother. "I said it was my birthday."

"Then you'll need to come get me again next weekend so I can take you birthday shopping."

"I'm sure Dr. Grovit will be able to get you a pass for the weekend. Your medical coverage only applies if you are in residence through the treatment period, but Dr. Grovit talks a good game."

My mother crossed her fingers and gave me a kiss. "I know, but I didn't realize how much I wanted out of here until our field trip today."

"We have to be careful," I reminded her. "We could find something awful." I hesitated as I thought about Loose Lizzy, the department

109

floozy. "If Dr. Wilson was right about the missing medications, this Liz James could have been a drug addict to boot."

My mother let out a whopping laugh. "Do I need to point out the irony? You were raised by a substance abuser."

She had me there. We were, of course, having this conversation in the parking lot of a rehab facility. "True," I admitted. "And you got yourself knocked up too."

"I did indeed," she said proudly. "Basically, I did everything wrong, and you still turned out fine."

I considered my mother's assessment of the situation alongside my father's generational DNA studies. My father suspected that nurture had more impact than nature. In the field of epigenetics, DNA could be manipulated by a subject's surroundings. To prove his hypothesis, my father had separated Teddy and Frank at birth, placing Frank in a low socioeconomic environment with uneducated parents. Yet Frank had thrived and if my mother was right, a child produced by me and my brother might have the DNA chops to weather a disadvantaged household.

A thread of hope.

We hugged goodbye and made plans for the weekend. With Frank's help, we hoped to locate Lizzy James quickly. It wasn't brain surgery. This woman was either raising my child or she wasn't.

TWENTY-ONE

KATRINA WAS STRETCHED OUT on the living room floor when I got home. Her stomach rose and fell with each controlled breath. "Am I boiling water?" I asked.

"Not yet," she exhaled and rolled over onto her side. "My back is achy, but I'm fine. How was your day?"

I laid down beside her and filled her in on Dr. Wilson and Liz James, but before I could cover my mother's theory that my kid was a fighter, capable of conquering a dysfunctional upbringing, Katrina started to bawl. Uncontrollable sobs followed incoherent babbling.

"Oh my god," I gasped. "Are you in pain?" Katrina had moved from her side to all fours, and I got right down on the floor with her. I had heard about women giving birth in this position. It didn't seem gravitationally possible, but what did I know?

"No," she cried, droplets of tears hit the knotty pine floor. "No pain. Help me up."

I pulled her to her feet and led her over to a secondhand couch I had picked up at the recycling center, based on a tip from Bob. Katrina dug into a large pocket on her maternity dress and produced a crisply starched, monogrammed hankie. This one had an O on it.

"I can't believe how self-centered I've been for the past nine months," Katrina said, wiping her nose. "This Lizzy James seems horrible. The whole thing is just horrible and here you've been taking care of me while Jonathan's been away. It should be the other way around." The tears started to flow, a veritable hormonal explosion. I looked at Katrina's hands—her fingers, normally slender, were puffed up like stubby cocktail franks.

"Wow, you look really uncomfortable," I said.

"See?" she wept. "I've been getting all the attention, but this birth is no more important than your child." Katrina placed my hand on her belly, and I felt her baby thump a foot or hand out at me. The immediacy of the sensation frightened me, and I yanked my hand away.

"It's still not real for you, is it?" Katrina led my hand back to her stomach, and I relaxed into the gentle rhythm of her swimming baby.

I studied the thin fabric covering Katrina's midsection. A yard of material and half an inch of skin and tissue were the only things that separated us from a full-term being. In less than two weeks, we'd be assigning personality traits to this baby. What a calm baby, a delightful or cranky baby, a good little sleeper, a huge eater and oh, that smile. Better yet, this baby would be responding to our prompts with a stretched out arm or tiny fingers curled around ours.

"My sketches," I sighed, recognizing the shortcomings in the drawings of my potential child. "They're completely one-dimensional, aren't they?"

"It's partially our fault," Katrina said. "It seemed so bizarre, this plot of your father's to steal your eggs. I think we haven't been taking it seriously in the last year. But now that I'm weeks away from having a baby, I can appreciate what you may have missed."

I nodded and borrowed a dry corner from Katrina's hankie.

"I think you'd have more success finding this child if you envisioned him or her as a whole person. A person with thoughts and interests and emotions. Not simply a physical rendering, but what they'd be doing and how they'd be acting."

I was twelve when my egg was taken. This kid could be sixteen now. I had no idea how to piece together the life of a teenage girl or boy, but the idea pried open that part of my brain that had been locked. It was as if I'd had a pounding headache that gave way to sublime relief, a mental breath.

"Jet black hair," I stammered as a vision formed behind my eyelids. "The woman outside of Bob's house had jet black hair. I remember her moving a strand of hair away from her face to get a better look at me." My sketchbook had slid under the couch. I couldn't get to it fast enough.

TWENTY-TWO

FRIDAY, APRIL 25

WITH MY MENTAL HEALTH week coming to a close and the beginnings of a sketch in my possession, I was eager to impress Frank with my progress. I took a few steps back from my easel. The hair wasn't dark enough, so I rubbed the charcoal hard against the canvas surface. The woman I remembered had bottle-black hair, cut in a tight pageboy. She was medium-height, five-six or -seven, and skinny, maybe a few years younger than myself. I drew the woman leaning in with one shoulder forward, because I was still convinced she had been moving toward me. The twinkle of a jangly earring peeked out from the sharp border of her bob. Unfortunately, I had to leave the oval of her face completely empty, giving her a ghostly appeal.

It would have to do for now, as I was confident the rest of my memory would surface soon enough. As Katrina had urged, I forced myself to see this person as a whole. The minute I stepped back and considered my peripheral memory, something appeared in the woman's hands. She had been carrying a paper bag. With one shoulder sloped, I remembered the bag had heft, and there were odds and ends spilling out of it. I thought there may have been plastic tubes. *Maybe supplies for one of Bob's dioramas,* I thought. I remembered the tubes because as the woman turned to go, one of the hoses got caught around her skinny jeans.

I scooped up my sketch and headed down one flight to Frank's makeshift office. From the staircase window, I could see Cheski and Lamendola pulling in. Perfect timing.

"Frank, I've got something," I said. I found a random nail on the wall, hung my sketch and pretended to model the canvas like Vanna White turning block letters. Cheski and Lamendola arrived in time to catch my television game show spoof.

"Asian?" Cheski asked, noticing the straight dark hair.

I thought about it. "No, but that's a good question. At least we know what she's not."

"Was she pretty?" Lamendola asked.

Again, good question. "I don't remember being turned off by her looks so no, she wasn't unattractive."

Cheski pulled a folded sheet of paper out his pocket. It was a photocopy of a Facebook page. "Is that her?"

I stared at the picture, a glam shot of a woman with too much of everything. The hair was black alright, so black it bled purple. Instead of a short cut, the salon-styled hair was voluminous and windswept, framing a perfectly drawn face, not with pencils but with make-up brushes.

"She looks like the aggressive perfume lady at a cosmetics counter," I said.

"But is it the same woman you saw?" Cheski repeated.

Frank leaned over my shoulder to grab a look. "Who is she?"

I shook my head. "That's not the woman I saw."

"Too bad," Cheski said, "because I think this woman is who Katrina saw at HG storage. Cheryl Goldberg."

"Another Goldberg cousin?" Frank asked.

"Go ahead," Lamendola urged his partner. "You're dying to tell them what we found."

Cheski tacked the Facebook image up on the wall next to my sketch. "Cheryl Goldberg is David Goldberg's wife. Harry Goldberg's cousin-in-law."

"What was she doing at Harry's place?" I asked and then stopped. "Ohhh," I said knowingly. "She wasn't breaking in, was she?"

"Breaking in the mattress Harry's got stored in the back office, maybe," Cheski laughed.

"Interesting," Frank said as he started his first lap of the day around the cramped room. "So Harry is having an affair with his cousin's wife. I knew there was something off about him. Do we think David Goldberg knows?"

"Maybe," Cheski said. "I'm just not sure if the bad blood goes any deeper than this affair."

"How'd you find out they were screwing around?" I asked.

"We've been driving through the industrial parking lot for the past two days," Lamendola said. "Yesterday we saw Harry arrive around noon and then a half hour later, a woman showed up with the scarf and sunglasses."

"Twenty-three minutes after that," Cheski chuckled, "Cheryl came out and Lamendola followed her home. We checked the address. The house belongs to David Goldberg."

"That doesn't necessarily mean Harry and his cousin's wife are having an affair," I reasoned.

"Yeah, it does," Frank said. "There's no other reason for David Goldberg's wife to be at his cousin's place of business, especially if the cousins don't get along. Now that it's come up, the mattress in the HG offices did catch my attention on our first walk through."

"Maybe it's for the night guard?" I challenged.

Cheski shook his head. "I checked in on Harry after David's wife left. I may be old, but I remember what a crumpled shirt and a flushed face look like."

"I wonder if Harry is sleeping with Cheryl to get information on his cousin's business. But even if that's true," Frank answered his own question, "it's inconsequential unless it links back to the Goldbergs being involved in a garbage scam that led to Bob's death."

"Otherwise, it is what it is." Cheski shrugged, his palms open. "Two small business owners that cut a deal with the wrong company. Just like Charlie described—the Goldbergs got stuck on the wrong end of a recycling shell game."

"But why are the warehouses empty now?" I pushed. "It doesn't make sense. In fact, do we even know that David Goldberg's warehouse *is* empty? That information came from Harry, but then again, he's sleeping with his cousin's wife. Maybe he lied about his cousin's warehouse."

Everyone with a badge in their pocket fell silent. No one had spoken directly to David Goldberg since Harry's warehouse was found empty. Lamendola walked out of the room with his cell phone in hand and returned within seconds. "Confirmed. The DG Self Storage warehouse is empty too."

I kept up with my questions. "Is it possible Harry emptied both warehouses to divert attention away from him and any association with Bob?" I pondered. "You have to admit that his closed-eyed reaction to Bob's name was sly."

"That's possible," Frank said as his eyebrows rose. "You know what else I'm thinking?"

We all waited.

"When Barbara left town, she dropped the duties typically reserved for a widow. There hasn't been a funeral." Frank took another lap. "Who else knows Bob is dead?" he continued. "There hasn't been anything in the paper."

"Harry Goldberg and all the workers at the recycling center are aware of Bob's passing," I said. "But some of them think it was an accident."

"I think the question Frank is getting at is when did Harry Goldberg know Bob was dead?" Cheski said, turning to Frank. "Did he know before us, and was he trying to clear out those warehouses before anyone linked the two events?"

"Exactly." Frank pointed at Cheski. "And then there's the doughy man," he added. "If he pushed Bob, then he is certainly aware of Bob's fate. In fact, since the news is not fully public, then the only people who know Bob is dead are those we've told and those involved." He motioned to my sketch. "If this woman knew Bob was dead, why would she be at his house?"

"Maybe she was looking for him? It's possible she didn't know he was dead," I said, thinking about the bag in her hand. "Maybe her intent was to give him the contents of the bag?"

We all stared at the drawing of the department store paper bag with a spaghetti-like string sticking out the top.

"It could also be evidence she wanted to hide," Frank said.

Cheski walked up to my sketch. "Are these tubes or elastic bands?"

"Why?" I asked.

Cheski gave Frank a forlorn look.

Frank sighed and sat down. "Bands are used to enlarge a vein before shooting up."

"You just can't drop the drug thing," I said angrily. "Can you?"

118

Frank was silent.

"The answer is in the garbage," I remind him as I abruptly removed my sketch from the wall. "Bob died in a twenty-foot mound of garbage. That's where our focus should be."

"CeCe is right," Frank said.

"I am?"

Frank laughed. "We all appreciate your ..." He paused to think.

Lamendola filled in the blank: "Enthusiasm."

"Good word," Frank said. "We all appreciate your enthusiasm, but now that you're working with us you'll need to get used to something we call 'contained speculation.'"

Cheski placed a fatherly hand on my arm. "You're a good thinker, CeCe. Try not to take our criticism personally." Cheski took the sketch out of my hands and rehung it on the wall. "Most police work is administrative. It's boring. This"—he nodded to his co-workers—"the part where we theorize, is the fun stuff. Keep an open mind and use the facts."

"It's what gets us to the best part," Lamendola said. "Nailing the bad guy."

Frank stopped pacing briefly. "And I think I've got a way to get us there. Let me tie up a few loose ends and we can meet tomorrow."

Cheski's face fell. "Tomorrow is Saturday."

Frank looked confused, as if weekends were a new invention or a word only recently accepted by Webster's. "Oh," he replied. "Is that a problem?"

Cheski shook his head.

TWENTY-THREE
SATURDAY, APRIL 26

As EXPECTED, THE LOBBY of the local police station at 11 a.m. on a Saturday morning was dead. Except for a down-and-out fisherman who had gotten drunk and drowned in the shallow bay a few years back, suspicious deaths were not a major issue in Cold Spring Harbor. With the high concentration of wealth, the town had its fair share of robberies, but those typically occurred on weekend nights and during major holidays when the wealthy traveled. Inevitably each year, the jet-setting crew returned home to discover their recently purchased cruise wear, neatly folded in their Coach suitcases, was the only clothing they had left.

It wasn't lost on me that I was connected to two local murders that had broken a kill-free stretch of over a century. Home values, thanks to me, had probably plummeted in the last twelve months, leaving my neighbors' investments underwater and my name quietly removed from any social register that hadn't banished me years ago.

I looked around the empty stationhouse. Since I was accounted for, the chance of a crime occurring was next to nothing. There was one man sitting on a bench reading the local paper, and he looked like he might have stopped by for the complimentary coffee.

"Jimmy?" I said as a face appeared over the newspaper. Missing was Jimmy's one-piece recycling center coverall and hard hat. I realized I had never seen him outside the recycling center, and it irked me that a change of clothing was enough to alter his appearance beyond recognition. I stared at him a little bit too long, causing him to shift awkwardly.

"I'm sorry," I apologized. "I didn't recognize you in street clothes."

"People see what they expect to see," he replied, rising to shake my hand. "Even if Bob had lost a hundred pounds, he still would have been a fat guy, you know?"

In fact, I knew exactly what Jimmy meant. Seeing isn't a function of the eyes. Our brains tend to interpret or distort information in a way that makes us comfortable. We see what we want to see or what others have told us to expect.

"I'm going to remember that," I said as I watched Frank approach us. Frank's gait had purpose, and although he rarely seemed to be in a rush, you could tell he never wasted a minute.

"Thanks for coming in," he said, leading us down the hall toward his office.

Charlie was already seated at Frank's round table, and I took his attendance as a good sign. Given Charlie's technological expertise, it meant Frank's primary interest was e-waste, not Bob's supposed drug problem. I came to that conclusion having taken Cheski's comments to heart—focus on the facts.

"I didn't want to meet at the recycling center, and I think you'll soon see why," Frank said, and turned to Jimmy. "Obviously, I've got waste-related questions so I'm going to jump right in. When was the last time the recycling center ran a printed e-waste take-back program?" Frank asked.

"Maybe two years ago," Jimmy replied.

"So these scavengers you told us about must be pretty hungry," Frank concluded. "Assuming the scavengers are still in the business of mining free garbage, the recycling center curbside programs were potentially one of their bigger suppliers."

"Sure," Jimmy said. "We were easy money for them. We did the advertising, and they received the profits. I imagine they've got other sources now, but they probably have to work much harder for it."

"How long do you think a scavenger holds on to e-waste before it's sold?"

"Small-time players get in and out fast," Jimmy said. "It's strictly quick money. I'm assuming scavengers move the product by the next day, maybe even that night."

"That's what I was hoping," Frank said, and then he proceeded to outline a very clever plan.

———

"The minute an item is deemed to have value," Frank explained, "a ski jacket, designer sneakers or an iPod—the door has been opened for crime. Even crimes that don't involve a tangible object involve the concept of value. The taking of a life, for example, or a person's dignity, in the case of a rape, is essentially the taking of value. What I've learned from the people at this table is that garbage, while useless to most of us, has value to some people." Frank let us sit on this point, but we didn't need any encouragement. With two Freegans in the room and the guy that now ran the recycling center, he was preaching to the choir. If anything, Frank was late to this game. We nodded in patient unison.

"Our gap in this investigation is that we haven't identified all the players who deem garbage valuable."

"Until it's not," Charlie said.

"True," Frank said. "With value comes risk, as objects can lose value due to external events. With risk comes the potential for loss or great profits. Either outcome is a motivator for crime. To create a list of suspects, we need to identify anyone who thinks garbage has value. We know the local recycling center is a legitimate player. However, we need a way to uncover all the related parties."

"But at this point, would these players raise their hand to identify themselves, if they knew a murder investigation that involved garbage was underway?" I said.

"That's what got me thinking," Frank said. "CeCe, yesterday you hypothesized that Harry paid to unload the warehouse in an attempt to avoid an association with Bob. It's possible other players in the world of e-waste have tried to lay low."

I nodded.

"We also discussed the fact that maybe not everyone knows Bob is dead."

"I'm a little lost," Jimmy responded. "But I'm guessing you've got a plan to bring these parties to the forefront?"

Frank's mouth curled slyly. "Oh, I've got a plan," he said, as he rose proudly and walked to the white board mounted on his office wall. Using colorful magnets, he tacked up a detailed street map of the town.

"We're going to bait the players," Frank said, "with something of value by staging an e-waste sting. Within the week, the recycling center is going to run a traditional curbside take-back program."

"Damn, this is good," Charlie said, nodding as his mind raced ahead. "We're going to fill the streets with recyclables, draw out the scavengers, and follow them. It's like a drug bust where the police ignore the small-timers but use them to find the kingpin."

"Yup," Frank replied with an extra air of confidence. "And, we're going to lace this garbage with whatever you tell me is highly sellable right now," he said to Charlie.

"I wondered why I was here," Charlie said as he rubbed his hands together conspiratorially.

Frank wrote a to-do list on the board. "Charlie, those leftover computers in the warehouse. We can use those as plants, right?"

"Can do," Charlie said. "We can also curb whatever the recycling center hasn't processed yet."

"And Jimmy," Frank continued. "The reason you're here is that you've got to make this look real. The center's employees can't suspect this is a setup. We'll map out a controlled area for pickup—a designated neighborhood where you think homeowners will actively participate. You'll need to set up a robo-call, but more importantly we'll need to post print ads. We can even run an ad in the local newspaper. The most important thing is that this needs to look legitimate."

"What about me?" I asked.

"I'm hoping your dark-haired lady makes an appearance," Frank said. "And I'm hoping your night vision is working."

Right, my night vision. My "seeing" ability. This was a real job, and I had to get my head together.

"It's Saturday. Bob has been dead a week and a day," Frank said. "Can we pull this off by Thursday?"

Charlie and Jimmy agreed to the deadline.

I raised my hand. "That's Katrina's due date."

Frank's face registered exasperation. "Babies either come early or late but never on their expected due date. In the meantime"—he glanced at his watch—"you and I have a date."

"We do?" I said.

TWENTY-FOUR

UNLIKE COLD SPRING HARBOR, the neighboring town of Huntington was actually a township representing five unincorporated areas and housing a population of close to a million residents. Cold Spring Harbor, with only five thousand residents, had a gourmet food store but no supermarkets. Our hamlet had no gas stations or mini-marts or anything that might imply convenience. You could, however, sample Long Island wines at one of three Cold Spring Harbor liquor stores while you waited for your speed boat to be winterized at the docks. The more mundane purchases, like aspirin, occurred somewhere among the suburban sprawl of Huntington. The border of the two towns was a real estate hot potato. The homes *appeared* equally as grand on both sides of the town line, but the housing prices dropped a few hundred thousand on the Huntington side. As you inched farther into Huntington, the town took on a more diverse reality. That means everyone didn't look alike—in a good way.

The Carmen House Apartments, a cluster of three-story brick buildings, were located on the east side of Huntington, as far as you could possibly get from Cold Spring Harbor. It was Huntington's first attempt, in the 1960s, to stratify housing needs. Set in a leafy, suburban area with single-family neighborhoods on either side, the Carmen apartments seemed revolutionary at the time. Fifty years later, natural wear and tear, as well as a revolving door of residents, showed the cracks. The buildings were, in fact, crumbling. The grassy green, now a dirt courtyard, seemed beyond landscape repair. And of course there were signs that meant nothing when taken individually, but told a story of poverty in cumulative display: a lone child's sandal, a broken tricycle, an overflowing Dumpster even I wouldn't approach on an empty stomach.

"Is this where scavengers live?" I asked, opening my sketchbook.

"Not quite," Frank said, as he parked the Gremlin under a shady oak tree. "This is where Lizzy James lives."

"Frank!" I yelled. "How could you not tell me where we were going?"

"How could you not tell me about this woman?" Frank's hands gripped the steering wheel, probably to prevent himself from hitting me. "You've done nothing but beg me to help you, yet you went off to play detective with Dr. Grovit instead of me. You realize I'm a detective, right? Did you think I wouldn't find out?"

"How *did* you find out?"

"It wasn't rocket science," he said. "Grovit called Harbor House and I picked up."

If someone were watching us, they would have seen two very angry people in a heated argument. My arms flailed and my mouth jabbered. The only problem was the accompanying audio. I hadn't actually said anything of merit, because I had zero comeback to Frank's accusations. He was dead-on. In my misguided zeal, I had gone on my wild goose chase without him.

Frank grabbed my circling hands and slapped them together in a prayer position. "Why are we doing this to each other?" he said, and then released me. "From day one, we've been challenging each other."

I started to speak, but again, I had nothing worthy to say.

"If this is going to work, we need to be honest," Frank said. "We've probably got some unresolved issues holding us back. I know I do."

I raised my eyebrows. I hadn't considered Frank's take on our relationship, as I had only seen him reacting to *my* histrionics. "Oh," I said softly. "I guess I haven't been listening too well, have I? Is something bugging you?"

Without much coaxing on my part, Frank admitted what was really on his mind. "Is something still going on between you and Charlie?"

Holy cow. Is that what he'd been thinking this whole time? Me and Charlie? *Ridiculous*, I thought, and then I looked at Frank. It wasn't ridiculous to him.

"No, but if I'm being honest, I could see why it would bother you," I replied. "My friendship with Charlie has crossed the line in the past, but it hasn't recently, and it won't going forward."

"Good," he nodded. "Your turn."

Hmm. Why did I challenge Frank all the time? Could it be I was frustrated that our physical relationship had stalled? It seemed like a shallow reason for all this angst, but I couldn't come up with anything better. I distracted myself by watching people come and go across Carmen House's courtyard, and I realized that any one of these people could be Lizzy James. Suspicion crept up my spine as I eyed a group of chatty women and immediately branded them guilty of something. The feeling of culpability was all too familiar. *Of course*, I thought. I'd felt it the day I met Detective Frank DeRosa, nearly a year ago.

"The night you first came to Harbor House," I said as I tilted my side-view mirror at an angle that allowed me to catch Frank's reaction. "Did you think I was involved in Teddy's death?" It had always bothered me that Frank might have been suspicious of me in the beginning of the investigation.

"Yes," Frank replied, his face remaining placid.

I was blatantly offended. "Why?"

"Because everyone I spoke to prior to meeting you described you as, well…" Frank slowed down as he tried to sanitize his recollections.

"Forget it," I murmured.

"No, that's the point. We need to clear the air," Frank replied and then continued. "You were described as the black sheep, the trouble-maker, a disappointment, and well, a bit eccentric. And then there was your attic. The piles of sketches, face after face after face. The whole setting was bizarre. And Harbor House, with the junky furniture and the broken down car…"

"Okay, okay," I interrupted, "I get it. I come across as a modern-day Miss Havisham."

"A younger, cuter version," Frank amended as he opened the car window. "And there it goes, right out the window."

"What?"

Frank pretended to brush something imaginary through the car window. "The tension. It's gone."

I smiled. Frank wasn't naturally funny, but when necessary, he could see the humor in a situation. He also had a habit of being right most of the time. We did have unresolved issues, but at his insistence, we had just remedied two. Charlie and I hadn't slept together recently, which I'm sure brightened Frank's day. I wasn't thrilled that Frank had initially considered me a suspect in Teddy's death due to an unfavorable first impression. I guessed, however, that by this point, we'd moved successfully past our preconceptions.

I smiled and asked, "What's Lizzy's apartment number?"

TWENTY-FIVE

I HAD AN EXCEPTIONALLY high tolerance for dirt, but I could not accept filth. Dirt was merely wrapping paper, an exterior coating easily removed to reveal a treasure. Filth implied continuous neglect, a ground-in lack of care or concern. I think people would be surprised to discover that recycling centers are clean, well-maintained facilities. Garbage isn't left to rot but rather processed and moved along quickly for further uses.

The hallway leading to Lizzy James's apartment, conversely, was filthy. The carpet was stained in colors I'd only associated with bodily functions, and the torn wallpaper revealed splotches of lung-threatening mold on the exposed plaster. My toes curled in disgust, and I practiced breathing through my mouth and out my nose. Thank God I didn't have asthma. If my kid had breathing problems in this environment, it wasn't from my gene pool.

"Gross," I coughed.

"I've seen worse," Frank replied as he stopped halfway down the hall.

"What's your plan?"

"She's got three kids, but they're twelve and under." Frank looked over his shoulder. "Your child needs to be older."

"Correction. My child and your niece or nephew needs to be older. That's one of our issues: your inability to accept that you're related to this child."

"Okay, you win," he conceded. "I'm wondering if Ms. James has been lying about the oldest one's age. That's why I want to get into the apartment," he said as he knocked on the door. "Or she's got a child she's never reported."

A hidden child? What if my undocumented child were sitting in this apartment watching television and drinking a Slurpee? I wasn't sure I could do this, but Frank had already knocked on the front door.

No response.

He knocked again. "Follow my lead."

Do I have a choice?

We waited longer than I could control my breathing exercises. Filth filled my nostrils.

"Whatta you want?" a voice called through the closed door.

"Ms. James?" Frank said, lightening his tone to increase his sweet quotient. "I'm here from Sound View Laboratories. It's been years, but it turns out there's an unclaimed paycheck for you."

Money, as they say, opens doors. In this case, it flew off the hinges to reveal a plump, full-breasted woman with a cigarette stuck precariously to her bottom lip.

"Bullshit," she snarled, pulling a wad of dry, damaged hair into a loose bun while she took a puff on her cigarette. "Dr. Prentice cut me off years ago." She threw her head back and stared at me under heavy lids, strands of limp locks falling back to her shoulders. "You're the daughter."

It wasn't a question. Lizzy James knew exactly who I was, because as my mother had noted yesterday, my father didn't hire stupid people. I watched as she walked back into her apartment. Her jeans were snug and traces of a swagger that twenty years ago might have turned a few lab assistants' heads sashayed across the room. She left the door open.

"I read in the paper about that crap he pulled last year." She extended a tobacco-stained finger toward Frank. "I recognize you."

"I'm a cop."

I shot a look at Frank as if to say, *That's the lead I'm following?*

Lizzy James blew smoke out of the side of her mouth, sat back into her couch, and crossed her shapely ankles, the only part of her that didn't appear bloated. She nodded for us to sit. "For the record, I loved that job, and I was really good at it."

I glanced back over my shoulder, eyeing Lizzy's soiled recliner. I held my breath and took the plunge. The chair's springs were loose, sending the slider back a few inches. Lizzy laughed as I pulled myself out of the spongy hole in the seat cushion. "So why did you leave?" I asked as I looked around the room hoping to spot a Sear's family portrait with a child that looked frighteningly like me.

"Dr. Prentice offered me something better," she said, and then corrected herself. "At least, I thought it would be better. Fewer hours, no commute, more money. Turned out the job was temporary."

Frank's wheels were churning. I could see, as his jaw rotated, he wanted to turn the conversation toward Lizzy's personal life and a reference to her children, but Ms. James was moving in a decidedly different direction.

"What was the job?" Frank asked.

Lizzy held her hand out, palm up, requiring Frank to reach into his pocket for a stack of twenties. With the agility of a card dealer, the cash disappeared into Lizzy's cleavage. I had always wanted to do that, jam a roll of bills in between my breasts and actually have it stick. We waited while Lizzy adjusted her blouse.

"Surrogate," she finally said.

I jolted, causing the recliner to roll backward about a half a foot. Had I heard correctly? Because it sounded as if my father had paid this woman to carry my baby. I glanced at Frank to see his Adam's apple bursting from his neck.

"Where's the child?" I asked, grabbing onto an end table for support.

"There is no child," Lizzy said as if I didn't understand the concept of a surrogate as a hired vessel.

"I know what *surrogate* means," I snapped. "Who did you carry the child for?"

"I don't know, but I can tell you they must have been pretty disappointed."

"Why?" Frank asked.

"Because I couldn't carry to term. The baby died at twenty weeks." Lizzy stubbed her cigarette out. "Your asshole of a father fired me. Said I was a bad carrier." She laughed raucously and pointed to the family photo I'd been looking for. Three kids all gussied up for Christmas stared back. "Bad carrier, my ass. Tell that to the rug rats."

Frank stood up without fanfare and walked out. What was the point of staying if there was no baby? Obviously, this wasn't what either of us had expected. As for myself, I'd played this moment over in my head so many times. I had cleverly constructed long and short versions of the Great Baby Reveal. In the long version, a well-meaning woman in mom jeans looks longingly at the baby she'd been raising and then unselfishly hands the infant over to me. In the short version,

I'm hugging the most beautiful baby in the world while Ms. Mom Jeans fades conveniently into the background. Never, in any of my fantasy soap opera moments, did I expect to find out my child hadn't survived to be born. Clearly, neither did Frank. For him, this was his only shot at a relative.

I dug deep into my short pockets. No money, of course; Freegans traveled light when it came to the green stuff. Instead, I snapped off the watch I'd rescued from a Dumpster a few months back. It was one of my better finds, requiring nothing more than some spit polish and a new battery. I handed it to Lizzy.

"I'm going to guess you were just as smart as those lab assistants."

Lizzy's eyes scanned over her squalid apartment. "I deserve this, don't I?"

"Why do you say that?" I asked as I moved from my death-trap recliner to the germ-infested couch.

"Because I'm smart, and I screwed up."

"Was it the drinking and the smoking? Is that why you lost the baby?" *My baby*, I wanted to say.

In an act of selflessness, Lizzy blew her secondhand smoke away from my face although the smell, strangely, was a pleasant relief from the stink of the apartment.

"No, I was completely clean. I wasn't taking the drugs I stole." She laughed at the memory. "I sold them, but your father caught me. He told me he had a better way for me to make money. The problem was that I had lied to get the first job managing the storage room in the lab. I told your father I was twenty-one when I was actually sixteen," she said, shrugging her soft shoulders. "That's why I lost the baby. I couldn't carry because I was too young. Despite what you may think," she said as she ran her hand down her curves, "my body wasn't ready at sixteen."

"You passed for twenty-one at sixteen?" I said in total amazement until I realized that Lizzy James currently passed for a woman in her forties at the ripe old age of thirty-two. I remembered what Jimmy had said earlier in the day about appearances. I had just assumed Liz James was older.

"I really wanted that surrogate thing to work out," she continued, "because your father promised me twice the money for the next baby if I carried well the first time. Apparently, a good first pregnancy is a requirement for surrogates."

You poor woman, I thought, *practically a child when my father sunk his claws into you.* Bright, savvy, healthy, and in need of money. What a find for my father. But like every scientist, he would have to put her to the test before she carried his prized possession—my egg and my brother's sperm. He must have impregnated her with someone else's embryo to test her viability before he risked implanting mine. If Dr. Grovit and Dr. Wilson were correct, Teddy and I had only supplied one fertilized embryo. He had to ensure the surrogate was viable. But Lizzy had failed. That meant the chance someone else had carried my egg still existed.

"Were there other surrogates?" I asked.

Lizzy rose and walked to a cluttered desk. From the bottom drawer, she located a folder and pulled out a wrinkled newspaper. "This is a newsletter from the lab, and this"—she pointed to a group photo on the cover—"is a picture of the lab assistants."

I took the newspaper and stared at the faces. I recognized Dr. Wilson with his red hair, as well as Lizzy. She was quite a looker at sixteen. "This woman," Lizzy said, indicating the woman next to her in the photo. "I don't remember her name, but I think she organized the surrogates."

I looked closely. Yet another woman's face to evaluate, but again, it wasn't anyone I had seen before. No matter. It was still a lead. I headed for the door, down one fancy timepiece but up a valuable clue.

TWENTY-SIX

IN THE FEW MINUTES I had spent alone with Lizzy, Frank had regressed to a full-blown hissy fit. From across the courtyard, I could see the signs of frustration as he circled the car.

"Stop your snuffling. She's not the surrogate," I said as we settled into the Gremlin. "My father had only tested her viability as a surrogate. Had she past the test, then he would have implanted my egg." I handed him the photo. "Lizzy thinks this woman knows something about the other surrogates. We passed a Staples on the way here. I want to fax this photo to my mother and Dr. Wilson."

Frank regained his composure and stepped on the pedal. "Thanks," he said.

———

The red-shirted man at Staples faxed off our photo in a snap while Frank successfully conferenced in Dr. Wilson and my mother. We moved to a quiet aisle in the store and put Frank's phone on speaker.

"Anybody?" I said.

"It's Carolyn Corey," Dr. Wilson said. "She wasn't a lab assistant."

"What was she?" Frank asked.

"Good question," Dr. Wilson said. "I'm not sure why she's in that picture. I just know she worked at the labs."

"Wait," my mother added excitedly. "I think I recognize her."

I clapped my hands and winked at Frank. I loved the new and improved version of my rehabilitated mother.

"I think this woman came to our house the day of your procedure," my mother continued. "It's the freckles. I remember thinking how young she was at the time."

I thought we'd lost the three-way connection as Frank shoved the phone into my hand. Then I realized we were all simply speechless at my mother's recollection.

"I remember," my mother broke the silence, "because this woman thought I was the patient, and yet there I was, with a half bottle of empty Chardonnay in my hand when she arrived. She seemed surprised to find out it was you."

I turned to Frank, who was pounding away at a Staples computer since I still held his phone. "Can we find her?"

"Done," he said. "She's a local obstetrician."

TWENTY-SEVEN

FRANK HANDED ME HIS phone as he started the car. "Dial the guys and put 'em on speaker."

"Hey boss," Lamendola said. "Can you meet us? We got a lead on an auctioneer that might know Bob. He owns a local pawn shop."

I had hoped our next step was Dr. Carolyn Corey, but Bob's murder came first so I didn't bother asking Frank. In reality, there was no urgency. Dr. Corey had no idea we wanted to speak with her and in all likelihood, she'd be doing the same thing tomorrow as she did last week and the week before.

The address of the pawn shop, located in the mid-island town of Commack, wasn't far from the Carmen House apartments and therefore within reach. Commack was famous for two things: Rosie O'Donnell's childhood home and the Commack Motor Inn, a sleazy hotel where teenagers and cheating spouses went to have sex. Besides these places of interest, Commack was a flat slice of Long Island good for farming and strip malls. Unlike the quaint shops of Cold Spring Harbor, Commack's shopping district spilled out for miles.

The pawn shop we were looking for was located on a main thoroughfare across the street from a large chain supermarket. I had a love/hate relationship with superstores, especially the type that sold food. I knew that for every oversized shopping cart stuffed with excessive calories, almost a third of the food would go uneaten and ultimately be trashed. This endless supply of wasted food was a nice supplement to my own shopping budget. Between Harbor House's farm and Dumpster diving at stores like these, my food expenditure was only a few dollars a week. Although I was always thrilled to find a box of cereal past its expiration date, knowing that perfectly good food had been tossed drove me crazy.

While we waited at the intersection, I spotted a mom with three small children maneuvering a top-heavy cart to her car. I was about to shake my finger disapprovingly at her empty calorie haul when Frank grabbed my hand.

"Save your judgment for the auctioneer," he said as we pulled in. "I'm curious to see if this guy is legit. Pawn shops are notorious for attracting shady people."

The store was bookended by the Happy Roses nail salon and a Laundromat. Nail salons. There was another commercial enterprise that made me question humanity. How can you relax when the person pushing your cuticles back is wearing a face mask to avoid inhaling toxic lacquer? I was about to take a jab at the nail place when Frank pointed to the window of the pawn shop. Lamendola and Cheski were at the glass counter trying on watches.

"Thinking about retirement?" Frank asked as we walked in.

"Can't come soon enough," Cheski replied and then added, "The auctioneer's name is Sally, short for Salvatore. He's taking a phone call in the back." Cheski handed Frank a watch to try on while I busied myself with Civil War memorabilia. I inched over to the jewelry

141

and a velvet tray of wedding rings. Strangely enough, I hadn't formed an opinion on weddings. I figured someday I'd make a commitment, and I assumed that when I did, it would be nontraditional. I had never, however, considered the meaning of a ring or the size for that matter. A row of sparkly diamonds smiled brightly at me, and for a split second I felt a twinge of consumerism creep up. For sure, I'd never find a diamond ring at the bottom of a Dumpster ... but hey, you never know.

Sally, the auctioneer, emerged from the back room. I don't know what I expected—maybe a fast-talking southerner with a checkered shirt and a cowboy hat—but it certainly wasn't this auctioneer. Salvatore Riggi was young, maybe early thirties, and dressed in business casual—slacks, a button-down, and no tie. He shook our hands calmly and repeated each of our names at least once and then offered us a seat at a pawned dining room table.

"I know you have some questions about my clients, and I'm happy to help. What do you need?"

"We have a couple of questions about storage default auctions, but first, maybe you could tell us how you came to own the store?" Frank said. By his question, I guessed Frank had been expecting a more seasoned pawn shop owner as well.

"Sure," Sally said, and then he went on to describe his unusual but rather lucrative career path. "I worked here in high school and through college, loading the heavier pieces to and from people's cars. It was grunt work, but I loved the idea that something amazing, a real treasure, could be found in boxes of junk."

My ears were burning while my heart melted. A fellow junk aficionado? I wanted to swipe one of the pawned rings and propose to Sally Riggi on the spot. Instinctively, Frank slid his chair closer to mine. Where had this guy been hiding all my life? Sally went on to explain his decision to major in art and his subsequent graduate degree in appraisals from Sotheby's. And an art major?! Could this get any better?

"At the end of the day, I didn't want to work in a Soho gallery selling overpriced art to overpaid New Yorkers. I wanted to dig for the good stuff. So I got a loan and bought out the owner of this place, who was ready to retire anyway. The auctions help me build a client list. I keep careful track of each bidder's interests and then I develop a one-on-one with the regulars. There's no magic. The key is to cultivate a personal relationship with each client, and as it turns out, I'm pretty good at it."

"When I called earlier," Cheski said, "I asked you about one of your clients. A heavyset guy?"

"Absolutely. Bob, the Outsider Artist. I don't do a lot of business in dolls, but when I stumble upon a cache, I call Bob."

"Have you seen any of his artwork?" I asked.

Sally's eyes lit up. "I was so impressed that I've tried to find him an agent. Actually, I owe him a call." Again, another person in Bob's network that didn't know he had passed.

"So you've been to the HG storage site?" Frank asked.

"Oh yeah. I've done maybe six or seven auctions for them over the years. Bob is always there."

Frank's jaw pounded away, and I knew he was evaluating the extent to which he could trust Sally Riggi. The signs were positive. The store was clean, organized, and professionally run. Sally seemed knowledgeable and forthcoming, and he had no hesitation meeting with us on short notice. We sat in silence for a few seconds until Frank delivered the bad news about Bob.

"Wow," Sally said. "I had no idea. I thought you were here to investigate stolen goods. I was prepared to open my books."

"That's good to know, but what we're looking for now is information about a murder," Frank said. "Is there anything else you can remember about your interactions with Bob?"

Sally opened a folder in front of him and ran his finger down the page. "I don't know if this will help, but recently Bob had been buying old computers. I think maybe he was working on a tech-themed art piece."

"How many computers had he purchased?" Cheski asked.

"What he'll do is wait for another buyer to take a whole unit, and if there's a computer in the unit, he'll buy it piecemeal for maybe twenty bucks. I've seen him buy three or four at a single auction."

"Does everyone know each other at these storage unit auctions?" I asked.

"The regulars know each other. Bob had a couple of buddies on the circuit, and recently his daughter tagged along."

Frank held his hand up to stop us from asking wild questions. "Did he introduce her as his daughter?"

Sally shrugged. "No, I just assumed it was his daughter." And then Sally the auctioneer went on to describe a young woman who sounded an awful lot like the skinny-jeaned woman from the recycling center.

"When was the last time you saw Bob?" Frank asked.

"About a month ago at a storage auction in Queens. His daughter was with him, and now that I think about it, Bob started buying computers at about the time his daughter joined him. Maybe a year ago."

———

We left Sally's pawn shop and headed to a coffee shop at the end of the strip mall.

"Oh my god," I said, reaching out for Frank's arm. "This is incredible. I didn't know Bob had a daughter."

"Actually, we don't know Bob did have a daughter," Cheski replied. "All we know is he's been seen with a young woman, but it's not a given that they're related. We already looked into Bob's background, and there's nothing in the public records that indicate a child."

"In Barbara's absence, who else can we ask?" Lamendola said.

"The fact that CeCe doesn't know," Frank said, "makes me think that Bob was either very private, or it's not his daughter. Most parents make reference to their children in conversation. Cheski's kids are out of college, and he still can't stop talking about them." Frank laughed.

This was true. I knew more about Cheski's extended clan of relatives than I did about my own family. This wasn't saying much since my family stories read like a textbook from a communist bloc country, heavy on the rewrite. But I had to agree with Frank. If Bob had a daughter, it was strange he had never mentioned her, especially since he'd been out and about in public with her.

"Talk to Jimmy tomorrow," Frank instructed. "He might be aware of a relative. And Barbara? She hasn't returned?"

Cheski ordered a bag of donuts and four coffees. I felt badly I didn't have money until I realized that a monetary transaction wasn't about to take place. Cheski's uniform closed the deal for free. Frank groaned and refused his donut and coffee.

"Well, we haven't looked too hard," Cheski said as he poured two packets of sugar in a paper cup. "Lamendola and I were wondering how long we should let it go. Barbara's been AWOL for a week. At what point is this a missing person's case?"

"As of now, we're the only ones missing her," Frank reasoned. "Usually a relative or coworker reports someone missing. The fact that no has come to us leads me to believe she's keeping in touch with the people who would miss her."

"So you don't think it's strange that Bob's wife goes missing with no forwarding address shortly after his death?"

"Cheski," Frank said, "you're a social guy. If you went missing for a few hours, half the town would call in a missing person's report. Remember the overnight stakeout we did at that Wall Street trader's house? You were getting a text every two minutes from family members. On the other hand, if I took a month off, who would come looking for me?"

"I would," I said, slighted that Frank thought he wouldn't be missed.

Frank rubbed my hand and whispered, "You'd be with me." I smiled and Frank continued, "I think Barbara's fine, but at this point we should track down a list of her local friends just to be sure. CeCe, can help you with that task?"

"Sure thing. I'll head over to the food co-op in the morning. Barbara does a rotation there once a month, and I'm sure she's friendly with some of the other volunteers."

"Can I come?" Cheski asked.

I blinked. "To the food co-op?"

"Yeah, I'm getting into it. You know, the alternative food thing."

Cheski's mouth was framed in sugary powder, and he dabbed his finger on his napkin to save the last few slivers of donut flakes. I wasn't sure he was an appropriate candidate for an organic market.

"For real?"

"For real," he said as we tossed our garbage. "I figure if I can cut my monthly spending, I might be able to retire earlier. Maybe I'll become a Freegan."

"As long as you don't cut into my diving territory," I laughed.

TWENTY-EIGHT

CHARLIE STOOD IN THE driveway when Frank and I returned. Without speaking, he handed us each a bandana and then instructed us to blindfold ourselves. Katrina waddled down the driveway and wiped her hands on a jelly-covered apron.

"Oh, go ahead," she said. "You'll love it."

"Does this have anything to do with the case?" Frank grumbled. "I'm not into games."

"It does," Charlie said as he secured the knot at the back of my head and pulled the flap down in the front so I couldn't sneak a peek.

"Where are we going?" I asked. "Are you taking us down to the water?"

"Hush," Charlie said. "There's a step ahead."

"Floor boards? Are we in the barn?" I banged my foot on the ground. "We're in the barn," I whispered to Frank. I heard the barn doors scrape along the gravel driveway as Charlie pulled them shut.

"On three," Charlie said as he snapped his fingers. "Remove your blindfolds."

Katrina shrieked with glee when she saw my delighted face. The entire barn was strung and lit with thousands of Christmas tree lights. In the middle of the off-season holiday extravaganza was a café table with two mismatched chairs, a bottle of wine, cheese, and crackers.

"The table was my idea," Katrina said. "Charlie paid full price for the wine, but I can't tell Frank where we got the crackers and cheese."

I laughed at Frank's expense and spun around the room, enchanted by the festive spirit. "What's the occasion?"

"A scavenger hunt." Charlie pointed to boxes of yet unopened lights. "Copper is at an all-time high," he said as he sliced at a green tangled cord with a pocket knife to reveal a thin line of copper. "Christmas lights contain miles of copper, and they're tops on a scavenger's list. Jimmy is putting a reminder on the flyers to check attics for old lights. This way the scavengers will be expecting to find lights."

"Did you ransack Rockefeller Center?" Frank said, clearly in awe of Charlie's own scavenging.

"Actually, I found a seasonal store still recovering from Hurricane Sandy. The owner had a basement full of damaged lights. The boxes had been soaked during the flood, but it turns out most of the lights are just fine. It's kind of a shame, because the scavengers won't even care if the lights are operational. They'll just cut them down for the copper."

"Very _____," I complimented Charlie. "But I'm not sure how the wine and cheese fits in."

Charlie shuffled awkwardly in place. "Technically, there's no connection, but Katrina got all hormonal on me when I tested the lights and before I knew it, the barn was strung."

"In the spirit of Freeganism," Katrina said, "it seemed wasteful to toss the lights in a few days without one last hurrah. So we decided that since it's almost the anniversary of Teddy's death, it might be better to honor his passing by celebrating you two meeting each other instead."

My hand rose to my chest as I recognized a crushingly bittersweet but tender moment. My earlier conversation with Charlie about Frank and Teddy must have had an impact, because it was obvious that he and Katrina wanted my relationship with Frank to work out.

"It was all Trina's idea," Charlie said as he and Katrina politely headed for the door. "Unplug the lights when you leave. I don't trust a hundred-year-old barn with these lights."

"Sure thing," Frank said. "And thanks."

TWENTY-NINE

I POURED US A second glass of wine and insisted Frank eat a few crackers. "They're totally fresh," I said as I happily crunched away. "So what do you think about this Corey lady?"

Frank reluctantly took a handful of crackers, but he politely avoided the cheese. "She'll know something. The problem is now she's in private practice, and I don't imagine she'll want to jeopardize her career by dredging up a questionable event from the past. It might be hard to get her to talk."

"Do you have a plan? We got pretty lucky with Lizzy James," I said. "I don't think a roll of twenties is going to cut it this time."

Frank pulled out his phone, dialed Dr. Grovit, and punched the button for speaker. As expected, Dr. Grovit's voice was preceded by the crinkle of papers. "Dr. Grovit here," he finally answered. Frank wasted no time introducing Dr. Grovit to our latest discovery—Dr. Corey.

"Did you know her?"

"I can't say I did. At any one point in time, the labs employ hundreds of people. William kept his pet projects and those involved close to the vest. If she's an obstetrician now, she must have had an

150

early interest in the field. Working with William on reproduction would have made sense."

"I wonder if she was recruited specifically for the study," I said. "It increases the odds she was aware of my father's relationship with Lifely."

We listened as Dr. Grovit clacked away at his computer. "I'm on the World Wide Web now, and I'm looking at her practice's website." Frank smiled at Dr. Grovit's outdated reference to the Internet. "She's got three partners and a swank address in Northport in a new medical building on the water." Dr. Grovit sighed sadly and then added, "The practice doesn't take insurance."

"I've never heard of that," Frank said, leaning into the phone.

"It's called boutique medicine," Dr. Grovit bemoaned. "I'm not a big fan, but it's the result of the country's recent move toward a more socialized medical system. The reimbursement fees to doctors are embarrassingly low and frankly, that doesn't work for doctors. The new medical model is to offer a narrow specialty to a select group of patients willing to pay out-of-pocket for individualized attention. From what I'm reading here, this practice handles only high-risk pregnancies for patients willing to pay the whole bill out-of-pocket. I'm guessing these doctors deliver ten babies a month, making them millionaires in a few years. Since most high-risk births are by cesarean, the doctor is almost never on call, which eliminates the worst part of the obstetric profession."

I thought about Katrina's midwife, Vicky. An overworked woman in her fifties juggling dozens of patients at a time and expecting no more pay than a few cases of homemade jelly. I wondered when the poor lady slept. "There's got to be an angle to get to Dr. Corey," I said.

Frank, who also felt the frustration, started to pace the barn.

"I don't think you're going to have any luck with this woman," Dr. Grovit said. "Her focus is making money, not making amends for something she may have done in the past."

"I read recently that New York State is looking into regulating the sperm bank industry," Frank said, fingering a bucket of unpackaged Christmas lights. "Is that true?"

Dr. Grovit hesitated. "Well, yes. There are real issues related to the unregulated sale of reproductive material over the last twenty years. But as I said, if this doctor isn't even taking insurance, I don't think she'll be concerned about her early role in the industry working at the Sound View labs."

"How so?" I asked.

"Think of it this way. A single semen sample could repopulate the world." Dr. Grovit laughed at the enormity of his statement. "Apocalyptic theories be damned. All you need are a few hundred people who are smart enough to avoid their first cousins and presto, you've got instant civilization. Strangely enough, even well-meaning sperm banks that understand how productive a single sample of sperm could be, never controlled for the distribution of the samples collected. That's why the product of purchased sperm, either a baby boy or a girl, could now have more than fifty siblings. The end result is so out of control, this Dr. Corey couldn't do anything about it now even if she wanted to. I think your best bet is to leave it alone."

Frank circled back to our café table and took a sip of wine. "But now this has become a modern medical problem for these children, hasn't it?"

"Indeed it has," Dr. Grovit said. "But again, I'm not sure how this information will get Dr. Corey to tell you about CeCe's egg."

Frank rubbed his face and leaned into the phone. "How about this: If a woman purchased sperm from a local bank, she likely lived near the bank, just like all the other purchasers. Assuming the recipients stayed in the area, their children are now of reproductive age themselves and could, in fact, be attending the prom unwittingly with their half sibling."

"Eww," I said.

"Weird, but also scary," Frank added. "The lack of regulation has now become a public health risk."

"A public scare. That's an interesting angle. You might be able to reach Dr. Corey's conscience with that argument," Dr. Grovit said. "But it's a stretch."

Frank grunted. He wasn't ready to give up. "How does a legitimate sperm bank account for the distribution of sperm to recipients?"

"Legitimate sperm banks gave sperm samples identification numbers. Now those ID numbers, as you said, have become very important to the grown children actively seeking out siblings from the same batch of sperm."

Frank thanked Dr. Grovit and hung up. "He's skeptical. I need someone who's motivated personally to help me form this argument." Frank picked up the phone, placed another call, and asked to be connected to Dr. Wilson, the doctor whose own sperm had been sent to Lifely simply because he had worked in my father's lab. Frank repeated his theory that untracked sperm posed a health risk in areas local to the banks themselves.

"I think it's perfectly believable to say the police department is working in conjunction with ..." Dr. Wilson paused while he thought of a credible cover for Frank. "Tell Dr. Corey you are working with the New York State Centers for Disease Control in an attempt to track and catalog unnumbered sperm to prevent the spread of genetic diseases."

"Wow," I exclaimed. "That works. It's totally believable."

"Let's not get ahead of ourselves," Frank countered. "I'm sure Dr. Corey is no dummy, and I still think it will be hard to get her to talk."

"If you don't want to raise suspicion, try this," Dr. Wilson proposed. "Tell Dr. Corey the Lifely case is closed, and those involved have already been punished, which is true. To take the heat off, she'll need to believe this effort is a follow-up to a public health issue with no existing criminal implications. But to put the pressure on, Frank should show up on a Tuesday, after lunch."

Frank raised his eyebrows. "Why Tuesday?"

"Doctors' offices are typically closed on Wednesdays, so appointments will be stacked tightly on Tuesdays. The doctors will also be squeezing in emergencies before the day off. Most pregnant woman panic when they know their doctors' office is going to be closed, so the phones will be buzzing. If the appointments are backed up—and they always are—the waiting room will be full by the afternoon."

"And a high-end boutique practice doesn't need a detective flashing a badge in a room full of pregnant woman," Frank finished.

I nodded at Frank. "It's Saturday; will you have time on Tuesday?" Frank looked around the well-lit barn. The scavenger hunt was scheduled for Thursday, and Charlie and Jimmy were about halfway through organizing the equipment. From what I could gather, Frank still hadn't finished the route's surveillance points.

"There's still a lot to do, but I feel like I need to make time for this," Frank said, and then he ended the phone call with Dr. Wilson. He came back to the table, sat down, and took another sip of wine.

"Tuesday it is," Frank said.

"This is crazy." I leaned in to kiss Frank. "I think we might actually find this baby."

"Don't go buying a car seat anytime soon."

154

"Given the kid's age by now, I'll be buying video games or a cell phone," I said, and then I took Frank's hand, "Admit it, you were pretty upset when you thought Lizzy James had lost the baby."

"I was," he confessed. "Losing the baby just wasn't a scenario I had considered. I don't want to disappoint you, but I've been betting on the fact that there *is* no baby, simply because there were so many junctures where your father's plan could have fallen apart."

"And what do you think now?"

Frank poured us another glass of wine. "The idea that your father tested Lizzy James as a surrogate for a more important delivery is troublesome. It lends credibility to your father's long-term plan. Before we met Lizzy James, we only knew part one of your father's plan: the retrieval of genetic material. Now, we know he had been testing surrogates."

Frank's acceptance of something I had taken as fact enticed me. I leaned in and kissed him again, this time passionately. He pulled back and raised his head toward the barn's roof.

"I don't suppose this place has a hayloft …?"

I wiped cracker crumbs from my lips and moved closer to Frank. The room was warm and twinkly, and I watched Frank's steady hand as he reached for his wine. I wasn't feeling all that steady myself as we clinked glasses. Frank returned my kiss, an experience heightened by the wine and sparkling lights. It was a long, deep kiss causing a sensation so heady, I thought for a moment I was passing out until I realized Frank had led me to the barn floor. Like a magician, Frank yanked the embroidered cloth off the café table to cover the wide wood planks.

"How resourcefully Freegan," I whispered as Frank kissed my ear. I melted. *Please don't stop.*

At that exact moment, Frank hesitated. He reached around to the back of his waistband. *His gun. He's about to remove his gun.* That seemed logical, but in our deep embrace, I didn't feel the telltale bulge at his back. I could feel a bulge, but I was certain that wasn't a gun.

A condom. Of course. As I leaned backwards and inched my way to a fully reclined position, my hand scraped along the pine floor. The nick on my finger I had earned free-falling into a mound of garbage reopened. I ignored the sting, but it reminded me of the great dig for Bob. My thoughts drifted to Bob and then to the woman with black bobbed hair.

"CeCe." Frank stopped midkiss. "You have to turn your brain off for at least five minutes."

"I can do that," I said as my chest heaved up and down. I grabbed at Frank's shirt collar and drew him closer. Then I closed my eyes and stared at the back of my eyelids as the remnants of Christmas lights played across my darkened vision. *Let it be,* I thought. *Let go.*

And I did.

THIRTY
SUNDAY, APRIL 27

CHESKI PICKED ME UP at nine in the morning for our culinary field trip. "You get how this works?" I asked.

"You gotta do the hours to shop at the co-op."

"Yup. To keep the prices down, individual members take turns working at the market. It's different for us. We sell our excess farm yield at super-low prices to the market and that gets us a membership. There's just so much you can freeze or can, and there's no way we'd dump it. As long as it's got a forty-eight-hour shelf life, the co-op will take it."

"How many hours would I need to work?"

"It's proportional to the volume of your purchases."

Cheski's face dropped; his eating habits could require him to work a sixty-hour week.

"I'm joking! Usually, it's no more than a few hours a month. The co-op has thousands of members."

Cheski's phone rang, and I answered it for him. Lamendola was on the line, jabbering at rapper speed.

"Are you kidding?" I said into the phone. Cheski poked me in the arm for information. "He was up all night going through the list of accounts Harry Goldberg finally found the time to send," I relayed. "Turns out Bob had a unit at HG storage. Unit 125."

Cheski slammed on the brakes and swung the car around. "Get Frank on the phone."

THIRTY-ONE

UNIT 125. EACH TIME Frank mentioned the number of Bob's storage unit, it took on the mysterious allure of Area 51, the Bermuda Triangle, or the grassy knoll.

We met Harry Goldberg outside unit 125. It was almost noon. Harry had a ring of keys jangling from a pair of ironed, designer jeans. A crisp crease ran down both legs. Now that I'd learned my own jeans were dreadfully out of style, I had a bit more sympathy for other people's denim dilemmas. Harry's pressed jeans, cut high on his hips, were as outdated as my own.

Frank wasn't focused on Harry's jeans. "This was information we needed to know last week," he spit at Harry.

"Give me a break," Harry sniped. "I have thousands of renters. How the hell was I supposed to know the guy that died was a renter?"

"How? Because we told you his name," Frank replied in disgust. "Just clip it."

Harry opened the arms of a bolt cutter and clamped down on Bob's lock. Frank pushed Harry aside and removed the remaining metal pieces and lifted the door.

"Hmmm," I said as I peered into the storage unit. "I guess I'm not surprised."

The interior of the unit was devoted to a single diorama, but instead of being constrained to the size of a shoebox, this scenario flowed over the entirety of the space save for one corner in the back for Bob's workbench.

"Mother of God," Harry said, shaking his head at the contents of Bob's storage unit. "I gotta get out of this business," he said, leaving Frank, Cheski, and me alone.

The unit was staged like a scene from a Tim Burton film. Bob had built an impossibly jagged mountain range that came up about waist high in the center of the unit. Teetering on the mountain's only plateau was a long narrow dining table covered with pounds of carefully sculpted food. Having seen Bob's work before, it was clear he wanted the viewer to feel a sense of overabundance. Piles of turkey legs sat next to towering chocolate cakes and bubbling mugs of an unidentifiable frothy mixture.

"This is getting weirder by the minute," Frank said. "What's with these people at the table?" The figures, or rather dolls, seated around the table were about a foot high. It looked like Bob had repurposed the dolls by interchanging their body parts. The effect was ghoulish, an odd gathering of misfits with strange deformities. It wasn't hard to notice that if the diners moved their chairs back an inch, they'd plummet down the side of the mountain. The only thing that saved the bizarre dinner party were the faces of the dolls. They appeared to be radiantly happy.

Frank narrowed in on a figure seated in the middle of the table. The miniature man, cloaked in a velvet cape, had his arms stretched out on the table with his head tilted to the side. The other diners, deep in conversation with each other, seemed to be ignoring him yet aware of his presence. Frank circled the table from every vantage point.

"This guy," he said as he identified another man-doll seated at the far end of the table. "I don't like him."

"Me neither," Cheski said.

"I'm guessing Bob doesn't want you to like him," I said. "Let's take some pictures. There's too much going on here to see it all in one viewing. Plus I'm getting the heebie-jeebies."

Just as I mentioned my skin crawling, a low, flat groan filled the storage unit.

"Perfect timing," Frank said with a smile. "The tuba lady has arrived."

Frank instructed Cheski to finish photographing Bob's storage unit as we headed in the direction of the music.

———

In the way a dog owner can resemble their pet, the tuba lady looked like her bulbous brass instrument. I guess if the goal is to force air through a centimeter-sized hole while balancing a twenty-five-pound hunk of metal between your thighs, you've got to have some heft to pull it off.

Frank waved to the tuba lady who was midstream in what sounded like the longest middle C in history. But who was I to judge? I couldn't even play the kazoo.

"Impressive," Frank said when she came up for air. "I'm Frank DeRosa. I work for the Cold Spring Harbor Police Department, and this is CeCe Prentice."

"What's your vice?" she asked Frank. "You look like a train guy to me, maybe Lionel?"

"Actually, I was into Bachmann N scale as a kid," Frank said as he shook her hand. "I'm not a renter. Unfortunately, I'm here investigating a murder."

"Is it Goldberg?" the tuba lady inquired as she rolled her instrument aside. "I'm hoping it's Goldberg."

Frank couldn't suppress his smirk. "Mr. Goldberg is just fine and nothing dangerous has occurred on the premise. However, our investigation has led us here. Mr. Goldberg mentioned you use your unit quite a lot and that you play with your unit door open. I was hoping you could tell us what goes on at the storage facility."

"Heats up faster than a South American mambo contest if I shut the door."

I considered the size of the unit, the size of the tuba, and the size of the tuba player and realized there was little room left for air circulation given the combination of space and mass. Door open seemed to be the only solution.

The tuba lady gave us a quick rundown of her "hood" as she called it. Bob, no surprise, was one of her best buds. Frank didn't tell her about Bob's death and as her admiration of Bob's talents escalated, I could see it was becoming increasingly difficult for Frank to break the news.

"Did you ever see Bob with a young woman? A woman with short black hair?"

The tuba lady shook her head. "No, never saw him with anyone, but this isn't his first unit. Originally, he was two blocks over. He moved here about a year ago," she said, laughing. "He says the view is better— as if a row of rusty metal doors was something to look at. I thought maybe he was flirting with me," she guffawed. "Some of these guys, you know, they're chubby chasers."

At the mention of a better view, Frank pivoted in place. From Bob's unit there was a clear shot of the warehouse. Frank pointed in that direction.

"Have you ever seen activity at the warehouse?"

The tuba lady nodded. "Big commotion recently. I couldn't hear myself play, and I'm damn loud."

"Was it the Groundsweep walkers?" Frank asked.

"Huh?"

"Were you aware that the warehouse was leaking toxins?"

"No, but then I guess the noise was worth it, because it took the movers three hours to empty the place."

Frank, a master of self-control, was visibly excited. "What did you see?"

"Nothing special." The tuba lady seemed surprised. "People move out of this place all the time."

Frank started up his iPad and walked into the tuba lady's unit. "Do you mind if I sit?" he said, pulling up an extra chair. "Were you aware of Bob's day job?"

"Sure," the tuba lady said. "He runs the recycling center."

"I guess we need to tell you that Bob died last week. It's possible he was murdered."

The tuba lady emitted a low note that sounded an awful lot like her instrument in need of tuning. I entered the unit and placed my hand on her soft shoulder.

"I'm sorry," I said as she sobbed quietly.

"We think there's a connection between the warehouse and Bob," Frank said. "It would be helpful if you could tell us what you saw."

She inhaled deeply. "There were two moving trucks. About an hour after the trucks arrived, a third showed up. That's when I left."

"Did you catch the name of the moving company?" Frank asked.

She shook her head. "It looked Chinese to me."

"Are you sure?" I asked.

"Trust me. I eat a lot of Chinese takeout."

Frank nodded as he jotted down the first of what could be an important clue. "Do you remember anyone in particular from that day?"

"Just Goldberg," the tuba lady said. "I called the office to complain about the noise, and he picked up."

———

Frank slammed the door of Bob's unit with such force I feared the cheerful dolls balanced in their chairs would tumble down the side of the papier-mâché mountain.

"I don't get it," I said. "Can't you lock Goldberg up?"

"For what?" Frank said. "Answering the phone at his place of business?"

"How about obstructing justice? He lied about Bob's unit, and he lied about the warehouse."

Frank's face cracked, and he started to laugh. "From sketch artist to rookie cop in less than a week."

"I'm just trying to help," I said as I threw my hands up in the air. "Why don't you give me something to keep me busy? How about something to sketch?"

Frank looked at me, and I could see he was thinking but not ready to speak. Instead, he fished around in a plastic bag, retrieving a new lock to replace the one Goldberg had clipped. He unwrapped the plastic covering, fiddled with the combination, and resecured the unit. Then he took a quick lap up and down the row while I stood in place and listened to the bellowing and, now, mournful moans of a tuba.

"Cheski's photo of Cheryl Goldberg," he said when he returned. "Can you draw a picture of Cheryl and make it look as if Katrina had gotten a good look at her and actually described her to you?"

"You want it close, but not exact."

"Yeah, can you do that?"

"Of course."

"Good," Frank said happily. "Because we're going to catch Goldberg in a lie. I'll drop you at home and give you a few hours."

THIRTY-TWO

My mother, on Sunday furlough, thanks to Dr. Grovit's persuasive use of medical jargon, rested comfortably on my attic futon. Katrina lay next to her, a human beach ball with limbs.

"How much is this going to hurt?"

My mother shrugged. "I opted for pain medication, before, during, and after."

"Yeah, like twenty years after," I laughed.

Katrina grimaced and rubbed her stomach. I could see that her present level of discomfort had weakened her resolve. "If it gets bad, I might consider taking something."

"I know this is going to be a home birth," I said as I tweaked the finishing touches on Cheryl Goldberg's nose, "but have you decided on the room?"

"The kitchen," Katrina replied.

"Nice, Trina." I nodded. "You really don't want Frank to ever enjoy a meal here, do you?" I brought my completed drawing and the Facebook picture over to the futon for comments. "Drawing first," I said as I held up my pad. I let Katrina and my mother eyeball a charcoal of

166

Harry Goldberg's girlfriend/David Goldberg's wife for a full minute. I had drawn Cheryl looking positively sultry, which I knew would get a rise out of Goldberg. Her scarf and sunglasses gave her image a Marilyn Monroe effect, as if she were hiding from the press. "Now, her actual picture." I revealed the Facebook photo Cheski had secured.

"The hair is different," Katrina noticed. "It's not as poufy."

"Cheski and Lamendola did a drive-by yesterday. Based on their description, her in-person look is not as dramatic as her Facebook glam shot."

Katrina propped herself up on her elbows. "So that guy I met at the storage place, he's having an affair with this woman? This is the lady I thought broke in?"

"Yeah, it's his cousin's wife," I confirmed. "You wasted a jelly sandwich on that loser."

"What a sleazeball," Katrina said, grabbing the slanted wall for support to reach a full sitting position. "And the day we saw him dancing around the warehouse, that was a total lie?"

"Can you believe it?" I said. "It was an act. He knew the warehouse was empty, and we think he knew Bob was dead too."

"Why didn't he just say so?" My mother was stating the obvious. It was a good question, and one we'd all been wrestling with since the tuba lady had tipped us off to Harry.

"If Harry was actually stuck with the e-waste as a result of the green washing scam," I explained, "then, unfortunately, he'd have to get rid of it under careful EPA supervision. That would cost him a mint."

"Isn't the disposal of a storage unit's contents the responsibility of the renter?" Katrina asked.

"If he could find the warehouse's renter, I'm sure he'd sue the renter for the cleanup. But, based on Frank's investigation, the company that rented the unit was bogus from the start." I gave my mother and Katrina the low-down on green washing, an eco-un-friendly scam. "I think it was cheaper for Harry Goldberg to pay to have it illegally removed and then feign surprise when the e-waste had mysteriously disappeared from the warehouse." I handed the drawing to my mother.

"It's good, honey," she said, reaching into her pocketbook, "but this is the woman I'm really interested in." She unfolded the dated newsletter of Dr. Carolyn Corey. "I guarantee this woman was at our house after your procedure."

I frowned. "I'm starting to lose track," I said, referring to the ever-increasing number of female faces we were juggling. Between Lizzy James, Carolyn Corey, Bob's maybe daughter, the skinny jeans lady, and Cheryl Goldberg, I was on visual overload.

I took the picture from my mother and studied Dr. Carolyn Corey. She seemed pleasant enough in the photo, and I noticed she had her arm around Lizzy James. For an office photo, the pose seemed somewhat personal. Were Lizzy and Carolyn friends? They appeared to be an unlikely pair, yet there they were, arm in arm. If it was Carolyn's job to manage the surrogates, then there must have been a certain level of intimacy in their relationship, although Lizzy James didn't let on to that when we met her. Was it possible Carolyn Corey felt badly for Lizzy, or was she more like my father, an opportunist on the lookout for an available and hopefully healthy uterus?

I was about to quiz my mother on Carolyn Corey's visit when Frank entered the attic. I loved seeing Frank in my attic studio, because he always appeared impossibly out of place. He wasn't artsy, so my canvases and supplies held no interest for him. And then there was his stature; he was too physically large for the space. Given the present company of a pregnant woman and his girlfriend's mother, he must have had a good reason for making the pilgrimage to my attic workspace. Especially on a Sunday, one of the few days he actually took off.

"I've been staring at this picture of Bob's diorama all morning, and I'm coming up dry," he said. "It needs an artist's interpretation." He handed his iPad to my mother, who held it at arm's length and squinted her eyes.

"So this piece wasn't with his others?" my mother asked thoughtfully.

"It's currently in a storage unit," Frank said. "Bob has a studio at his house that appears to be his main work area. There are easily eight dioramas at his home studio."

"Is there room for one more at his home studio?" my mother asked as she scrutinized the photo.

"This piece"—Frank pointed to the picture—"is pretty big, but I'm guessing he could have made space at home."

"What are you getting at, Mom?"

My mother placed the photo on her lap and addressed Frank. "When CeCe's father and I started to have problems, I painted the most godawful canvases with painfully transparent messages. I was a one-trick pony, churning out paintings of a screaming woman with her hair on fire." My mother posed for us by running her fingers through to the ends of her hair and stretching her mouth. "Unlike a diary, a piece of art isn't so easy to shove in a drawer, so I hid them in the basement boiler room." She laughed at her own expense. "They're probably still there."

"Do you think Bob hid this diorama from Barbara?" I asked

"I don't know," she said as she brushed her hair back into place. "Maybe he just ran out of room? Regardless, I do think the change of venue is odd. Usually an artist gets in a groove in a certain locale."

She moved her hand across my workspace to prove her point. My attic was my sanctuary. It's where it all happened.

Frank nodded. "It's a very good point, Mrs. Prentice. I wondered why Bob would lay down hard cash for the extra space. It seems out of character for a Freegan opposed to spending money, but if he really needed privacy, this may have been his only option."

I pulled up an artist's stool for Frank and cracked the window. In seconds, the room filled with salty breezes moving south off Long Island Sound. I glanced at the farm below, knowing full well we were completely behind schedule. Up until this year, Katrina, her boyfriend Jonathan, and Charlie and I had been able to maintain the rows of vegetables and fruits entirely on our own. Jonathan's decision to return to medical school, Katrina's upcoming birth, and my relationship with Frank had left the fields sadly underfarmed over the last few months.

During the winter, Charlie and I had built a portable greenhouse out of recycled plastic tarp and PVC piping. At one hundred pounds, the eight-by-ten-foot house could be lifted by two people and rotated over in-ground crops to extend the growing season. We were testing sweet potatoes this year, which required the painstaking process of cultivating slips, or shoots from existing potatoes. The leggy shoots, soaking in water, should have been in the ground and under the protective sheath of the new greenhouse a week ago. If we let the farm go any longer, we'd be fully dependent on Dumpster diving, a total turnoff to Frank. Worse, I'd have to get a job to generate cash for the basics, like food.

My mother studied the diorama. She pulled it close to her face and then slid it back like the arm of a trombone. I heard her counting. Then she asked Frank to advance the frames so she could look at more photos from different angles. Again, she counted.

"It's *The Last Supper*," she said matter-of-factly. "At least I think it's Bob's version of *The Last Supper*."

My mother's revelation was enough motivation for Katrina to sit up again. She grabbed the iPad and counted out loud. "She's right. There are twelve people in this picture, plus this one guy who seems to be the focal point."

My mother laid her finger on the man in the velvet cape. "See how his arms are stretched open on the table, and he's staring into the distance. Now, look at the other twelve people. They all seem to be in clustered discussions, except for this man here."

We crowded around Frank's iPad. Frank used the tips of his fingers to enlarge Bob's rendering of the unknown man. Close up, his face had been sculpted in a wry, almost shit-eating grin. It reminded me of a chess player uttering the fatal word: *checkmate.*

Frank poked at the photo. "He's got some pounds on him."

"Damn," I said. "What if he's the doughy man? What if he's Bob's betrayer, and Bob knew it?"

Frank panned over to the man in the velvet cape, his palms pointing to heaven. He narrowed in on the figure's exposed arms, but the photo blurred. "If the one in the cape is Bob, then maybe the other people in the picture are real too. I wonder how close Bob came to depicting their actual features."

"I feel like Bob wanted this diorama discovered," I said. "I feel like there are answers in this piece of art."

Frank stood up too quickly and beaned his head on the tilted ceiling. He pointed to Katrina. "Please don't have this baby in the next few days. Give me another week of CeCe's undivided attention." Then he turned to my mother. "Are you free for an afternoon of culture?"

My mother smiled at her newfound freedom. "Let's go."

THIRTY-THREE

SUNDAY AFTERNOON AT THE storage facility turned out to be a circus side show. The tuba lady honked away at an endless tribute to John Philip Sousa while a body builder with skin-splitting muscles pumped iron in a unit only slightly larger than his shoulder span.

"He seems fit," I said as the rippled man bounced a medicine ball against his unit's metal interior. For his neighbor's sake, I hoped grandma's china wasn't in a box against the shared wall.

Frank smirked. "Sure, now your vision returns."

"I never said I was blind."

We walked down the storage row and watched as a half dozen renters puttered about their units, shoving cardboard boxes into the airless spaces. My mother, a snob at heart, tilted her nose so high I thought she might flip over backward. This was not her idea of an adventure.

"It's like a trailer park without running water," she commented. "How long will this take? Norma is taking me shopping later."

Frank fiddled with the lock on unit 125. A wad of stale air seeped out when the unit opened. My mother, desperate to cut the visit short, walked up to Bob's diorama, grabbed a figure off its chair, and turned it over.

"Mom," I yelled. "What are you doing?"

"Maybe Bob labeled the dolls."

Frank moved quickly to the table following my mother's lead. It seemed sacrilegious to dismantle Bob's art, but at the end of the day, Bob was dead. If his art contained clues, then he'd left them for a reason.

Frank picked up a young girl with long braids who looked to be about twelve. He tilted the little girl to the floor and looked at the bottom of her feet. "T. First initial?" Frank pondered.

My mother picked up the man with the cape. "No letter," she said. "Makes sense if this one is Bob. He wouldn't need to label himself."

I leaned over Bob's shoulder and pointed to the braided girl's chair. "Look, her chair also has a T on it. That's probably how he coded the layout."

Frank took out his iPad and started snapping pics of the figurines' faces, feet, and chairs. Sure enough, each doll had a single letter on their foot that corresponded to the one on their chair. I looked carefully at each of the dolls. None looked like the woman with black hair and skinny jeans.

Frank lifted the doughy man. "If we're right about the first letter corresponding to the person's name, then this guy's name starts with an L."

I stared closely at the doughy man's face. "He bothers me," I said. His face, no bigger than a half dollar, was unlikable. "In the photo he appeared to be gloating, but now that I'm looking at him, he seems weak."

My mother sidled up to us. "It's his mouth. Look how chin is set back into his face. It's crumbling, like a baby's shivering lip."

I nodded. "Let's put him back in his seat and see what his body language says."

Frank placed the doughy man back in his assigned chair. Unlike some of the other dolls, whose legs were casually crossed or stretched, this man's feet were planted firmly on the floor. His left hand, hidden under the tablecloth, was balled in a fist.

"What do you think, Mom?"

"I feel like I'm stating the obvious, but if Bob placed this man at the table, it means he was part of Bob's inner circle, and all of these people were Bob's followers."

Frank lapped the table. "If they followed Bob that means they all had something in common."

"Garbage?" I said, but it didn't sound convincing. "I don't see a little girl or the doughy man Dumpster diving. Also, we know that Bob was connected to the skinny jeans lady, but there's no one at the table with short black hair."

I stepped outside the metal box for some fresh air and an unobstructed view of the warehouse.

"Hey, Charlie's here," I said. "Let's take a break."

We walked over to the warehouse accompanied by the tuba lady's music. I felt an urge to swing my legs and march in formation. My mother rolled her eyes and jabbed at her watch.

"Soon," I whispered.

"Hey," Charlie said, giving my mother a peck on the cheek. "This is a nice surprise." Charlie's flattery provided just enough attention to buy a few more minutes from my mother. "Frank, I'm glad you're here. There's something I want to show you."

"Did you find something?"

"Maybe," Charlie said as he started to unscrew a panel on one of the computers. "You know how we're using the extra computers from

174

the warehouse and the bin at the recycling center to beef up the scavenger hunt?"

Frank nodded. "I'm assuming you've been cherry picking the pieces most valuable to the scavengers."

"I have," Charlie started, "but I'm noticing something different between the two sets of computers. I'm not sure if it's relevant."

"Let's hear it," I said.

"Well, to pick the best computers for the scavengers, I had to pop the backs off to make sure they hadn't been stripped. I'll show you." Charlie started to unscrew and remove components from a computer.

"I'm guessing these warehouse computers were already stripped for the good stuff," Frank said. "It would make sense given the miraculous disappearance of the waste. Someone must have considered the computers valuable."

"Right? That's what I thought. Except the warehouse computers are completely intact." Charlie pointed to the interior of the computer he had just dismantled. It could have been filled with parts from a Mr. Coffee machine for all I knew about computers.

"See?" he said.

We all shook our heads. We were lost.

"These computers," Charlie said patiently as he pointed to various pieces of plastic and metal with a small screwdriver, "have all the parts needed to run. If we plugged them in, they'd probably be usable. However, the computers from the recycling center were all missing their C drives."

"Well, then I guess they'd been picked through," I said.

Charlie shook his head. "If you're interested in recycling the parts of a computer, you go for the motherboard. That's the electrical panel that connects the computer's devices, and it's the part with the most amount of copper wire. The C drive is useless to a scavenger."

"So someone opened the back on all of the computers at the recycling center and pulled out the C drive, but left the motherboards?" Frank confirmed.

"That's correct."

"I can't stand it any longer," my mother whined. "What's a sea drive?"

"A leisurely car ride along the coast." Charlie laughed at his own joke.

My mother pouted.

"The C drive," Charlie said, making a C shape with his hand, "is the computer's main storage device. When you hit Save, that's where the information goes, like a virtual file cabinet."

"Okay," Frank said slowly. "Isn't it recommended that an owner remove the main storage device before recycling so their personal information is not compromised?"

"Sure," Charlie replied. "But no one ever does it. It's the same thing with shredders. Shredding machines sell like hotcakes, but I'll bet half are still in their boxes while people stupidly load their garbage pails with everything from their bank account numbers to their credit card statements. That's why the missing drives caught my attention. I went through seventy computers from the recycling center and every single one was missing a C drive. That's not typical. People are lazy. I thought maybe Bob removed the drives to protect the users, but then where did the C drives go?"

"Did you ask Jimmy?" Frank said.

"I did, but he didn't know anything about it."

I remembered Bob's tool kit, the one Jimmy had retrieved from the garbage heap. Was Bob removing the C drives from the recycling bin? And if so, why?

Frank nodded his head a few more times and then said, "So I show up at the recycling center with a computer. I hand it over to Bob, and because I'm not a techie, Bob volunteers to remove my C drive and then hands it to me for safekeeping. I go home with the C drive."

My mother raised her hand. "May I?"

"Be my guest," Frank replied. "Maybe someone with absolutely no computer knowledge can explain this."

"People don't leave a recycling center with garbage," my mother said. "Only my daughter takes stuff home. For the rest of us, the whole point is to leave the garbage at the recycling center. I'd be furious is someone handed me back a hunk of useless metal and told me to take it home after I'd gone out of my way to dispose of it properly. Not that I'd actually go to a recycling center, but you get the idea."

I smiled at my mother. It was amazing how logical she could be when she wasn't looped.

"Maybe Bob smashed them," I suggested. "I thought you were supposed to take a hammer to your drives."

"You can," Charlie replied. "And some people do, literally, smash them, but don't you think Jimmy would remember Bob taking a sledge hammer to a bunch of computer components? Plus you have to clean up the crushed pieces, or it just makes more garbage."

"Jimmy said that nonprofits picked through the computers bins for secondhand use."

"Well, if they did," Charlie said, "they'd be lugging back a useless shell, because none of Bob's computers had C drives."

Frank rubbed his face so hard I could hear the stubble on his cheeks scratching the palms of his hands. "Ten years ago I would have immediately accused Bob of involvement in an identity theft scam, but I'm fairly confident that's not the case."

"How do you know?" Charlie asked.

"Because nowadays, people are more aware of identity theft. If there was a localized uptick in identity theft, the police department would know by now."

"Shouldn't we confirm with the people who dropped off their computers?" I said. "We've got Bob's receipt pad."

Frank's eyes slid to mine. "That we do," he said as he lifted his phone.

THIRTY-FOUR

WE RETURNED MY MOTHER home in time for her and Norma to do some serious damage at the stores in town. It was a beautiful afternoon for window shopping, and a beautiful day for a stroll. Although I had spent most of my life embarrassed at my parents' wealth, I couldn't hide my love for the grounds of the Prentice estate, especially enticing in the spring.

"How about a walk?" I asked Frank. "It'll clear our heads."

Frank took my hand, and we headed to the back of the house. A lovely stone patio surrounding an intricately tiled pool showcased the well-groomed yard. About half an acre of perfectly manicured grass stretched north to the Long Island Sound and ended in a densely wooded area with miles of horse trails connecting to the next estate.

"Come on. I'll show you where I used to hang out to plot my escape from the Prentice prison."

"Some escape. You ended up a few miles from your parents' house."

"Pretty lame, huh?" I admitted as I led Frank toward the trails. We chatted for about twenty minutes along a winding path until we came to an enclave of pine trees. Years of fallen needles covered the ground like a carpet. In the middle of the area was a circle of tree stumps and the remnants of a fort built from reclaimed plywood.

"A witch's coven?"

"Not quite," I said as I sat down on the stump I had always considered mine. Teddy, Charlie, and I each had our own chunks of wood. It somehow didn't surprise me that Frank unknowingly chose Teddy's stump.

We sat quietly for a few minutes. My thoughts ping-ponged between Bob's bizarre diorama featuring the doughy man and Frank's upcoming surprise meeting with Dr. Carolyn Corey. Although he seemed encouraged on both fronts, I wondered if our leads were long shots. Did Bob really feel threatened by the doughy man, and did he actually leave prescient clues in his artwork? And then there was Dr. Corey, a high-end obstetrician. Even if she knew what my father had done with my genetic samples, what was the chance that a baby had been born and that this doctor knew the child's whereabouts now?

"Is this whole thing nutty?"

"There's always a point in an investigation where nothing and everything makes sense."

"I guess we're there now."

"That's why we can't lose sight of the facts."

I liked facts. Although I was an artist, I had always chosen to draw reality. I didn't have a head for dreamy landscapes, but I certainly had an eye for faces, and the doughy man's expression got under my skin. "From what we learned this morning, Bob knew the doughy man, and most likely he was aware the doughy man was trouble."

"But if your mother is right, then the people at the table all had something in common with Bob, and that would include the doughy man." Frank contorted his brow. "But as you said, they can't all be Dumpster divers."

"Or Olympic swimmers."

"Or famous chefs."

"Or strippers," I added. My last comment made me think of Lizzy James, the failed surrogate of my would-be baby. "Hey," I said. "What if the people at the table were all related to Bob? Like extended family?"

Frank's mouth dropped while he considered my observation. "Now that's an interesting thought. What if they weren't family, but had something in common that made them like a family? Maybe that's why they were sharing a meal."

"And how about that meal?" I asked. "Why was there so much food?"

"Well, we know Bob liked food."

"True, but this seemed excessive."

"No," Frank corrected. "It seemed hopeful. Remember the harpoon? It was enlarged, like the food. I wonder if hope is an artistic theme for Bob."

"I like the theme of hope. It's consistent with Bob's upbeat personality. Maybe the people at the table were all hoping for the same thing?"

"See what happens when you focus on the facts?" Frank said. "I think I'd like to go back to Bob's house to see if we can get something out of the other dioramas."

"That's a good idea," I said. "Let's keep going. What else do we know for sure?"

"We know Harry Goldberg is a liar," Frank said without hesitation. "He knew Bob, and he mostly likely knew Bob was dead before we did. He also found a way to empty those warehouses."

"Hence, the warehouses are connected to Bob's death."

"That sounds about right."

"How about Dr. Corey?"

Frank rose, walked over to Charlie's stump, and sat down. "Different case, different seat."

"Whatever works for you. So what do you think about Corey?"

"Few people remember details from more than fifteen years ago. To make matters worse, I'll be catching her off-guard. She's likely to get defensive. I may just tell her why I'm there and leave my card."

"No," I blurted out. "That's not good enough."

"Let's be realistic. What can we expect to get out of her in a ten-minute surprise meeting?"

Now it was my turn to take a quick walk around the woods. I stretched my legs and wandered over to the old fort. As kids, we had covered the interior with leftover silver foil wallpaper, and the floor was a patchwork of discarded linoleum. The fort's archaeological evidence supported my early interest in repurposing materials. I remembered an intense feeling of satisfaction when we lugged what had otherwise been designated for the trash to the woods. Teddy and Charlie thought I was crazy, but once the fort was complete, I had the last laugh.

The fort made me think about Dr. Corey and her interest in working in my father's lab. It had been no mistake that her career path led to obstetrics with a specialty in high-risk pregnancies. My father's work must have dovetailed with her goals to better understand genetics and obstetrics.

I explained the link to Frank. "I don't think my father's lab was just a summer job for her. There had to be a greater benefit. What if she assisted his long-term epigenetics research? Think about it. We know what my father was doing. He's admitted it to us, yet we've never found any documentation."

"We never asked," Frank replied.

"True, but since scientists are in the business of studying and documenting, we know it's somewhere."

"So the question I want to ask her," Frank continued, "is whether she had access to documentation related to your father's study. How was the research data collected and stored? I can ask the question as if I already know that's what she'd worked on."

"That's what I'm thinking, and it matches what Dr. Wilson remembered."

"But he didn't remember what her role was in the labs."

"That's my point. He didn't remember, because she probably didn't have a day-to-day role, like washing the beakers. Assuming her job was to track and document, then that would give her a reason to have contact with the surrogates. It would also coincide with my mother's memory that my father wouldn't lower himself to handle administrative tasks. Dr. Corey was probably the one who arranged the transport of the samples to Lifely."

"Okay, and maybe that's why Dr. Wilson didn't know what Dr. Corey did, because he and the other lab assistants would have flipped out if they knew their sperm was being sent off without their permission."

I nodded.

Frank turned his head up to the sky and scanned the woods. "I like this thinking spot. Can I borrow it sometime?"

"Yes, but now I need you to return to your first seat." I helped Frank up and led him back to the other stump.

Frank did as I directed. The moment he sat down, I returned to our original topic. There was something about the diorama in the storage unit that bothered me.

"We haven't talked about the ID tag. I drew the doughy man with a tag, but the man in the diorama wasn't wearing a tag."

"You're right. I still need to follow up with more local companies that use tags," Frank said. "May I add to your list?"

"Go for it."

"I need to talk to David Goldberg. We know Harry is a liar, but we don't know enough about his cousin David."

"All we know is that David's wife is sleeping with his cousin, Harry."

THIRTY-FIVE

THE HATCHBACK OF THE Gremlin was packed with enough shopping bags that I actually worried they would be the straw that broke the car's back. My mother and I were returning to rehab where, for the remainder of her stay, she'd be the best dressed patient in group therapy.

"You wouldn't believe the whining," my mother lamented about the group. "You just can't believe what passes for a crisis these days. There are two or three girls about your age who think their parents' divorce is worthy of their self-absorbed drama."

"I can't see you sharing during these sessions."

"What would I say? *My husband was instrumental in my son's death? My son was adopted and separated from his twin brother, but he didn't know until months before he was murdered?* These people have no idea what drama is."

"How about *My daughter eats from garbage pails?*" I suggested.

"Now *that* I mentioned."

"Mom," I yelled.

"You have to say *something*. You can't just sit there in silence or you'll lose privileges."

"But my Dumpster diving had nothing to do with your drinking," I retorted.

"Of course it didn't, but you should have seen their faces."

"Let me guess. You're saving up the story of my egg theft to wow them on your last day?"

My mother smiled slyly. "Maybe."

I pulled into the front drive of the rehab and turned off the key. The sun hung low in the sky, and I could almost feel the grapevines in the distance soaking in the last of their solar vitamins. Tomorrow, I promised myself, I would work on the farm. If I wedged Katrina in a comfortable chair, she could strip the sweet potatoes of their new tubers while I did the planting. There was too much going on to think ahead to the harvest. By the time the sweet potatoes were grown, my mother would be out of rehab, Katrina would have a baby, and I might have a child—or rather, a teenager. My mother would be a grandmother, which seemed inconceivable at the moment. How many kids visit their grandmothers in rehab?

My mother looked sadly at her new home. "It's as if none of these people ever enjoyed their poison."

"Come on, it's only a few more weeks." I emptied the trunk and carried my mother's packages into the lobby. On Sunday night, a so-called free time, patients gathered socially in the small meeting pods on the main level. A few waved to my mother, and she smiled back blankly, that same fake smile she had offered me as a kid when she was more interested in her refill than my homework. The only available table had an opened bottle of water and a half-eaten bag of chips on it. I moved the discarded food aside and set down my mother's new spring wardrobe. I looked around the room to make sure I caught the eyes of my mother's fellow patients. Then, I picked up the chips and started to munch.

"You are doing this on purpose," my mother hissed.

I reached for the bottle of water to wash down the chips.

"You wouldn't," she said.

"I won't if you promise to stop using me as your emotional crutch in therapy. You've got to get to the real stuff if you want to get better." *The real stuff*, I thought. If I truly considered the real stuff in my life, I'd be a permanent resident at this facility. I inched my hand closer to the water bottle until my mother caved.

"You win," she said, and I put the bottle down.

I gave her a hug, which she graciously returned. "Seriously, Mom. I want you back."

———

I returned to Harbor House around ten that night. Frank, Katrina, and Charlie were in the barn enjoying the last of the Christmas lights. Frank had reverted to his traditional six-pack of beer while Charlie looked like the before picture for the brochure of my mother's rehab facility. Katrina had her legs propped up on a cardboard box. Her shoeless swollen feet looked like she'd been smashing grapes in an Italian winery for the last nine months.

"Trina, I think Frank was kidding when he asked you to give him a week." I rubbed her toes. "Feel free to have this baby whenever you want."

"I'm never doing this again," she moaned.

"One and done," Charlie chimed in and Frank laughed. Clearly, I had arrived late to the party.

"Okay," Frank said as he passed out scraps of paper and pencils. "I've come up with an investigative game. I'd like you to write down possible links between the people in Bob's diorama and Bob. To assist you, I'll display the photos we took of the artwork." Frank fired up his iPad and placed it on the table.

"What do we get if we win?" I asked.

"The respect of the tax-paying public." Frank shrugged. "It's what keeps me coming to work every day."

I was intrigued by Frank's motivation to serve. On some level, I felt that people like Bob and I were also serving, but our public extended beyond the borders of Cold Spring Harbor. Global sustainability, an unwieldy goal, had to start at a local level. Try telling that to my neighbors whose garbage I regularly pillaged.

Katrina made a useless attempt to bend over and reach for the iPad. "It's such a diverse group." She squinted at the picture. "There's children, young adults, and seniors in this picture. I can't see them participating in the same thing given the differences in their ages and physical capabilities."

"Unless it's something like singing," Frank said. "The funny thing about vocal ability is that it's not dependent on the singer's appearance, like an athlete. People of all shapes and sizes can have amazing voices."

"So they're in a band." Charlie chuckled.

"How about Mensa?" Katrina said. "IQ is detectable at a young age. That would give the little girl a reason to be at the table."

"It's possible. Bob always struck me as a smart guy," I said, and then added. "In keeping with the concept of how they think, maybe their commonality is an idea, a shared philosophy?"

"Like a religion?" Charlie said.

"Please don't say cult," Frank added. "I don't have the energy to infiltrate a cult."

"Then how about a church choir?" Charlie countered.

The singing angle seemed plausible. Music had a way of bringing people of various ages together, although Bob never hummed more than his favorite Sesame Street tune. Besides, there was nothing else in the diorama to indicate music. I'd need a treble clef fashioned out of a discarded paper clip to go with the music theory.

"We need more options," I said encouragingly. "What else can a diverse group of people share?"

"Art?" Frank asked. "Or maybe collecting?"

"That's true," Katrina said. "I collected recipes as a kid."

"If this was some type of group, I'll bet they communicated or maybe even met online," Charlie said. "Most clubs have email chains, or they congregate in chat rooms or on groups sponsored by search engines."

"Damn." Frank lowered his beer. "We only checked Bob's work computer, because we thought this was strictly work related. We never checked to see if Bob had a personal computer at his house."

I looked at my watch and then remembered I had given it to Lizzy James. "Isn't it late, Frank?" I said. "I need to sleep, and Bob's house isn't going anywhere."

"Tomorrow?" Frank asked Charlie.

"I'm there," Charlie slurred.

THIRTY-SIX
MONDAY, APRIL 28

I WOKE UP THE next morning feeling energized. In the past few days, we'd made an enormous amount of progress, and I felt like my contributions had made a difference. Frank and Charlie were headed to Bob's house in search of his personal computer. With my finished sketch of Cheryl Goldberg, Harry would have a hard time denying that the woman spotted at his office door was his cousin's wife. Small cracks, Frank said, would lead to big breaks. We also had a witness, the tuba lady, who could place Harry on site the night the warehouse had been emptied. Finally, we had a good feeling that the doughy man was represented in the diorama, and assuming Bob had labeled the dolls as we suspected, the doughy man's name most likely started with an L. Most importantly, I had remembered that the skinny jeans woman had black hair.

I dug through my closet and came up with a backpack that I stuffed with my sketchbook, some pencils, a water bottle, and a jar of peach jelly. I tiptoed out the front door to the barn, retrieved my bicycle, and pedaled south on Shore Road, where I made a quick right into the neighborhood of Laurel Hollow. It was a lovely area. On a map it mirrored Cold Spring Harbor like the matching wings of a butterfly. Laurel Hollow's nearest neighbor was the Sound View labs, and many of the homes in the area belonged to doctors and researchers associated with the famous laboratory. As I neared my destination, oncoming traffic picked up, but that was to be expected since it was seven a.m. on a Monday morning.

About halfway through the maze of streets, including two or three wrong turns, I stopped in front of a grand Colonial with carved columns supporting a circular-roofed portico. Map in hand, I stared at the circle mark I had made last night after Googling Dr. Carolyn Corey's home address. Getting a glimpse of Dr. Corey on her way to work was just the type of move that would piss off Frank, but I couldn't resist the temptation. Clearly, I couldn't wait until tomorrow when Frank was scheduled to see Dr. Corey.

There was a shiny BMW in Dr. Corey's driveway and a wooden play set in the back yard. I looked around the neighborhood and realized I was insanely exposed. If my purpose was to get a peek at Dr. Corey, standing without purpose in the middle of the street would trigger a phone call to the police by an observant neighbor. With my luck, Cheski would be on call and actually arrest me. Truth be told, I had no intention of spying on Dr. Corey; I simply wanted to see the woman responsible for sending my fertilized embryo to its final destination.

I buried my head in my map, which I figured would buy me a few minutes posing as a lost biker. Just when I had memorized every esoteric symbol on my map, Dr. Corey's across-the-street-neighbors, a suited couple with travel coffee mugs, shuffled out to their own BMW. As soon as the neighbors backed out, I cycled down their driveway and pulled my bike behind an overgrown azalea bush. My hiding spot had an unobstructed view of Dr. Corey's house.

By 7:45 a.m., I still sat in a pile of dirt picking sticky azalea blossoms off my shorts. For all I knew, Dr. Corey had delivered a baby in the middle of the night and wasn't even home yet. I rose to stretch my legs when a beat-up Honda Civic pulled up in front of Dr. Corey's house. I scrambled forward through the bushes to get a better look. Three women got out of the car. One of the women opened the trunk and took out a vacuum cleaner. In my new position, closer to the street, my only cover was the neighbor's mailbox.

The woman emptying the trunk instinctively turned in my direction. "CeCe!"

"Norma?" It was my mother's housekeeper. "What are you doing here?"

Norma hurried across the street and shoved me farther back into the bushes. "I'm sorry, I'm sorry," she repeated over and over until I felt like slapping her across the face. "I tell you later."

"When later?"

"Come to the side door when you see the car leave."

I waited patiently while Norma, and the two other cleaning women entered Dr. Corey's house. A few minutes passed, and Dr. Corey came outside with two adorable girls who looked to be about two and four years old. A year ago, I would never have been able to guess a child's age, but my excessive sketching had honed my age-detection skills. Both girls had thick, dark hair and medium skin—unlike their mother, whose face was the map of Ireland. It was brief, but I got a good look at Dr. Corey. *Harmless*, was the first word that came to mind. By all accounts, she was patient with her children and took the time to listen to one of the girls tell what seemed to be a meandering story. She strapped each girl into their car seat and through the back window of the car, I could see her tenderly kiss her daughters. *Darn*, I thought. *Why can't she have a witch's nose with a mole the size of quarter on her chin? Or a glass eye and a limp?*

I waited until Dr. Corey drove slowly away before scurrying across the street to the side door.

Norma waited for me. "I'm sorry," she repeated.

"I get it," I said. "You're sorry."

"Really, I'm sorry," she said again.

"Why would you be sorry?" I asked. Wasn't that supposed to be my line? I wondered why I didn't feel more guilty hiding out in a stranger's driveway to spy on a doctor I had never met.

"How did you find out?" Norma said, opening the door for me as I followed her inside Dr. Corey's house. "I should listen to your mother. She said you were the smart one. Did you follow me?"

I tilted my head. This didn't made sense. Why did Norma think I had followed her, and why the hell was she so dreadfully sorry? She seemed to think I understood, but I was completely lost. I decided to go along with her misinformation to see where it took me.

"At first I wasn't sure it was you," I said, "but then I began to wonder …"

"See, I knew I should say no to your father."

My father? The same one who'd been in exile for the past year since he'd been accused of facilitating my brother's murder? This was too weird even for me to bluff my way through. I hadn't seen or heard from my father since the trial six months ago, and although he ultimately did not take the fall for my brother's death, the shame had forced my dad out of town. I had no idea where my father had relocated. All I knew is that my mother's bills got paid. Of course, I hadn't made a single attempt to find him, and my mother hadn't been back in the land of the sober long enough to really question this arrangement.

If I had to guess, I'd say my father was in Europe. He had always enjoyed the finer things in life, as if he considered himself royalty. For this reason, I'd imagined him strolling through Bruges or sipping coffee in the south of France. It had been a convenient dream from which I sensed I was about to wake.

"Norma, can we sit and talk?"

The house, a cookie cutter version of every other upscale Long Island McMansion, had the requisite marble countertops, stainless-steel appliances, and enough tech equipment to blow a circuit breaker or two. It was unimpressive in its sameness. It was, however, exceptionally clean, and that was Norma's handiwork. It concerned me that she'd had contact with my father, and although I didn't truly know where her loyalties lay, her affection for my mother had seemed genuine in the past. I hoped this was still true, because I couldn't keep up this charade much longer.

"I didn't follow you," I admitted. "I was just riding for exercise when I saw you."

Norma seemed confused by my explanation. "Just riding?" she asked.

I nodded, and she went back to unloading the dishwasher. I walked over to a corkboard covered with family photos and studied the pictures. "Do you work here?" I asked.

"I'm mooning, and I'm so sorry."

"I think you mean moonlighting." The drinking glasses clinked at her touch. My visit had made her nervous. "Did my father get you this job?"

"Ohh," Norma groaned. "He called me when your mother went to rehab. He still pays me for your house, but he pays me more every week to come here. How can I say no to good money?"

I wasn't sure it was *good* money, but I kept that to myself.

The kitchen was in the back of the Colonial. From the table I could see straight down the center hall, through the windows lining the front door, and across the street to my bicycle, which, despite my attempt to hide, was in full view. It wasn't just my bicycle that stuck out like a sore thumb. My father's motivation to place Norma in this job was an oversized red flag.

"Has my father been here?"

Norma nodded. Her guilt crushed her, but there was nothing I could say to make her feel better. She likely needed the money, but she also knew this arrangement my father had orchestrated wasn't kosher. My guess is that fear played a factor too. I watched Norma fiddle with the spray attachment at the kitchen sink. I figured this would be a bad time to introduce her to the financial benefits of Freeganism as a form of self-sufficiency.

"He came in the house?"

"Yes."

"What did he do?"

"Same thing as you. He looked at the pictures on the board."

"How about this: We pretend this never happened," I suggested. She nodded.

"Except for one thing," I added. "For my mother's sake, you need to let me know when my father contacts you, and I promise you won't get fired." The last part was a lie. I couldn't protect Norma from my father.

Norma frowned as she rinsed out the coffee maker. "Okay, I do it for your mother."

Back outside, I retrieved my bicycle from the neighbor's yard and started to pedal toward my final destination. I got what I'd come for: a firsthand look at Dr. Carolyn Corey. I also got a bit more than I intended. I could have biked cross-country and still not found the time to solve the new problem I had just created for myself. How was I supposed to tell Frank that my father had found Norma a job working at Dr. Corey's house without revealing that I had been spying on Dr. Corey? I couldn't ignore what I had discovered; it highlighted that Dr. Corey was on my father's radar, and that seemed like a very bad turn of events. Frank, of course, would be too savvy to buy my "biking for exercise" story. I wrestled with the idea of telling Frank that Norma had a come-to-Jesus moment and voluntarily told me about the arrangement, but then Frank would want to speak to Norma, and I was sure she'd unravel under his scrutiny.

I passed the Cold Spring Harbor train station and congratulated myself on never succumbing to the drudgery of a daily job. I considered a detour by the platform to see if the bagel guy had thrown out any day-olds, but it was unnecessary. Norma had packed a snack for me from Dr. Corey's kitchen. Instead of stopping, I pressed on, biking up and down hills that looked an awful lot flatter on my map.

About twenty minutes into my ride, I turned into a neighborhood I had never been in before. The houses weren't on par with Dr. Corey's, but the streets were nicely laid out with quaint Cape Cod–style homes, many of which had been renovated and expanded over the years. I rode as far into the neighborhood as I could in search of a public path at the end of a cul-de-sac, as indicated on my map. I found the path easily and rode through the woods until the path became too bumpy, forcing me to walk along side my bike.

There were a few splits in the trail that required left or right decisions, but before long I spotted the roofline of the recycling center. I leaned my bike against a tree and climbed up a few branches. From my perch, I had an aerial view of the path that connected the recycling center to the neighborhood I had entered. One thing that struck me was the lack of options or exits the path allowed. Although there were turnoffs and forks, all roads led either to the neighborhood where I had entered or to the recycling center. I wondered if the skinny jean woman had a car. Was it possible she saw Bob being threatened by the doughy man, got scared, and ran toward the woods to avoid detection? Maybe she retrieved her car later. Or was it possible she arrived and departed on foot? If she had left by the path, she may have had a car parked in the neighborhood I had just ridden through. That would make sense, since she seemed to be on foot the day I saw her at Bob's house. The other possibility was that she made her way to the main road. From there, she might have been able to hitch a ride . . . except that no one bums a ride in the suburbs, even Freegans.

I rummaged through my backpack and tore the wrapping off an organic fruit bar courtesy of Norma. I washed it down with a child's juice box. *What a waste of individual wrapping,* I thought. *Doesn't anyone drink from a reusable glass anymore?* The bendy straw was so thin that the sucking started to give me a headache. My squeaky slurping caught the attention of a dog, who found his way to my tree and proceeded to bark incessantly.

"Hey," the dog's owner apologized when he caught up. "He doesn't bite."

I climbed down the tree to greet the man and his dog. Not that I had much of a choice, but I allowed the dog to slobber all over the last bite of my fruit bar. It tasted horrible anyway and that's coming from someone who eats out of a Dumpster.

"What were you doing in the tree?" the man asked. "Are you lost?"

"A bit. I wanted to see if there were other ways out."

"One way in and one way out."

I pointed back to the neighborhood. "Do you live over there?"

"I do," the man said. "First house at the end of the path. It's really convenient with the dog."

I patted the dog on the rump and climbed back on my bike. "Do you think I'll see anyone else today?"

"Nah, not during the workday. In the late afternoon, you get teenagers. But that's it."

THIRTY-SEVEN

Snack consumed and legs rested, I continued on my way. The wooded path quickly evened out, and I was able to bike the rest of the way to the recycling center. My ride had come to an end and I still hadn't figured out how to tell Frank I had stalked Dr. Corey. Worse, I had to tell him my father had gotten to Corey first. I chained my bicycle to a fence just in case someone might think it was garbage. The bicycle had, in fact, been garbage at one point until I rescued it.

The recycling center was quieter than usual, and I noticed Jimmy supervising the repair of one of the sorting machines.

"I don't suppose you brought a ten-inch rubber belt with you?" Jimmy asked from his hunched position.

"Not today," I said. "May I speak with Marissa?"

"The pickers are on break until I finish this up. Check the lunch room."

The lunch room was packed, but I spotted Marissa and asked her to step outside with me, and she willingly agreed. My sketch pad was opened to reveal my latest version of the doughy man. It was a long shot, but I had used the close-up photos of Bob's doll to develop my sketch. The challenge, of course, was to tone down Bob's satirical exaggerations to create a more lifelike rendering. Almost like undoing a caricature. For example, the doughy man doll, upon closer inspection, had huge ears and droopy eyes. In Bob's interpretation, the man looked like a bloated hound dog. I took those features and drew them realistically. Bob's doll also had a particular hair style, the thinning combover. For the viewer to see the receding hairline, I had to draw the face slightly downward and to the side.

"Is this the man you saw?"

Marissa was a detail-oriented person. I knew this already by her attire, make-up, and jewelry, and as I had hoped, she studied the photo carefully.

"The hair. It's good," she confirmed. I had felt confident about the hair, but Marissa's acknowledgment cinched it. Bob's diorama had delivered.

"I want to ask you about the man's badge." I pointed to my chest. "Have you seen anyone else with a badge at the recycling center? A badge like the man wore?"

She shook her head no.

"One more question. Do all the workers leave at the same time each day?"

"Yes. Some drive home, and some of us walk to the road and wait for the bus."

"So a bus comes by?"

"Yes, I take the bus, but I missed it that day, and I had to wait for another."

"When you left, were there cars in the parking lot?"

Marissa's eyebrows rose. "Well," she said slowly. "If I had recognized one of the cars, I would have asked for a ride. I hate missing the bus. I guess I didn't know any of the cars or I would definitely have asked for a ride home."

That made sense. When you're reliant on public transportation, missing a bus is a big deal. I believed that Marissa did, in fact, check the parking lot for a coworker's car in order to avoid waiting for a later bus.

"Think hard," I urged.

"I remember being sad I'd missed my bus." Marissa opened her mouth and placed a neatly painted nail on her chin. "Now that you say it, I think there was only one car in the lot and I didn't recognize it."

"And Bob didn't drive a car to work?"

"Mr. Bob walked."

That would leave only the doughy man and the skinny jeans woman with transportation needs. Assuming the workers had left for the day, there should have been two cars, unless one of the two people had walked.

"Are you sure there was only one car?"

"Maybe."

I thanked Marissa and handed her a jar of jelly from my bag.

———

My plan had been to return home by the same route, but I figured a quick ride to Bob's house wouldn't kill me. I was interested in the trails surrounding Bob's house. Could the skinny jeans woman have moved undetected from the recycling center to Bob's house on the day I saw her? I turned into Bob's driveway.

Frank's car was parked ahead. I'd forgotten he'd wanted to check Bob's home computer for participation in a social group or network. I rode so slowly my bicycle almost tipped over. Turning around was an option, but that seemed even more childish than hiding behind a bush to spy on Dr. Corey. If only I could think of a lie that made me look good from Frank's perspective.

I chose to ignore the inevitable tongue lashing and headed to Bob's house. What I had discovered at Dr. Corey's house was too important to hide.

"Hey," I said, pushing the half-hinged metal door from the frame. "Anybody home?"

"In the kitchen," Charlie said.

Charlie and Frank were both standing, arms crossed, staring at a computer on the kitchen table.

"Where did you find it?"

Frank shifted from side to side. "It was in his art shed."

"Is there a password?"

"*Recycle*," Charlie said. "It took less than thirty seconds to figure out."

Charlie sat down at the table and slid the cursor to an icon, branded with the capital letters OL. "Are you all familiar with this site?" he asked us. "It's called Other Life, or OL for short."

"Is that the social site where you make a better, but cartoony version of yourself, like a new-and-improved you?" I asked.

"Yeah, it's called an avatar," Charlie said as he clicked on the icon.

"Then you socialize with other new-and-improved people in computer-generated fantasy locales," I added.

Charlie laughed. "Pretty much. Basically it's a series of virtual worlds you join and then hang out in. The worlds are designed for interest groups, like tattoo aficionados or motorcycle enthusiasts. This way the user can interact with other people who have the same hobbies or jobs or interests."

"So what groups does Bob belong to?" Frank asked.

"That's where I'm getting lost," Charlie said as he poked at the keyboard some more. "Bob is maxed out at ninety-two worlds, way more than anyone can keep track of, even if you were able to create a super-improved avatar version of yourself."

"What's Bob's avatar look like?" I asked, assuming Bob would have refashioned himself in to a svelte, athletic man. I'd never created an avatar, but an inch or two in height would be my personal priority. Charlie hit a key, and Bob's Other Life avatar filled the screen.

Hmmm. Not what I expected.

In addition to Bob's many hobbies, he now seemed to have a fascination with all things medieval. Although not a king or a serf in rags, Bob's screen-self looked like he'd be right at home at a jousting competition. His avatar was stout, but not grossly overweight, and sure enough, the avatar sported Bob's standard welcoming smile. I guessed the velvet cape from the diorama was inspired by this jousting theme. Under Bob's avatar was a fictitious map. The red pin points suggested the locations of Bob's movements through his virtual worlds. Quite the traveler, our Bob. I hadn't seen him leave the recycling center in years but online, he was a regular Phileas Fogg.

A text box popped up in the corner. *Hi, Bobin. We missed you.*

Within seconds, text messages filled the margins of the screen. Most asked Bob, or Bobin, where he'd been and welcomed him back to whichever virtual world they were connecting from. Virtual Bob, it turned out, was a popular guy.

"Holy cow," I said as I sat down. "More people who think Bob's alive."

"Charlie," Frank yelled, "stop typing!" Charlie lifted his hands as instructed. "I need to think," Frank said.

"This is freakish," I whispered to Charlie. "It's like he's still here."

Charlie nodded and then rested his hand on the mouse to scroll through the messages. "Not yet," I said, and pointed to Frank, who had moved from the kitchen to the porch to the yard. "Let him walk it off. He'll come back with a solution."

We waited. My stomach growled. Apparently Dr. Corey's fruit bar wasn't sufficient given my lengthy bike ride. I rose, reached for a kitchen cabinet, and grabbed a box of opened whole grain crackers.

"Hungry?" I offered a few dry, brown squares to Charlie.

Charlie's face was glued to the screen. "I'm pretty sure Bob's got a better stash than dry crackers. Where's the scavenger in you?"

Charlie was right. Organic crackers hadn't pushed Bob to his peak circus weight. I was missing the mother lode of snack supplies. I tore through Bob and Barbara's cabinets like I hadn't eaten in days. Cups, plates, medicines, baking supplies. "Jackpot!" I yelled as I opened the narrow door on a floor-to-ceiling pantry. The shelves were lined with boxes of cookies—the good kind with fancy names that sounded like places you could never afford to travel to and containing no more than twelve cookies per bag. Two additional cookies and you'd likely use up your fat allocation for a month. I scanned the shelves and settled on a chocolate chip brand that, based on the picture, had more chip than cookie. My mouth watered as I separated the filmy layers of parchment between each wafer.

By the time Frank returned, there was one cookie left in the bag.

"The messages in the margin," he said, pointing to the screen. "Did they load when you logged on?"

"Yup," Charlie confirmed. "If I scroll back we should be able to see some history of conversations he had before he died." Charlie scrolled up passed about thirty new welcome-back messages. "Here," he said, running his finger down the screen. "Bob had been in conversation with these people over the last few weeks."

"Don't click. Let's print screen so we can read the messages." A printer in one of the bedrooms kicked on, and I ran in and took the sheets from the tray.

"Besides *someone is trying to kill me*, what are we looking for?" Charlie asked.

"Any conversation that seems deeper than, *Hey, how's it going?*" Frank replied.

With that, we dove into Bob's message log. One thing was clear, the back and forth between Bob and his friends was short, almost superficial. Most repeated the same phrase—*still working*—until a few exchanges later where the friend would tell Bob they were *looking for a new job*. Bob always replied the same way: *Three to five days*. Regardless of the virtual world where the avatar resided, all the interactions were similar.

"Wait, I found one," Charlie said. "It says, *Recycle on Thursdays.*"

The sugary remnants of my last cookie turned sour in my mouth. "Oh god, Thursday was the day Bob was pushed."

"The avatar goes by the nickname the Maid," Charlie said as he scrolled over the messenger's screen name. "This message is from a medieval princess." Sure enough, the Maid's thumbnail looked like a character from a Disney movie.

"Is she online now?" Frank asked as he continued to scan the list of previous messages.

"She is," Charlie said as he waited for Frank's instructions.

Frank tapped on the computer sheet. "On the Wednesday before Bob's death, the Maid wrote *Recycle on Thursdays*. She posted the same thing last Wednesday. If she'd attempted to communicate with Bob, it means she didn't know he'd died the week before"

"Is it possible the Maid is the skinny-jeaned woman? She was at the recycling center on Thursday."

"It is possible," Frank said. "She may have seen Bob arguing with the doughy man, but she may not have known the outcome. Maybe she's been looking for Bob and that's why she showed up at his house a few days later."

"We need to make a move," Charlie said. "The reason people are on these sites is to socialize. If Bob's avatar doesn't communicate soon, people will know something is up."

"So she can tell Bob's online?" I asked.

Charlie pointed to a graphic in the upper right-hand corner of the screen. "This box keeps track of who has signed in or out. It's almost like watching the door of a bar on a Friday night to see if your crush has come in."

Frank circled Bob and Barbara's kitchen table. "It's possible *Recycle on Thursday* was code to schedule a meeting. The skinny jeans woman might have been on her way to meet Bob when she stumbled upon him with the doughy man. If Marissa was right about what she saw—that the skinny jean woman was running away—then she might have known Bob was in trouble."

I offered Frank the last cookie. "Why didn't she do something?"

He took a bite and said, "I don't know, but let's see if we can draw her out. Type *Recycle on Thursday,* and we'll see if we can get her to show up again this Thursday."

Charlie, posing as Bob's avatar, posted the message. Bob's message bubble hung in the air for no more than a second before the Maid abruptly logged off.

"Damn," Frank said. "We scared her off."

"But look what we started," Charlie said as the screen filled with messages sent from avatars visiting from one of Bob's many fantasy worlds.

Each message, although not identical, escalated in intensity.

Lost job.

Need new one by next week.

Please help.

"What the hell?" Frank whispered, and then turned to Charlie, frustrated. "Log out."

THIRTY-EIGHT

I GAVE CHARLIE MY bike, and he offered to ride it home so Frank and I could meet with the Goldbergs. David Goldberg's storage facility, our first stop, was a quick drive from the recycling center. Laid out similarly to Harry's place, it had one distinct difference—it was well-kept. There were flowers planted outside the main office, and the internal streets were clearly designated with names like Park, Madison, and Lexington Avenues. Fresh white lines gave the parking lot a sense of order, and the office looked welcoming, with a smiling attendant at the counter.

Frank made no move to exit the car. I knew the messages on Bob's screen bothered him. He turned to me and said, "There was a certain level of desperation in those messages."

I nodded silently, allowing Frank to think out loud without interruption.

"The timing appeared urgent. I don't know what the 'job' represents, but these people seem to think that Bob can deliver something within the week. What could Bob have that these people wanted?"

I shook my head and reached for the door handle. "I don't know, but I still feel like this is connected to the warehouses. Let's see what we can get out of David."

We approached the facility's main office. Frank held the door for me and a tinkling, cheery bell announced our arrival. Frank, distracted by Bob's messages, ignored the customer-friendly environment and cut right to the chase, flashing his badge at the counter attendant and asking for David Goldberg. A nice-looking man, about ten years younger than Harry, strolled casually out. I was confused. If I had to choose between Harry and David, I'd definitely go for the latter, yet Cheryl had married David and was cheating with Harry.

"Can I help you?"

Frank repeated his credentials and nodded to the hallway behind the front desk. David invited us in to his office and offered us the chairs facing his desk. His workspace was organized, the plants by the window were thriving, and his face, a placid canvas, showed no sign of nerves.

"We're following up on the toxic warehouses," Frank said. "We've already met with your cousin."

"Is there some type of additional clean-up I need to do?" David asked. His hands rested calmly on his desk. "If so, I'm fine with it, although Harry will blow a gasket if he's required to shell out another penny."

Frank leaned back in his chair. We already knew the Goldberg cousins didn't get along and that Harry's business dwarfed David's single location. I figured Frank was about to use this knowledge to get David's back up and crack his composure.

"I guess that's how your cousin's chain grew," Frank said in an obvious attempt to insult David. "He watches every penny."

"Yeah, well he's going to need a magnifying glass to find those pennies, because he's broke," David laughed. "You know Harry is hard up when he calls me asking for money." I watched David's eyes smile in concert with his mouth. I'd been drawing faces long enough to know that a genuine smile envelops the whole face, like I'd just seen. Based on his facial cues, David Goldberg was for real.

"He's broke?" I asked.

"Harry snatched up a bunch of storage places during the height of the recession only to find out that people don't store their junk when they're broke. They sell it or chuck it or simply stop paying the monthly bill."

I looked at Frank. Harry had portrayed David as a visionless businessman living on a shoestring. If I was right about David's relaxed attitude, then this cousin rivalry was a one-way street. "The auctions," I said.

"That's one way to get rid of it," David confirmed. "I chose a different strategy. I lowered my prices to keep my long-term customers from defaulting." He shrugged. "A unit earning something is better than an empty unit. I got this place free and clear from my grandfather and every dollar goes straight to the bottom line. All Harry's got is debt and empty units. He acts like he's got money, but he doesn't."

"How did the Eco-Systems deal come your way?" Frank asked.

"Harry brought me the deal, actually. Made me pay him a finder's fee to boot."

Frank rose and shook David's hand. "How much debt are we talking about?"

"Millions, unfortunately," David said as he led us to the door. "I heard he's got an expensive girlfriend too." And then he winked.

Frank thanked David for his time, and we headed back to the car.

"David knows his wife is having an affair with Harry," I said.

"That he does," Frank confirmed, "and I'll bet he thinks Harry's current financial bind is fair payback for ruining his marriage."

"What's your take on him?"

"I think he's a straight shooter," Frank said as he started the car. "I wish we'd spoken to him earlier because now we know Harry is carrying millions in debt and that helps establish motive. Financial stress makes people do stupid things."

I shook my head in agreement wondering if now was the right time to tell Frank about Norma's "mooning" job. Frank's observation about money as a motivator seemed like a perfect segue to explain Norma's decision to take a second job offered by my father.

"I need to tell you something," I said.

Frank swerved the car slightly. "You slept with Charlie?"

Gee, I thought. *I'd almost rather own up to sleeping with Charlie than admit to Frank that I've been playing super-sleuth on my own again.* "I haven't slept with Charlie," I said quickly, and then I described how I discovered Norma had been hired to clean Dr. Corey's house.

Frank nostrils flared, and I watched as he tightened his grip on the steering wheel.

"You're mad."

"At you?" he said. He slowed the car down, found another parking spot, and then turned to me. "I'm not mad at you. If it makes you feel better, I budget for things like this."

"You … what?"

"I know I can't control you," he said. "Instead, I've started to anticipate that eventually you'll step over the line."

I wasn't sure what to make of Frank's assessment. Did he think I was impulsive and he'd forever be picking up the pieces of the messes I'd be certain to make? Or was he working around my quirks because he genuinely valued our relationship?

"So you're not mad?" I asked slowly.

"If it were Bob's case, I'd be furious, but your missing egg is not a police matter. I expected your curiosity might get the best of you."

I leaned over and pretended to rub the frown marks out of Frank's forehead. "You're mad."

"I'm not happy." He removed my hand. "But it has nothing to do with you. There's a reason your father is watching Dr. Corey, and I'm going to bet it's because Corey knows something about your egg. This crazy experiment of your father's never came out at your brother's murder trial, and I suspect he's been concerned it could resurface. I'm guessing your father wants to bury it for good."

The word *bury* was a poor choice of words. If there were a child—and by now I was convinced there was—he or she would be living proof of my father's perverted sense of morality. "Oh God, what if he gets to this child before we do?"

Frank started the car and pulled back into traffic. "Now you understand the frown marks. Your father is smart, and he's always one step ahead." Then Frank grinned and added, "I'm having enough trouble staying one step ahead of you."

———

Harry Goldberg had already been notified that Frank wanted to meet with him again, but Frank wasn't about to make it easy for Harry this time around. The meeting had been scheduled for the police station.

"I'm dropping you at home," he said. "I'll need your sketch of Cheryl Goldberg."

"Seriously? I'm not coming with you?"

"There's no need for you to meet with Harry."

I realized that if I hadn't stalked Dr. Corey, Frank would probably have allowed me to show Harry the sketch myself. I suspected I was being punished for my activities earlier in the morning. I grabbed my backpack and pulled out my sketchbook. "Can I still come with you tomorrow to see Corey?"

Frank hesitated.

"I'll wait in the parking lot," I bargained.

No response.

I decided to up the ante. "I'll wait in the car, and I won't get out."

"Fine. I'll pick you up tomorrow," Frank said.

I leaned in and kissed him. "Don't lose my sketchbook."

I watched Frank drive away, feeling strangely naked without my drawing pad. I walked over to the farm and made my way up and down the rows of neatly planted vegetables. Pockets of weeds brushed up against my legs and I realized the tasks ahead were more than I would be able to handle alone in the coming weeks. The farm, although pristine today, would soon show signs of neglect. Bob's death had consumed my attention, and at this time of year, every lost day mattered. There was one option I'd considered—opening the farm to people interested in organic farming in exchange for a take of the harvest. The food co-op seemed a likely place to advertise, and since my first attempt to visit the co-op with Cheski had been derailed, maybe I could kill two eco-friendly goals with one stone.

THIRTY-NINE

CHESKI HELD THE DOOR of the food co-op open for me. All the amenities typically associated with large-scale food retailers were absent from the store. The co-op didn't provide carts or bags. To hold costs down, lighting was dim and signage was limited. If you can't recognize a carrot, you probably need to eat more went the theory. None of this seemed to bother Cheski.

Cheski looked around the store and smiled. "I like it here," he said happily. We shopped the aisles and periodically Cheski picked up something interesting, sniffed it, and then put it back in place. "Did I ever tell you my grandfather owned a mom-and-pop grocery store in Queens? I used to bag groceries as a kid."

"Then you'll fit right in," I said. I pointed to a man in a stained apron stocking fruit. "He's one of the managers. Why don't you start by talking to him about Barbara? I'm going to hang my sign."

The woman at the customer service counter stamped my hastily prepared flyer and gave me the key to the glass-enclosed community board. I'd considered making the rounds with Cheski to inquire about Barbara's whereabouts, but I figured I should stick to what I knew—

sketching, Dumpster diving, farming, and jelly making. It bugged me that Frank had been "budgeting" for my behavior, as if I were a loose cannon, capable of blowing up his investigation at any moment.

I watched as Cheski moved easily through the store, listening patiently as people answered his questions. Cheski was an experienced cop, and it showed. Listening seemed to be one of my weaker qualities, and I noticed how Cheski gave ample time to each person he interviewed. By the time he got to the bread racks, he turned and gave me a thumbs up. I hurried over.

"So?" I asked.

"Barbara's got relatives in Wyoming," Cheski said.

"And you think you can find her? It's a pretty big state."

Cheski grabbed a loaf of whole grain bread and yanked off the end piece. "Easily. It's a big state but also the least populated in the union. I'll dig up her maiden name and start making calls." He bit down on a chunk of bread and smiled. "Delicious."

I handed Cheski a membership form, which he promptly filled out. As he dotted the I in his last name, his phone trilled.

"It's Frank," he whispered. "Harry Goldberg cracked. Your sketch of Cheryl did the trick."

FORTY

Frank was strutting around the police station when Cheski and I arrived. He returned my sketchbook and planted a well deserved kiss on my cheek.

"Yes, Harry is nearly bankrupt," Frank confirmed. "He admitted to the affair with Cheryl, and yes, he knowingly rented the warehouse to Eco-Systems without doing his homework." Frank smiled broadly and ushered us into his office. "According to Harry, he had no idea he'd get stuck with the equipment, but at the time he was happy to get cash he desperately needed." Frank held up the sketch of Cheryl Goldberg. "Of course, he denied all of this until I revealed your sketch and explained that our eyewitness appeared to remember a few more details since the day we had originally met. I thought he was going to pass out when he saw the drawing of his cousin's wife. You nailed it, CeCe."

Cheski continued to chew on his loaf of bread, which he now dipped in a cup of stationhouse coffee. "Did he arrange to have the warehouses emptied to avoid the EPA fine?"

"He lawyered up after I told him the tuba lady could place him at the storage facility the night the equipment was moved."

"Shoot," I said. "So he's not talking?"

"Never say *shoot* in a police station," Cheski laughed.

"Darn," I corrected.

"I knew he'd lawyer up," Frank said, "but I did get one more piece of information out of him before he shut down. He said Bob had approached him about moving the equipment to the recycling center."

I clapped my hands. "So he did know Bob! And Bob knew there was recyclable equipment in the warehouse. I feel like we're nearly there."

"Hold your applause," Frank said as he rose and approached the white board. He picked up a marker and wrote *Bob* in the middle of the board. Then, like a bicycle wheel, he drew spokes emanating from Bob's name at the center point. "This only comes together when we understand the connection between Harry, Bob, the doughy man, the skinny jeans woman, and the warehouse."

"And all the diners at Bob's diorama table," I added.

Frank fell silent and then drew more spokes and said, "And that's not counting his online contacts." He drew a tight circle around Bob's name. "Bob is at the center of something. I'm not sure all of these people are necessarily connected to each other, but they all have something in common with Bob."

Cheski slurped the last of his coffee. "What's our next move?"

"I'd say finding Barbara is now a priority. She might have insight into Bob's relationships."

"Already on it," Cheski replied.

"Today is Monday," Frank said. "The false recycling drop is this Thursday, which gives us three days to tighten up the surveillance plan. These scavengers are part of the bigger garbage puzzle, and we need to root them out and work our way up the recycling food chain. If Bob was interested in the contents of the warehouse, then we are too."

Lamendola poked his head into Frank's office. "I think I found something," he said, and I noticed his grimace. Lamendola placed Bob's notepad on the table, the one that had fallen out of his pocket into the garbage heap. Then he put an identical notepad next to the first one.

"When people dropped off their computers at the recycling center, Bob gave them a receipt. The receipt included their name, address, phone number, and a price estimate of the item being dropped off, in case the item was picked up by a nonprofit and then claimed as a tax deduction." He pointed to the first notepad. "This one fell out of Bob's pocket. The other one I found on Bob's desk at the recycling center. I called the first twenty names in each book." Lamendola paused and swallowed. "Every person in this book"—he pointed to the pad from Bob's pocket—"is dead."

Cheski coughed up a chunk of bread.

"That's insane," I said. "Unless the book itself is old, how could they *all* be dead?"

"That was my first reaction, but on some level, it makes sense," Lamendola explained. "From what I could uncover, in almost every case, a family member got rid of the deceased's belongings. It's not unusual to clean house after the death of a family member. I was, however, surprised to see something valuable like a computer being tossed, so I asked the relatives why they had dumped it. Many said they didn't know the password, or if they were able to log on, the experience seemed too personal. Regardless of the reason, the owners are dead and their computers ended up at the recycling center."

Frank's jaw started to grind. I wanted to pass him a piece of Cheski's bread just to give his teeth a cushion. "Bob removed the hard drives," he reminded us. I had nearly forgotten what Charlie had discovered about the computers earlier. The consoles at the recycling center were missing their hard drives.

"Why the hell would Bob want a dead person's hard drive?" I asked, and then turned to Lamendola. "What did these people die from?"

"I thought about that too, but I couldn't establish anything consistent about their deaths. I also called the people from the notebook I found in Bob's office—alive and well, with no issues to report to the police."

Frank picked up Bob's pocket notebook and leafed through it. He shook his head in silence.

FORTY-ONE
TUESDAY, APRIL 29

TUESDAY COULDN'T COME FAST enough for me. The anticipation woke me before dawn and, like a real farmer, I headed out to the field. By nine o'clock, Charlie and Katrina had joined me. In record time, Charlie and I repaired our homemade irrigation system, which ran, during a good season, on collected rainwater. Once the water leads were cleaned, we moved on to our homemade fertilizer. We had five compost barrels that required regular churning and I begged Charlie, as I did every month, to handle this task. Oddly, for a loyal Dumpster diver, composting triggered my heave reflex. Dumpsters actually get emptied regularly, while compost bins are designed for intensified rotting over a relatively short period of time. Even spinning the lid open made my esophagus flutter, not to mention the colonies of fruit flies that seemed to materialize out of thin air. I volunteered, instead, to weed.

Katrina moaned to me from her lawn chair. "I feel bad I'm not helping."

I rose from my squatting position and stretched. "This time next year your baby will be crawling up and down these rows with you in hot pursuit. Take a load off while you can."

"Ce," Katrina started, and then hesitated, "does it feel strange to possibly have a child you never carried?"

I glanced over at Charlie, who was now repairing a hole in our portable greenhouse. Men like Charlie, the type I labeled "players," never seemed to be bothered by the existence of unclaimed children. For all Charlie knew or cared, he had more kids than a Mormon elder.

"Seeing you pregnant has actually helped," I said. "You're a living case study for me and based on what I'm observing"—I pointed to her water-logged feet—"I think I dodged a bullet."

"You and your jokes," Katrina said. "Be honest."

I walked over to Katrina's lounger and sat on the edge. "In a few more days, you'll begin the process of raising your child with an emphasis on the things you hold true. I know you'll be an amazing mom, and your child will benefit from your knowledge and compassion." I paused and considered my non-birth baby. I'd invented the description *non-birth baby* since I guessed no one had established a word for people like me and my child. A person could be a donor, a birth mom, an adopted mother, one of two mommies, one of two daddies, but had anyone coined the term for moms that had involuntarily not given birth to their own child?

"I'm a little sad I've missed my chance to be an amazing mom," I admitted. "If this is for real, my kid is already a teenager." I rolled my eyes. "Unfortunately, I can't think of a worse time to meet someone new."

Katrina cringed. "I had bad skin and braces at that age."

"I was one screw-up away from boarding school," I said, and then shook my head. "Let's hope this kid takes after Teddy and not me."

We finished our chores at noon, and I dashed upstairs to wash up before Frank arrived. The newsletter with Dr. Corey and Lizzy James's group picture had collected dust on my desk. I stared at the photo of the lab employees. Why did these women, from two totally different backgrounds, appear so chummy in the photo? I held the picture up to the natural light streaming through the attic window. It was hard to believe Lizzy James was only in her teens in the picture. Based on this photo, I'd have easily pegged her for her late twenties. I thought back to Jimmy's comment that Bob could have lost weight and people would still have seen him as heavy. Perception is easily manipulated, and unless the outcome is exceedingly far from our expectations, our brains tend to go along with what we want to see.

Frank tapped on the Gremlin's horn to alert me to his arrival. I shoved the newsletter in my backpack and headed downstairs.

"Big day," I said as I buckled my seatbelt. "I could barely sleep. How about you?"

"Slept like a baby," Frank said.

"Aren't you excited?"

"The chance of this woman handing us an address for a child we're not even sure exists is minimal. I'm planning on pushing her, but realistically, I think you're setting yourself up to be disappointed." Frank backed the car down the driveway.

I frowned at him. Maybe he was having a bad day.

"What do *you* think we're going to get out of this woman, anyway?" Frank asked me.

"My father certainly believes he can get something out of Dr. Corey, and I'm not about to settle for less."

"You're a bulldog, you know that?"

"Frank, we're talking about a human being. It's not like I lost an earring. For God's sake, I lost a kid, and you've lost a close relative."

"Fine," he conceded. "But you promised to stay in the car."

"I won't even take off my seatbelt," I said as we pulled into the medical practice's very crowded parking lot. "Dr. Wilson was right. Dr. Corey's waiting room is going to be packed with a bunch of women as uncomfortable as Katrina." I shooed Frank toward the front doors and said, "Go ahead. Work your magic."

I watched as Frank entered the building, and then I undid my seatbelt and stepped out of the Gremlin. After counting to a hundred—enough time for Frank to find Dr. Corey's office and approach the receptionist—I pulled out my phone and dialed the office's main number.

A friendly receptionist answered, and as I pretended to make an appointment, I heard her falter. *Someone just flashed a badge.* Frank's booming voice registered over the receptionist's anxious panting through the phone. His presence, it seemed, had caused quite a stir. I hung up so Frank could command the receptionist's full attention.

I circled the border of the parking lot a dozen times before Frank emerged. Unfortunately, I was at the farthest point from the car, where I was supposed to be sitting, when he reappeared.

"Sorry," I said as I caught up to him. "I felt cooped up. What did she say?"

"All the right things." Frank shrugged. "She's a perfectly nice lady and was completely on board with the line I gave her about a public health issue and untracked sperm. Historically, the labs have always kept detailed files, and she'd be happy to return to the labs to piece together the coding system and the shipments to Lifely."

"So, she basically admitted to helping my father move genetic material to Lifely."

"And she was quick to remind me that, at the time, it didn't seem to be such a big deal," Frank said. "She's right on that point. The industry was in its infancy, and the protocols hadn't been established. In truth, the industry is just now getting up to speed with the genetic implications of a single donor's sperm being made available to hundreds of women."

"What about Lizzy James?"

"Just what we thought. She knew Lizzy was bright, and she was aware she'd had a rough home life. It seems she had simply reached out to a coworker in need. She said she was relieved Lizzy ultimately failed as a surrogate."

"Did you ask her about my egg?"

Frank turned away from me. "That's where it got weird." He cleared his throat. "I didn't mention you specifically, but she said the person to speak to about egg extraction was Dr. Grovit. She admitted to handling the sperm, but not the eggs. She said eggs were his domain because extraction required a licensed doctor; at the time, she hadn't yet earned her degree."

Dr. Grovit? I was dumbstruck by Corey's accusation that Dr. Grovit had been involved at a higher level. From the beginning, Dr. Grovit admitted the guilt he felt knowing my father had crossed ethical lines. He hadn't, however, mentioned that he'd had hands-on involvement in my father's studies. He'd always presented himself as an innocent sidebar to my father's activities. "I don't believe Corey," I stammered. "My mother insists *she* came to our house. Why the hell would Dr. Corey come to check on me if she wasn't involved? And," I added, "why would Dr. Grovit lie to us if he knew more? He's been nothing but helpful this whole time."

Frank titled his head and spoke loudly, as if English wasn't my first language. "Has he? Or has he simply perpetuated the confusion? Dr. Grovit led you to Dr. Wilson, who knew very little. When we asked Grovit about Corey, he said he didn't remember her, and yet she seems to be the key to this puzzle."

My mouth twisted, and I could feel the muscles in my neck locking.

"Ce," Frank said, "I've always thought it was strange Dr. Grovit didn't know more. Think about it. He tried to steer us away from Corey, insisting she wouldn't know much."

Frank was right. I had expected too much, and now I had received more than I could handle. The idea that Dr. Grovit had lied about his involvement broke my heart, but as Frank had mentioned, it was likely Dr. Grovit had known more all along. Although frustrated and distracted, I spotted a decidedly unpregnant woman moving quickly from the side door of the medical building.

"Hey, there's Corey," I said. "She's leaving."

Frank slid down in his seat taking me with him.

As it turned out, my spying on Corey had worked to our advantage because I knew she drove a BMW. We waited, hidden below the dashboard, until the roof of Corey's BMW glided by us, and then we rose from our crouched positions.

"Quick," Frank said as he opened his car door. "Let's switch seats. Corey won't recognize you. You drive." We did a record-breaking Chinese fire drill around the Gremlin and swapped spots. Frank returned to his hiding position under the dashboard.

"This is crazy," I complained as I started the car. "I don't know how to tail a suspect."

"Just don't pass her, and you'll be fine." *That part I get,* I thought. *It's the inevitable car chase that ends in a fiery crash that worries me.* Given the Gremlin's current condition, it didn't need a collision to self-combust. It could do that all by itself.

I caught up with Dr. Corey's BMW, leaving a buffer of at least one car between us. Although she stuck to the speed limit, I noticed her foot was heavy on the gas pedal. At intersections, she revved the engine to catch the yellow lights before they changed. Dr. Corey, it appeared, was in a hurry.

"I can't believe she ditched a room full of highly-hormonal patients," I said, glancing down at Frank. "You must have freaked her out."

"You wouldn't have guessed it by her demeanor," he said. "Look at the road, not me. And don't lose her."

Dr. Corey followed local streets from Northport through Huntington, in the direction of the Sound View labs. "She must be headed to the labs," I said. "Maybe there's something in the files she doesn't want us to see first."

"Stay on her ass."

I looked at my watch. It was 3:07 p.m., and a line of yellow school buses had inched their way into my lane. "Damn," I cursed and yanked at Frank's sleeve. "I need help. The buses are blocking my view."

Frank rolled down his window and attempted to bend his neck out the window and around the traffic. "She's making a right." He grabbed the steering wheel and directed it toward him. "Down this street and left." I followed Frank's instructions and sped through a residential area, only coming to a pause at a stop sign.

"I think she's avoiding the buses too," I said, moving out behind the BMW. "This is a back route to the labs."

We followed for a few more miles, and I relaxed when I realized all I had to do was make it to the labs and my cop boyfriend could handle it from there. As much as I wanted to find out what had happened to my egg, I wasn't prepared for this level of confrontation. Frank slunk back down in his seat, and I allowed three or four cars at a time to pad the distance between the Gremlin and Dr. Corey's BMW.

We were in the home stretch when Dr. Corey hooked a left and drove north. *What the hell? Where is this woman going?* "We need a backup plan," I said as my heart rate increased. "She's not headed to the labs." Within minutes, we were the only cars on the road. The Gremlin backfired loudly, and I watched as Dr. Corey glanced in her rearview mirror.

"Stay with her," Frank repeated.

We passed the railroad tracks following the route I had biked the other day.

"She must be going home," I said, but as we approached the turn for Dr. Corey's Laurel Hollow neighborhood, she cruised past her street. My mind raced to visualize the local roads and logical destinations, but Corey had already rejected the most obvious places.

Instead, Dr. Corey drove in the direction of the train station. Traffic picked up, allowing other cars to put some distance between us. I blew out my breath slowly.

"What?" Frank asked.

"Nothing," I replied. In truth, I had a bad feeling about this joy ride. The BMW's directional flashed, and I followed suit.

Frank peered over the dashboard. "Where are we?"

I made a right, slowed down, and pulled over in front of a compact Tudor-style house. My hands were shaking, and it took an extraordinary amount of effort to press the brake pedal. I silently begged the Gremlin to give out, once and for all. Frank bolted upright, and we watched as Dr. Corey's car disappeared ahead of us. "What the hell are you doing? Now is not the time to lose it. Keep driving."

I looked blankly at Frank. "Sure," I said and restarted the car. It didn't matter that I could no longer see the BMW ahead; I had already been in this neighborhood. Another school bus turned onto the street about a half of a mile ahead of us.

Frank slammed the dashboard. "Shit, we're going to get stuck behind a damn bus again. Move," he hollered at me.

Without the BMW to follow, I continued to drive, making two lefts and a right until finally Frank turned to me. "How do you know where we're going?" Just as he asked the question, the BMW reappeared at the end of a cul-de-sac, parking in front of a modest white house with blue shutters and stuffed planters spilling over with hardy geraniums. I parked at the neck of the cul-de-sac's entrance.

"Come on," I said.

I led Frank behind a row of houses until we emerged in a patch of woods across the street from the BMW.

"This is the entrance to the trail that leads to the recycling center," I said. The wind blew east and a faint odor confirmed our location. I stared at Frank. The only color in his face was the shadow of his stubble.

He jogged a hundred feet down the path in the direction of the recycling center and then back to me. Frank motioned toward the path. "You're saying if I follow this trail, I'll end up at the recycling center?"

"I biked it the day I met you and Charlie at Bob's house."

"And this is the path Marissa saw the skinny jeans lady run toward when she left the recycling center the day Bob died?"

I nodded. "There are a bunch of interconnected trails but only one way in and one way out. Based on Marissa's account, this is the direction the skinny jeans woman was headed."

"You're sure?" he pushed.

I told Frank how I had climbed a tree for an aerial view of the trails. I then explained that the front entrance, where we had driven into the recycling center from the main road, was the only road for cars. By foot, there were lots of paths, but they were interconnected and had only one exit—the exact spot where we were standing.

"You learned this the same day you discovered Norma at Corey's house?"

"Yeah."

Frank shook his head. "You're nuts. You know that?"

"It didn't seem crazy at the time, but now I'm not so sure." I ticked off the facts on my fingers. "The skinny jeans lady knew Bob. She knew where he lived, and she saw him the day he died, which was the exact moment he argued with the doughy man. Then, she ran through these woods." I told Frank my theory about the cars in the parking lot the day Bob died. "Marissa didn't remember lots of cars in the parking lot the day she missed her bus. She said it was possible there was only one car—I'm guessing it was the doughy man's car. If so, the skinny jeans lady was most likely on foot. I believe she was on foot again when I saw her at Bob's house a few days later. That means she must have entered the recycling center through this path. It's the only foot-path with an exit."

"Can you catch a bus in this neighborhood?"

"Not unless you want to ride a school bus," I said. "But she could have been parked in this neighborhood."

"Or she lives here," Frank said, and turned back to the house Dr. Corey had entered. The house, although small, oozed charm. It had a fresh coat of paint and a weed-free lawn. If the skinny jeans woman lived here, she must have been a regular at Home Depot. In fact, the house was so friendly, I had a hard time imagining evil lurking behind the front door.

Frank, I realized, thought otherwise as he grabbed me by the shoulders. "Go back to the car and wait."

I knew full well I wasn't about to obey that order. I returned to the car, waited half a minute, and doubled back. When I returned to my spot at the head of the trail, Frank had already pressed the doorbell of the blue-shuttered house. He stepped down into the manicured bushes and peered in the living room window. When the doorbell appeared useless, he banged on the front door hard enough that I could hear it from across the cul-de-sac. The scene was absurd; we had seen Corey enter the house minutes earlier. It was as if Frank's banging screamed, *Nice try, but we know you're in there.* Frank grew increasingly frustrated and, just when I thought he'd put his fist through a window, I spotted Dr. Corey sneaking around the side of the house to avoid Frank. Car keys in hand, Corey made a dash for it while Frank, clueless to the turn of events, continued to pound on the front door.

I charged from my spot and screamed Frank's name. He swung his head in my direction and picked up Corey in his peripheral. He sprinted across the front lawn in an attempt to intercept her, but she was surprisingly fast. After making it safely to her car, Corey tore up the road with Frank in useless pursuit behind the BMW.

The school bus, I thought. I hoped it had finished its route and the children were home safe, because Dr. Corey was on a mission.

"She's gone," I yelled.

A defeated Frank walked back to me, breathing hard, just as a familiar dog bounded from the path. "Don't worry. She doesn't bite," I said to Frank. I whistled to the dog, who recognized me as his source of tasteless fruit bars. The dog's owner came trotting from behind while his dog slobbered me with kisses.

"You again," he said, smiling. I shook his hand and introduced Frank.

"Do you know the people in the white house?" Frank asked.

"Sure. The Goffs. Nice people," he said, and then squinted at me. "By the way, I didn't buy your story about climbing the tree."

"Your dog loves me." I shrugged. "How bad could I be?"

The man turned to Frank. "I wouldn't be happy if you gave the family any trouble. One of them passed away recently, and they've had a rough go of it."

Another dead person within walking distance of the recycling center. *How convenient,* I thought as a shudder ran through my body.

Frank pet the dog. "I understand your concern, but it's a police matter," he said, and then added, "now."

Frank's last word hung precariously in the air like a boulder on the edge of a cliff. When we left Harbor House this morning, my egg wasn't a police matter. The surprise visit at Dr. Corey's office, also not a police matter. Even tailing Corey through the suburbs of Cold Spring Harbor was nothing more than an off-duty cop and his girlfriend seeking answers to a personal drama.

But now—*now* that the trail leading away from the recycling center, where a man had been murdered, led directly to the house where the woman who was closest to the answer about my egg had just fled … I was convinced that there really was a connection between these events.

The man started to turn away when Frank flashed his badge. The action surprised me because I knew Detective Frank DeRosa wasn't one to throw his badge around lightly. The ruse he had pulled earlier in the morning, telling Dr. Corey he was investigating uncatalogued sperm donations, had probably stretched the limits of his straight-laced conscience. This was a cop who turned down free coffee and donuts.

Yet here he was, his badge on display for the dog owner to see. It could only mean one thing: Frank, too, believed that the blue-shuttered house held clues to Bob's murder. With his game face on, Frank asked, "When does the family get home?"

The dog's owner stared at Frank's badge.

"You're a cop?"

"Yes, I am."

The man reattached the leash to the dog's collar and started to walk back to his house. "Kelly gets home around six thirty," he said without turning around.

It was all I could do not to ask the dog owner about Kelly. Could Kelly be the skinny jeans woman? My mouth opened, and Frank flashed me a look. "Let him go. We'll come back this evening."

"What about Dr. Grovit?"

"That's our next stop."

FORTY-TWO

DR. GROVIT LIVED IN a modest Victorian home in a historic section of Huntington, a short walk from the town's bustling main drag. Not unlike the disarray of Dr. Grovit's medical office, the house's landscaping was severely overgrown, and there were piles of corded newspapers stashed in a corner of the porch.

The front door was open, allowing us to see through the carved wooden screen door through to the kitchen. Dr. Grovit was seated at the table. He was so still I thought maybe he'd had a heart attack. We entered without knocking and walked quickly to the kitchen. Dr. Grovit's wife had passed away a few years ago, but her death didn't seem to warrant the current chaos of the kitchen. The sink was loaded with dirty dishes, piles of papers covered every available surface, and trash overflowed from a garbage can.

"Dr. Grovit," I said, taking a seat, "what's wrong?"

He shook his head sadly. "Did Corey remember me?"

"She did," I said.

"I wanted to tell you myself."

I looked up at Frank. He leaned against the kitchen counter, arms crossed over his chest. He wasn't pleased.

"I wanted you to meet with Corey." Dr. Grovit lifted his head, and I could see he'd been crying. "I want you to find your child," he said, reaching out to a pile of yellowed papers. He leafed through a stack and said, "I've searched through everything I could get my hands on to help you." Frustrated, he let the loose papers drift to the floor.

"Then why did you dissuade us from talking to Corey?" Frank asked.

Dr. Grovit pointed to an empty glass on the counter. Frank filled it and walked it over to him. "Why didn't you want us to talk to Corey?" he repeated as he dropped the glass down. Dr. Grovit took a long, slow drink of water.

"The day before you called about Corey, William came by."

My stomach heaved. "Here? My father was here too?"

Dr. Grovit's eyes flashed. "Where else has he been?"

"To Corey's house," Frank answered.

"Oh my god," Dr. Grovit moaned. "He must be serious."

"About what?" I grabbed Dr. Grovit's hand. "You have to tell us what you know."

"You must believe me, Constance. Nothing has been more important to me than helping you find your child. Now that you've spoken to Corey, you understand that I was more involved in the extraction than I led you to believe. Unfortunately, I still don't know what happened after the procedure occurred, but I felt confident we could still locate the child. Selfishly, I figured by the time anyone truly understood that I was in the operating room the day of your procedure, it would be overshadowed by the joy of finding your child. Your father, on the other hand, is not as willing to let things go."

Dr. Grovit took another sip of water and continued.

"Please believe me. I don't know where your child is, but I believe you're getting close." His hands shook and a droplet of water worked its way along the aging creases at the corner of his mouth. "Your father told me that if I gave you any more information about the child's whereabouts"—Dr. Grovit paused—"he'd hurt the girl."

Frank sat down next to me, pulled me into his chest, and repeated the only important words from Dr. Grovit's confession.

"It's a girl," he whispered in my ear. I had a daughter.

FORTY-THREE

IT WAS PAST SIX thirty, and Frank and I sat in the Gremlin outside the white house with the blue shutters. Corey, not surprisingly, hadn't returned to work after Frank chased her down the street. Nor had she returned to her own home. With no leads on Corey's whereabouts, our only option was to speak to the residents of the house.

"Am I the only one who thinks the skinny jeans woman will turn out to be this woman the neighbor with the dog told us about?"

Frank scrolled through his iPad. "Kelly Goff. According to my notes, the neighbor said her first name was Kelly." He looked from the trail to the house and back again. "I'm wondering if this Kelly woman is the surrogate," he said, and then turned to me. "There's got to be a reason Corey was in this house."

"Maybe Kelly is the adopted mother," I reasoned. "Maybe Corey is concerned that since the transfer wasn't legitimate, the adoption could be overturned. Maybe she's kept in touch with Kelly and tried to warn her."

"On the other hand, if Kelly *is* the surrogate," Frank said, "then there's no guarantee she knows the family that received the baby.

That would mean we've still got a ways to go until we find the child, and in this race, our competition is your father."

I stiffened at Frank's observation. "I can't believe I'm about to say this, but if that's the case, then I'd advocate backing off from this search. Clearly, my father doesn't want me to find my child. If we step back, maybe he'll stop and she'll be safe."

Frank shook his head. "At this point, we can't assume your father ever does the right thing."

I looked at the house. It was perfect. If my child had grown up in this home, I can't say I'd be disappointed. As much as I wanted to meet her, I'd rather she be safe than at the mercy of my father. I forced myself to believe Frank. Regardless of my actions, my father would continue to search for the sole purpose of eliminating the evidence of his twisted plan.

"I'm thinking about the picture of Corey with her arm around Liz," I said. "I wouldn't be surprised if she had befriended some of the women involved in the fertility exchanges. What I don't get is how any of these people are related to Bob's murder. Outside of this home's proximity to the recycling center, I don't see the connection."

"The connection to the murder *is* the location. Being in the vicinity at the time a crime occurs is a core requirement for a witness and murderer."

"So you think maybe the skinny jeans woman, or Kelly, as I'm going to call her now, was a witness?"

"Like the neighbor with the dog, she probably walks the trails and fell upon something that made her run home," Frank said as he opened the car door.

I thought about Kelly Goff. Did she have any idea that in addition to being an inadvertent witness to a murder, she was about to be questioned about a fertility scam?

"Since Corey is currently at large," Frank said as he headed for the house, "this is all we've got. Let's see where it goes."

―――――

Frank rang the bell, and the door opened immediately. A hefty man in his early fifties greeted us. He still held his briefcase, and his suit jacket hung halfway off his shoulder. Frank identified himself as a detective and asked for Kelly.

"I'm Kelly," he said, placing his bag on the foyer floor.

Frank shook his head in disbelief. "You're Kelly?"

So much for our theory about the skinny jeans woman with short black hair living in the blue-shuttered house. I turned to Frank and shrugged. Then I looked back at the trail leading from the woods to the cul-de-sac. Where had this woman run to? I counted the houses on the street—there were seven. The skinny jeans woman could be living in any one of these homes or maybe, as we had first theorized, she had left her car in the neighborhood and then made her getaway.

"That's right. Kelly Goff. I've lived here for twenty years." He led us into a cozy den with a stone fireplace. Frank and I sat down in a pair of soft leather chairs while Kelly remained standing. I glanced quickly around the room, hoping to spot a photo of the skinny jeans woman, but there were no pictures of a female with short black hair. The neighbor had mentioned that someone in the house had passed away. Maybe the skinny jeans woman was Kelly's new girlfriend and it was too early in their relationship to warrant a photo.

"What's this about?" Kelly asked.

"Do you know Dr. Carolyn Corey?" Frank asked.

"Carolyn is my sister-in-law."

My ears lit up, and my nails dug into the chair's leather arms. Carolyn Corey and Kelly Goff were related. I wondered if Corey had been afraid to return to her own home after Frank's visit. Her brother-in-law's house may have seemed a safer haven.

"Is there something wrong with her?"

Frank ignored the question. "And your wife passed away?"

Kelly frowned. "My *husband* passed away. It's been two years, and I don't know what I'd do without my sister-in-law's support. Has something happened to Carolyn?" He swiped at his mouth a few times, and I could see he was agitated.

Before Frank responded, Kelly Goff took a giant step toward me and stared directly into my eyes. "Excuse me. What did you say your name was?"

"CeCe," I said. "CeCe Prentice."

He nodded and then walked quickly to the stairs. For a large man, he moved swiftly, taking two steps at a time. We felt his heavy vibrations overhead as he moved from room to room.

Frank looked at me. "We can't afford another runner," he said, and then he directed his voice toward the stairs. "Mr. Goff," he called. "We're coming up."

We found Kelly seated on an antique iron bed made up with a vintage quilt in a patchwork of purples and pinks. Kelly Goff's weight caused the ancient bed to sag, and a pile of stuffed animals had rolled to the lowest point around his thighs.

"She's not here," he said, and then he lowered his head and wept.

"Do you mean Dr. Corey?" I probed while Frank ran to find tissues. I took a shot in the dark. "Is this where she stays when she visits?"

"No," he said. "My daughter is gone. She should have been home by now. I assumed she was upstairs studying."

Frank returned with a box of tissues. My voice was thin, but I repeated what Kelly had told me. "He says his daughter is gone."

Frank walked over to Kelly and knelt by the bed. "How do you know she's gone and not at a friend's house?"

Kelly shook his head. "It's Thai Tuesday, our father/daughter night. We'd normally be heading out the door for Thai now."

"How old is your daughter?" Frank asked.

Kelly inhaled swiftly, as if woken from a trance, and looked at Frank. "She's sixteen."

At that moment, my legs gave way like my hamstrings had been sliced with a knife. I lunged for the desk and crumpled into a chair. Two gay men, one sister-in-law with a medical background, a free egg, and a container of Teddy's sperm: the exact ingredients required for a test-tube baby. In a billion years, I would never have guessed the outcome unfolding in front of me, yet it was entirely plausible.

I stared at the man. "You asked me my name. Why?"

Kelly Goff wiped his tears and looked at me. "Because I know two men can't produce a baby." He blew his nose and continued. "Since the first day I held my daughter, I've worried that someone, a woman, would surface and lay claim to her. Carolyn told me I was crazy. But then, about six months ago, she came to me. She said she had read something in the paper that made her nervous."

I turned to Frank and mouthed, *The trial*. He nodded.

Kelly stared at me. "I'm assuming you're her."

"Maybe," I said, leaving the door open to speculation. "Only a blood test can confirm." But deep down I knew Kelly was on to something. I didn't need my blood drawn to know that Kelly Goff's child was my child, Teddy's daughter, and Frank's niece.

"Carolyn had always been vague about the baby's biological origins," Kelly continued, "but we assumed that since she worked with the labs, it was legitimate."

"Did you use Lifely's fertility services?"

He seemed surprised that I knew about Lifely.

"Initially, yes," he stammered. "Carolyn introduced us to the center. It wasn't easy for two gay men to adopt a white baby twenty years ago. We also weren't on the fertility clinics' radars at the time. In New York State, paid surrogacy was and still is illegal, which severely limited our choices. At that point, we'd already wasted years getting rejected by mainstream options. We were thrilled to find Lifely. They were progressive. We went pretty far through the process and paid ten grand for preliminary paperwork. And then one day, Carolyn showed up with another solution."

"She had found a surrogate for you?" I said as my mind immediately raced to Lizzy James. I wondered if my father and Corey had been competing for Lizzy's uterus. "Had your sister-in-law found you a surrogate?" I repeated.

"No," Kelly said. "She was pregnant. Carolyn was our surrogate."

My face fell into my hands. Carolyn Corey had carried my child? Why me? Why my child? Why had she stolen my baby and given it to her brother and his husband?

Frank handed us both a tissue. "Tell us again why CeCe's name interested you."

"After years of downplaying my concerns, Carolyn recently told me someone by the name of Prentice might come around asking questions. By Carolyn's description though, I thought it would be an older man."

So Carolyn Corey knew my father was on to her and that after sixteen years, he'd come back to erase the evidence of his unethical plan to manipulate my family's genetic tree in the name of science. That's why Corey had run. She, too, could be implicated. And now she probably also feared my father, afraid of what he might try to do to the child she had carried to term and then given to her brother and Kelly. Surely Dr. Corey, as a former employee of the Sound View labs, had read about Teddy's death in the papers and the subsequent coverage of the trial. Frank's unannounced visit to her office and his questions about Lifely must have set off a red flag. When Frank left her office, I guessed Dr. Corey had put a simple plan into action—intercept her niece before the girl returned from school and move her to a safe place.

"Dr. Corey might think you're working with my father," I said to Frank.

"I realize that," Frank replied as he paced the small bedroom. "She might think your father has a cop in his pocket, and she certainly won't come forward if she believes that to be so."

"I'm not so sure she'd go to the cops, anyway," I countered. "It doesn't help her credibility that she stole my egg," I said, and then I turned to Kelly. "I'm sorry, there's more here than you realize."

"What about the school buses?" Frank asked. "When we were here before, the bus was still making stops. Corey was in her BMW and heading toward the bus. She might have met her niece at a bus stop farther up the road while we were still talking to the neighbor."

"That's what I was thinking. If that's so, then at the least we know the two are together," I said.

Kelly Goff breathed a sigh of relief. "But where are they now?"

"We don't know," Frank said. "But we're going to find out."

I moved gingerly from my chair to the bed and placed my hand on Kelly's. "What's your daughter's name?"

"Gayle."

"Gayle," I said as if trying the name on for size. "Like a storm."

Kelly smiled and squeezed my hand. "We had no idea when we named her, but as it turned out, she's a bit of a hurricane." He paused, and then as if to apologize to me, he said, "She's difficult, but in a good way."

No apology required, I cheered to myself. My most notable quality, a challenging personality, had just been assigned to my daughter. Little did Kelly know it was the greatest compliment I had ever received. Having spent years lamenting the differences between myself and my brother Teddy, finally I had proof that at least one other person on the planet shared my traits.

Kelly opened his wallet and produced a school photo of his daughter. I gulped a pound of air. The girl in the picture had long, straight blond hair, just as I'd had at that age.

"She's got my hair," I said proudly.

Kelly frowned. "Well, the hair has proved to be a bit of drama. A whopper of a fight," he said. "Her hair was as smooth as silk and the color of fresh wheat. Now it's dyed black, and she's got it cut in this severe-looking bob."

"What?" Frank yelled.

Kelly seemed surprised at Frank's outburst. For all he knew, it was just hair.

I yanked my sketchbook out of my bag and flipped to the faceless woman with the short-bobbed hair, whom I had seen outside of Bob's house. "Hair like this?"

Kelly nodded yes.

I turned the pages again to the sketch of the calves. "How about pants like this?"

"Always," Kelly said. "That's what teen girls wear."

I reached for Gayle's picture and stared directly into the eyes of my own daughter. Upon closer inspection, I could see that Gayle bore a familiar resemblance to my own mother. Elizabeth Prentice had a regal, almost handsome appeal, and I recognized the similarity in Gayle's face. Unlike a giggly teenager, my daughter's image had an air of maturity. With her jaw raised and her shoulder's square in the frame, this girl could easily pass for a woman in her early twenties.

"Shit, Frank," I said. "*Gayle* is the skinny jeans woman. I must have seen her in family photos at Corey's house and not recognized her with her natural blond hair. I think she looks a bit like my mother in this photo."

Frank was silent for a moment and then said, "Your father has been in Corey's house and has seen photos of her as blond too. He doesn't know to look for the new black hair." Frank turned to Kelly. "When did she color her hair?"

"About two months ago."

"My God," I said. "Her rebellion might have saved her from my father."

Frank asked Kelly to come to the window. He drew up the shade and pointed in the direction of the recycling center. "Do you know what's over there?"

"The recycling center," Kelly said.

"Does your daughter ever hike on the trails?"

"Not that I know of," Kelly said, "and I would be furious if I found out she had been in those woods. That's where the high school deadbeats hang out to smoke. In fact, that's why I thought you were here at first. We've had issues with kids starting fires in the woods."

Frank regarded Kelly for a moment. I couldn't decide if Frank was confused by Kelly's answer or annoyed that the man was unable to own up to his daughter's questionable actions. "You've got a daughter who by your own admission had disobeyed your rules, and you still think she hasn't been in those woods for the drug scene?"

Frank was back on the drugs theory and at this point, I couldn't blame him. We knew how Gayle was connected to Corey, my father, and myself, but we had no clue how or if she was connected to Bob. The only definitive fact was that a female matching Gayle's description had been seen leaving the recycling center in the direction of the trails on the day Bob died, and conveniently, she lived where the trail ended.

Kelly Goff had a good two inches and fifty pounds on Frank, not to mention the wrath of a father whose daughter was missing. He turned to me and said, "What would you say if I described a pre-schooler who refused to eat meat when she found out how it was processed, a sixth grader who refused to attend school on the day women received the right to vote, and a young woman who sent a video with a personal plea for gay marriage to the goddamn Pope?"

I swallowed hard. "I'd say she sounds an awful lot like me."

"If she was in the woods," Kelly said in a firm voice, "it wasn't be-cause she was up to no good." And then he turned to Frank. "Don't misinterpret my daughter. You need to get a handle on who this kid is, because although she doesn't walk the straight and narrow, she always has a purpose."

Before Frank could apologize, Kelly's phone buzzed. He fumbled in his pocket for his cell and read a text. "It's Carolyn. She wants to know if Gayle is with me."

Frank grumbled, and then turned to Kelly. "Can you come with us?"

FORTY-FOUR

Kelly was surprised when we pulled up at Harbor House.

"Where are we?"

"I live here," I replied.

"Why aren't we at the police station?"

"It's a long story," Frank said as we made our way into the house. "I need to make a few calls. I'll meet you two upstairs."

I led Kelly into the conference room and opened the windows. The room was stuffy, but the cool night air brought the temperature down. It was almost eight o'clock, and the last sliver of sun had plummeted below the horizon. It was officially nightfall, and Gayle, my sixteen-year-old non-birth daughter was missing.

"I'm overwhelmed," Kelly confessed. "This is a horrible way to meet my daughter's biological mother."

I pointed to the conference table, and Kelly and I sat down.

"Can I ask you a question?"

Kelly nodded.

I was about to ask if Gayle was a happy child, and then I changed my mind. "Is she connected?"

Kelly smiled. "She's the most present person I know."

———

Frank entered the room. He was sensitive enough to realize that Kelly and I had just had a moment.

"All good?" he asked, and we nodded.

"Okay. According to her high school, she was in attendance today, and she was seen on the bus at dropoff," Frank said. "It sounds like Dr. Corey missed the connection at the bus stop. I think maybe Gayle saw CeCe and me at the house and got spooked. Kelly, I need you to contact all of her friends and their families. Cheski and Lamendola are on their way, and they will help you make the calls. She must have taken refuge somewhere."

"I can do that," Kelly said, although he seemed completely spent at this point.

"One more thing," Frank said. "Has Carolyn said anything else besides texting to ask if Gayle is with you?"

"No. I've sent her about a hundred texts, but she hasn't replied."

Frank said, "Before I send out an Amber Alert, I'm going to ask you one more time. Is there any reason Gayle would be in the woods that connect to the recycling center?"

"If she had been, she never told me about it."

Frank pulled out a chair and sat down. "Had you ever been to the recycling center with Gayle?"

"No," Kelly replied and then hesitated. "Mike, my husband, handled most of the household duties. But now that you're asking, I believe Mike was friendly with the guy that runs the place. I think he might have even come to Mike's funeral."

Had I heard right? "Mike knew Bob?" I asked.

"Big guy, right?" Kelly said.

"Did Gayle know Bob?" Frank asked.

Kelly stood up abruptly. "I don't know why you're asking me these questions. My daughter is missing, and my sister-in-law is in hiding. Why the hell do you care about the fat guy at the recycling center?"

"Because he's dead," Frank said. "And we think Gayle witnessed his murder."

Kelly slumped back into his chair. His frame, although nowhere near the size of Bob's, filled his seat and then some. However, in his present defeated form, he looked as though my mother could have taken him in an arm-wrestling contest.

"We also suspect she was friendly with Bob. She had been seen with him more than once around town."

"What?" Kelly yelled. "Where? Where could my daughter have possibly been seen with the guy from the recycling center?"

Frank hesitated. The one thing Kelly didn't want to hear was that his daughter had been seen at a bar or motel with Bob. The truth, however, was even stranger.

"It seems they were attending storage unit auctions together," Frank said.

For Kelly, the comment about the auctions came out of left field and drained his face of expression. His cheeks dropped as if Frank had physically punched him with the news of his daughter's strange activities. "But then how is my sister-in-law involved?"

"We don't think Carolyn is involved in Bob's murder. We do, however, think she's trying to keep your daughter's identity secret."

"From whom?" Kelly said, and then made a stopping motion with his hand. "Forget it, I understand," he said to me. "Carolyn wants to keep Gayle away from your father. He was the one in the local papers last fall, the former head of the Sound View labs. If I remember, he may have used the labs' resources unethically."

"Yes," I confirmed.

"So you two think my daughter—who just happened to witness a murder at the same point your father, after sixteen years, has chosen to find her—is in danger?" Kelly chuckled sadly. "I don't believe it, and I'm going to repeat what I told you earlier. If my daughter was at the recycling center, she was there for a reason. She's not an outdoorsy kid, and she wasn't hiking in the trails for exercise. I also don't believe your father suddenly decided to reappear in her life at the same time she supposedly witnessed a murder."

Frank shifted uncomfortably in his chair. We had come so far in this investigation, but we were tripping over holes. Kelly was right. The facts didn't add up. What were the odds Gayle had simply strolled by the recycling center at the exact moment Bob was being pushed? Even if they had been friends, the timing seemed odd. I was also curious about my father's involvement. Why would he choose to step out of the shadows to find Gayle now?

"What does your daughter do in her free time?" Frank asked.

Kelly groaned. "Honestly, I don't know anymore. Mike was a stay-at-home dad, and he managed Gayle's afternoons. When he died, our family began to deteriorate, and I lost Gayle to her computer. That's why Thai Tuesdays are so important. She spends way too much time on those virtual social sites."

At the mention of social sites, Frank's eyebrows shot up. "Where's her computer?"

"In her backpack," Kelly replied. "That's another reason I knew she wasn't in the house. Her best friend, that damn computer, wasn't on her desk."

I reached for Frank's arm and pointed to the door. Cheski and Lamendola had arrived and sat down to help Kelly contact Gayle's friends. Frank and I stepped into the hallway.

"Let's get out of earshot," he said.

Frank and I headed up another flight to my attic studio, where one of my first drawings of the skinny jeans woman was propped up on my easel.

"I think Gayle knows Bob," I said. "I think Kelly is right. If she was at the recycling center, then there must have been a connection between Gayle and Bob."

"And we know they both spent time online."

"Not unusual for a teenager," I added.

"But odd for someone like Bob," Frank said. "We also know that Bob had an online conversation with someone named the Maid, to establish a meeting time at the recycling center."

"At the exact time Bob had the encounter with the doughy man."

"Is it possible that Gayle is the Maid?" I asked. "Was the social site their channel of communication?"

"It's possible," Frank confirmed. "Bob was a grown man. Whatever their relationship, he wouldn't want to leave a trail on Gayle's phone."

"Okay," I paused. "We also know they were collecting computers."

Frank nodded. "And that one of Gayle's dads was at least friendly with Bob." Frank reached his arms toward the ceiling and grabbed for a beam, stretching his shoulders and back while he processed the seemingly disconnected information. "The recycling sting is tomorrow night. We've got to get this right. We've got to find out why Gayle and Bob were collecting used computers."

"We will," I said. "We have to. She's real, she's scared, and I think she's gotten herself into something she can't handle." I walked over to Frank and hugged him, unable to let go. His body felt firm and safe—all the qualities I struggled to maintain.

He released his arms from the rafters and held me for a minute. Then he peeled me off his solid torso.

"We'll have time for this. I promise," he said, kissing me lightly on the lips. "For now, we need to find Gayle."

We made our way back down the attic stairs when I heard Katrina call for me. I rushed to the first floor expecting to find Katrina with an amniotic puddle at her feet. I wanted to smack Frank for shrugging off the arrival of this baby. I was just about to ream Frank when I saw that the floor below Katrina's bare feet was dry as she stood holding the front door open.

Katrina held her stomach with one hand and pushed the screen door forward with the other. Dr. Carolyn Corey walked into Harbor House.

———

I recognized her because I'd stalked her. Still, her presence rattled me, and I could see she felt the same way. Given the events of the day, none of us felt great, but Corey was a hot mess. Her hair, a halo of ratted frizz, framed the bursting bags under her eyes. Part of me wanted to punch her. To grab her matted rat's nest, slam her against the wall, and demand answers to questions that had plagued me for the last year. Instead I put my arm around Corey and led her into the library.

"My brother-in-law texted me and said he was here."

"Where is Gayle?" I asked. "Has she contacted you?"

"About an hour ago," Corey croaked, her voice raw with emotion. "That's why I came. I want to see Kelly. He needs to know she's safe." The three of us moved into the library. "Gayle wouldn't tell me where she was, but she said she was okay."

"Do you believe her?"

"I do," Corey said. "She's pretty savvy for a sixteen year old." She paused and looked at me. "You were no dummy yourself at that age."

Quite an ice-breaker, I thought. By making a direct reference to my life, Corey all but admitted our connection. Her veiled diplomacy, however, wasn't sufficiently forthcoming for Katrina.

"Why did you take CeCe's embryo?" Katrina demanded as she accelerated to the punch line.

"Look, I came here to help Kelly find my niece," Corey replied. "I'm not sure we need to rehash history right now. Besides, I think we all have a good idea what happened at the labs."

"Are you kidding me?" I said. "I was twelve. I have no idea what happened."

Corey rose to leave. To be polite, I grabbed her hand and not her hair. "You can't leave. The details may help us find Gayle."

"Fine, if you think it will help," she acquiesced and resumed her position on the couch. When she lifted her head, I could see the pain in her face. Her mouth was pulled down at the corners, and her brow was heavily creased. With a good night's sleep and some serious salon treatments, I'm sure Dr. Corey could pass unnoticed in a crowd. Tonight, she looked like a refugee. "I don't even know where to start," she mumbled.

"Tell me about the day of my procedure."

Corey's frown increased. This was sensitive ground. She sighed and started from the beginning. "Your procedure had been completed by the time I'd arrived to work. I had been under the assumption that the morning patient was William's wife, your mother, but the detail on the medical chart indicated otherwise." Corey stopped, and her mouth hung open as she recalled what would turn out to be an unpleasant day for both of us.

"Go on," I urged.

"According to the birth date on the chart, the patient, as you mentioned, was a kid." Corey's chin trembled. "I was horrified. I felt as though I was the only one who had seen the discrepancy. At first I thought the birth date was a typo, but your father's blinding passion for his genetic research had begun to make me nervous in the months preceding your procedure. He had become increasingly obsessed with his studies, aloof in a way, and I didn't think I'd get a straight answer if I had asked directly. So I drove to your house to see for myself."

"That's why you came over," I said. "You weren't there for a follow-up medical exam. You were checking up on my father to see if the patient was really twelve."

Corey nodded. "When I saw your mother with a glass of wine in her hand, I knew for sure she hadn't been the patient. I'd suspected as much. The chart had been correct and that meant only one thing. William was out of control, and he had used his children in a live experiment. I literally threw up in your bushes on my way out."

"Did you know he had been prepping Liz James as a potential surrogate for my embryos?"

"I was eventually able to piece that part together."

While Corey and I had been "catching up" in the library after our sixteen-year hiatus, Frank and Kelly had found their way back downstairs.

Kelly hugged the last bits of oxygen out of his emotionally drained sister-in-law. He looked at me and then back to Corey. "Is CeCe the donor?"

"Non-birth mother," I corrected. "For the record, I didn't donate voluntarily."

Kelly sat down next to his sister-in-law. "Carolyn, help me understand what happened."

Corey had gnawed a chunk out of her lip, and I could see it was becoming increasingly difficult for her to tell her brother-in-law the truth. From what I could recall from the photos in her house, the Corey-Goff clan were a happy bunch, and Carolyn had been instrumental in the creation of the family. She took one of Kelly's hands and placed it over her heart so he could feel the pounding. Hell, I could practically see her heart thumping from across the room.

"The egg was harvested without CeCe's knowledge when she was very young. Once I realized how sick CeCe's father truly was, I became hell-bent on protecting the future of the embryo," Corey said, and then turned to me. "Your father wasn't interested in bringing a new life into the world; he wanted a test subject to study, and he had planned to make damn sure your fertilized egg would come to fruition. I worried that the child would be forced into a life full of disadvantages simply so William could prove out his DNA thesis." Corey took a deep breath. "I figured the only place this life would be safe was with me. Physically *with* me."

The room fell silent.

"After the fertilization," she continued, "I had twenty-four hours to make my decision about implantation. I suspected William had already arranged a surrogate through Lifely, and I couldn't let it happen."

My throat tightened, and I asked a rather insensitive question. "Why didn't you flush it?"

Corey fiddled with her collar to release a thin gold chain with a tiny cross dangling from the bottom. "Irish Catholic," she said. "If the fertilization hadn't occurred, I would have discarded the material, but I couldn't make myself do it after fertilization. Mike and Kelly seemed like an obvious choice for parents. I was young, unmarried and still in medical school, but my brother and Kelly were"—she turned to Kelly—"perfect."

Like their house, I thought. The neat and tidy house at the end of the cul-de-sac, a stone's throw away from the recycling center. One look at Kelly and I felt certain Gayle had had a jump-start on a good life. I still wasn't sure what had brought us to this point, but I was determined to find out.

I stared blankly at Dr. Carolyn Corey. Had she stolen Gayle or saved her? At this point, Gayle didn't seem safe. In fact, I'd go so far as to say my daughter's life was now in jeopardy.

"Do you realize CeCe's father is looking for Gayle?" Frank asked.

"I do, and I think that might be my fault too," Corey confessed. "When I read about the death of CeCe's brother, I worried that the memories might stir up your father's interest in relocating the embryo. William had no proof at the time, but he knew your genetic material had gone missing right after it was harvested. For the remaining months I worked at the labs, I hid my pregnancy and played dumb, which I'm not very good at." Corey shrugged. "I couldn't hide my disgust, and I'm sure William suspected I had something to do with the missing embryo."

"Did he accuse you of taking the fertilized embryo?" I asked.

"I'd put him between a rock and a hard place. He knew the only reason I'd take the embryo was if I thought he had planned to do something inappropriate with it. He couldn't approach me because I could have called his bluff. It probably drove him crazy." She paused and then smirked. I could see the idea of upsetting my father had pleased her. She continued, "The problem is that six months ago, when your brother's trial was in full swing, I panicked. The implantation was an event I had buried years ago, but I felt I could no longer hide it once I realized your father might be thinking about it too. I wondered if the trial had stirred up your father's memories, so I told Kelly *and* Gayle that a man named Prentice might come around asking questions." She paused. "I thought giving Gayle the information would protect her."

"You told Gayle?" Kelly bellowed. "Why would you do that? You know your niece. If you didn't tell her the whole story, she'd try to figure it out herself."

"I realize that now," Corey said, "and, I think that's exactly what happened. I don't think William searched for Gayle until she started to look for him, and I know she made it at least as far as Liz James."

"Gayle found her way to Liz?" Frank asked.

"She did," Corey said. "I hadn't heard from Liz in years, and then she called me at work and told me Gayle had appeared at her door."

"Holy cow, Frank," I said. "That's how Liz James knew I was my father's daughter. She saw the players line up, and she knew this would come to a head. She bided her time and then bribed anyone connected to this lunacy." I looked at my wrist again. Damn, I had really liked that watch. I swung my watchless arm in frustration. "Well, now we know why my father stepped forward. Gayle's curiosity lured him out of hiding."

"The timing is right," Frank conceded. "It coincides with your father hiring Norma too."

"My new cleaning lady?" Corey asked. "She just started with us."

"Yeah." I advised Corey, "You might want to change your locks unless you want an unannounced visit in the middle of the night from my father. I'm guessing he's pretty annoyed with you."

Frank stood and paced the library. He pulled at his mouth but kept us waiting.

"Frank?" Katrina nudged.

He stopped and crossed his arms across his chest and said, "I'm going to bet your father has discovered his granddaughter's weak spot: her relationship to Bob," he said. "He's had a few months head start on us, and he's probably aware of what Gayle has gotten herself into at the recycling center. If we don't figure out what Gayle knows about Bob's murder, your father will get to her before we do."

"Now I believe you," Kelly said to Frank.

———

Frank sent an exhausted Carolyn and bewildered Kelly back to their respective homes, holding out hope that Gayle would return to one of the two houses before morning.

Before they departed, Frank turned his attention to Corey. "So all Gayle said was she was safe?"

Corey nodded and added, "She admitted she'd gotten herself into a bind, but she felt confident she could fix it."

"Those were her exact words?" I said.

"Pretty much," Corey answered. "She also said she knew where to hide so that William couldn't find her."

I waited for Corey and Kelly to leave before I addressed Frank. "I'm afraid Gayle is trying to solve Bob's murder on her own."

Frank frowned and scratched his beard. "It appears that way, doesn't it?"

FORTY-FIVE
WEDNESDAY, APRIL 30

THE CHRISTMAS LIGHTS WERE bundled, and a few dozen computers were stacked and ready for transport. Between the decoy recyclables and the e-waste neighbors were likely to dump at their curbs, Jimmy expected the route to be chock full of choice pickings for hungry scavengers. According to Jimmy, the scavengers would case the area during Wednesday's evening hours and return after dark, before the scheduled Thursday-morning pickup. Although there was no law against taking curbside garbage, scavengers didn't want the hassle of having someone call the police, because it would slow them down. Hence, scavenging typically occurred during the cover of nightfall. Frank had arranged for five unmarked cars to cover the streets in hopes of spotting the scavengers. Once the scavengers were identified, Frank hoped they'd lead us further up the garbage pyramid. Frank wasn't interested in a two-bit scavenger; he wanted the guy that was buying in volume, enough to fill a warehouse. Although not endorsed by the Cold Spring Harbor police, Charlie and I had planned on taking the Gremlin out for a spin after dark.

"You're sure you'll be okay?" I asked Katrina as I gave her belly a pat. What I guessed to be a foot kicked back at me. Boy, this kid was impatient. "Hey, you," I yelled at Katrina's mid-section. "You're not done cooking yet."

"I think tomorrow is my day," Katrina said as she helped Charlie load the car with snacks of an unhealthy variety for the stake-out. "If this baby were any lower it would need shoes," she quipped, handing me a bag of unopened candy. A bag of unopened anything was a rarity at Harbor House.

"Where did this come from?" I asked.

"Whoops," Charlie said, pointing to the recently purchased bags of candy. "The candy would be my fault. I had an uncontrollable fit of consumerism."

"I think I can ignore it," I said as I opened the bag and shared some treats with Katrina. "We'll be back before daybreak," I assured her before climbing into the car with Charlie.

We turned out of the driveway and headed to the center of the square-mile area Frank and Jimmy had drawn out on the town map. As we entered the Recyclable Zone, as Charlie insisted on calling it, it was obvious the extensive preparation had been worth the effort. Almost every house had a neat pile of tempting trash just begging for a scavenger to haul away.

"This rocks," I said as I eyed the garbage. "You know, we could actually use some Christmas lights."

"Don't worry, I kept a few boxes for us," Charlie said as he chomped through a bag of heavily seasoned chips.

We passed Cheski and Lamendola and moved on until I found an unmanned street. I parked the Gremlin and turned off the lights.

Charlie dusted his hands off and lit up his phone. "If someone spots us, we'll pretend to make out."

I laughed casually, but I was so nervous about where this sting would lead, I would have made out with Bob's murderer if I thought it would help. "Angry Birds?" I said, glancing at Charlie's phone.

"Nope. I created an avatar for myself on the Other Life site, and I've been trying to track the Maid. Charlie shook his head, indicating his frustration. "I don't think she's been online since the day we scared her off."

"If I were Gayle, I'd have created a new avatar by now."

Charlie looked at me. "Ce," he said, "that's an epic thought."

And it was. I realized we had been insanely remiss in not considering the possibility that Gayle, my hair-altering biological daughter, could have taken on a new virtual identity. If the Other Life site was a communication tool for Gayle, then she'd still need to be on it to further her effort to solve Bob's murder.

I leaned into Charlie's phone to see the Other Life home page. "I'm not even sure what to look for," I said.

Charlie took a deep breath and exhaled. His breath smelled like barbecue sauce, and I had to admit, it was a bit intoxicating—in a drunk fraternity party sort of way. "Frank's gonna kill me for this," Charlie said, punching the pad on his phone, "but I'm going to log on as Bob for a minute to see if I can root her out with her new identity."

"You can't do that," I said as I grabbed the phone. "You'll scare her off again."

"If Bob doesn't send a message, she may not notice his avatar has signed on."

"She'll know!" I yelled and made another play for the phone. While Charlie and I were wrestling for the phone, I caught sight of a car moving slowly down the street with its lights off. I took Charlie's face in my hands and kissed his chip-laced lips. Without breaking the kiss, I forced his head to the right so I could see over his shoulder and out the car's back window. Charlie, thinking my aggression was rough foreplay, stuck his tongue in my mouth.

I pushed him back. "Dude, this is the undercover part. It only needs to *look* real." Then I tilted my head at the car inching along the road.

Charlie wiped his mouth and adjusted the rearview mirror for a better view. I rested my head on Charlie's shoulder, as if the lovers had taken a breather. "Roll down the window," I whispered.

A cool breeze entered the car and night sounds filled the Gremlin. Luckily for us, the scavengers stopped at the house nearest our car. Of course, the fact that we could see them meant they could also see us. Charlie put his arm around me and nibbled at my ear. "Just keeping it real," he chuckled. "Wouldn't want to blow our cover."

I allowed Charlie a tiny bite out of my ear lobe as I studied the car. "Dodge Caravan with New York plates," I said. Charlie licked my neck, and I pinched his arm. "Cut it out," I hissed. Charlie reached under my shirt and around my back, feigning an attempt to unsnap my bra. "Nice try. You know I never wear a bra."

"Just checking," he panted in my ear, and I shoved him when I heard chattering from the direction of the scavenger's car.

"They're speaking Chinese," I whispered as I tucked my t-shirt securely into my shorts. "The tuba lady said the truck that emptied the warehouse had Chinese lettering."

Charlie turned his phone back on and snapped some pictures, and then he texted Frank. Within seconds, Frank texted back. The other police vehicles had all spotted the same thing. The scavengers were all Asian.

"What else did Frank say?" I asked.

Charlie read Frank's text: "*Great undercover work, Chuck. Now take your hands off my girlfriend and bring her home.*"

"Come on."

"The last part is true. He wants me to take you home."

"No way," I said, voice rising. One of the scavengers stopped loading their car and glanced in our direction. Charlie took the opportunity to kiss me again. As the car pulled away, Charlie released me. It took a second longer to disengage from our embrace than I would have liked, but I chalked it up to tension and an excessive amount of sugar.

As soon as the scavengers were out of sight, Charlie jumped out of the car and ran over to the nearest house. I watched as he bent down and searched the shell of a computer. He jogged back with a few empty boxes in his hand and loaded them into the trunk. "The computer's been stripped and the Christmas lights are gone."

"What about the hard drive?"

"Intact," he said as he pointed forward. "Let's see if we can catch up to them."

———

I drove slowly enough to not arouse suspicion but fast enough to catch a boxy Volvo station wagon combing the street for recyclables.

"More scavengers," I said as the Volvo's brake lights indicated the car was about to stop. "What should I do?"

Charlie said, "Roll slowly."

As we came up behind the wagon, my nerves kicked in, and the overwhelming smell of junk food in the car triggered a wave of nausea. Charlie rolled down his window and leaned out.

"Good haul tonight. Huh?" Charlie called out to one of the scavengers filling the trunk with boxes of Christmas lights. Charlie pointed to our hatchback crammed with boxes. The Asian man nodded quietly. Charlie turned to me and mouthed, *Stop.* "Are you headed back to Chinatown?" Charlie asked, and the man nodded again. "See you there," Charlie replied giving him a thumbs-up.

The man smiled. Just one big, happy family of scavengers.

Well," Charlie said as he dialed his phone. "At least now we know the scavengers' final destination."

"How did you know they were going to Chinatown?"

Charlie laughed. "Racial profiling at its worst."

I heard Frank's voice through Charlie's phone. "Got anything?"

Charlie told Frank about his exchange with the scavenger. He hung up the phone and reached for the bag of candies. "Road trip," he said.

"Seriously?" I asked. "Are we really driving to Chinatown?" Charlie offered me some sweets, and I slapped his hand. "I'm freaking out over here. You're not nervous?"

"No," Charlie said, looking down at his phone.

"Can't you at least be nervous for me?" I asked. "My daughter is in trouble and the only lead we've got is *Chinatown*. Have you ever been to Chinatown in the middle of the night?" I prattled on, my frayed nerves making me sound exactly how I felt—scared and helpless. I swatted at Charlie's hands again as he played with his phone.

He held his cell up in the air like a bratty boy torturing a shorter sibling. "I'm not worried," he said, "because I think I've got a lead on the Maid." Charlie held up his phone to reveal an Other Life virtual world, squeezed into the frame of his cell phone. "I think she's using the name Marian now."

"As in Maid Marian," I said slowly. "And what had Bob been calling himself?"

"Bobin," Charlie reminded me.

"Bobin and Maid Marian," I said. "Why the Robin Hood reference? Are they giving garbage to people who don't have garbage?"

"The swelling masses of the garbage-poor," Charlie joked as he gestured to Frank's car.

We pulled next to Frank, and he instructed us to park. "Any chance I can get you to go home?" Frank asked me. I shook my head and moved to the back seat of the Gremlin while Frank took the driver's seat. He started the car and checked the gas gauge. That's when I knew we really were headed to Chinatown.

"Frank," Charlie said when we were finally situated, "I have something to tell you."

The idea that Gayle had taken on a new online persona in attempt to solve Bob's murder was scary and exciting at the same time. If the avatar names Bob and Gayle had chosen were references to the story of Robin Hood, then it was possible Bob and Gayle had attempted to right a wrong. I wondered if, like the GroundSweep organization, they were reporting toxic sites or recycling infringements to government officials. Given Kelly's description of his daughter, a little girl who wrote a letter to the Pope to stop what she thought was an injustice, it was entirely plausible. As for Bob, he had spent his whole life advocating for a better environment, hence the theme of hope in his dioramas. Frank would be thrilled with what Charlie had found.

"Tell him," I said to Charlie.

"I tried to kiss CeCe," Charlie said.

Thank God I was seated in the back, because my face felt like I had swallowed of bag of Red Hots. What was Charlie doing?

"It was stupid," Charlie continued. "I thought a parked couple wouldn't arouse suspicion." Then he help up his hand, still red from my slaps from fighting over the phone, as evidence of my virtue. "The girl's got balls," he said, and he then turned to wink at me.

"You're an asshole," I moaned. "Frank, he's exaggerating," I said, "but he does have something on his phone that requires your attention." Of course by now, I realized what Charlie had done. He recognized my feelings for Frank were genuine and by taking the grenade up-front, neither of us would have to worry if Charlie slipped up about our make-out session at a later date. I guessed that Charlie, too, had felt the old energy between us lighting up again, and he wanted to shut it down quickly. It was a risky move on his part, considering Frank's job entailed cutting liars down to size. I hoped, as I'm sure Charlie did, that the minute he revealed what he had found about Gayle, Frank would be too distracted to delve deeper.

"I haven't been slapped yet, but I'm sure it will be my turn soon," Frank replied. "What do you need to show me?" And with that, the three of us hovered over Charlie's phone.

"I opened an account and created my own avatar. I went back to the virtual world where Bob's avatar still stands. At first, because Bob's avatar wasn't active, he hadn't attracted many visitors. Earlier tonight, however, I noticed a female avatar by the name of Marian standing next to Bob. When I looked at Marian's profile, I could see the avatar had been created only a few days ago."

"Is she communicating with anyone?" Frank asked.

"When someone approaches Bob, she repeats the same thing. *Hold on, short delay.* As if she's speaking for him." We fell silent.

"She's trying to fill in for Bob," I said.

Unfortunately, we still had no idea what filling in for Bob meant.

FORTY-SIX

ON A GOOD DAY, the Queens–Midtown Tunnel, a snaking underground passage connecting Long Island to Manhattan, is a deathtrap. A claustrophobic's nightmare, the width of the seventy-year-old tunnel had been measured and marked well before SUVs hit the road. With no shoulder on either side and no breathing room between cars, the only saving grace of the tunnel was its relatively short length.

I counted to two hundred in my head and exhaled deeply when the bottom of a billboard appeared on the horizon. Frank pulled out of the tunnel and made two left turns toward the southbound ramp for FDR Drive. We took the exit for Houston Street, a major east/west thoroughfare, and then turned south again. From there, we were within striking distance of Canal Street, the entrance to Chinatown. Although quiet at 4 a.m., early signs of life seeped into the streets. I watched as a hunched-over man with a threadbare broom swept the entrance to a storefront while a fresh seafood truck rumbled past.

"Now what?" I asked.

"Cheski and Lamendola are on their way. They're tailing one of the minivans," Frank said. "This central part of the neighborhood is only a few square streets, and I'm betting that the e-waste is being carted to a block with less tourism than Canal or Mott Streets. There's got to be a loading dock somewhere. I think we need to find a building or a warehouse with its own parking lot."

Charlie pounded away at his phone. "Head back to Bowery," he said, looking at a map. "The street isn't as dense, and I can see open space between some of the buildings."

Frank steered the Gremlin back toward Bowery, and as Charlie had indicated, the through street was more industrial than downtown Chinatown. Gone were the colorful lanterns and Chinese-styled architecture, replaced with dingy gray buildings.

"Bingo," Frank said as he pointed to a convoy of cars pulling into a parking lot between two commercial buildings. An unmarked car rolled by, and I waved to Cheski and Lamendola. Frank found street parking, a surprisingly manageable task in downtown New York at the crack of dawn.

"Time for you guys to get out," Frank said to Charlie and me.

"What's your plan?" I asked.

"I'm going to follow these cars and pretend I'm selling the contents of the trunk to whoever is buying."

"The boxes are almost empty," Charlie said. "It's just leftovers."

Frank pointed to the glove compartment. Charlie opened it up and pulled out a mass of heavy copper wire.

"There's about fifty dollars of wire here," Charlie said as he passed it to Frank.

"I know," Frank said, and then he pointed to me. "Stay on the sidewalk away from the entrance."

I nodded and got out of the car with Charlie, his blond curls catching the first rays of sunrise. "Like we don't stick out, standing on a corner in Chinatown at five in the morning," I moaned to Charlie as Frank drove away.

"We could make out," he offered.

"Shut up," I said as I grabbed Charlie's arm and drew him closer to the side of the building. We watched as Frank drove slowly into a parking lot wedged between what looked like two factories left over from the era of the Triangle Shirtwaist Fire. An Asian man directed Frank to an empty spot, and I watched as the minivan drivers parked their cars and released their trunks. A set of garage doors opened and an exceptionally tall Chinese man in a suit walked into the parking lot. He shook some hands, and I noticed his limbs were so long, the arms of his suit jacket appeared to have shrunk. His bare wrists revealed a seriously sparkly watch, and I wondered if we were dealing with the Chinese mafia. I mentioned it to Charlie.

"I don't even know if there's such a thing as the Chinese mafia," Charlie whispered back.

He had a point. We were out of our league.

Charlie's phone buzzed. "Boogers," he sighed as he answered the phone. "Katrina's contractions are starting."

"I knew this was going to happen. Have her call Norma," I instructed. "I'm sure Norma can come over and wait with Katrina until Vicky arrives to midwife."

―――――

I glanced back at the suited Chinese man. He worked the parking lot, stopping by each car to make small talk with the scavengers. As he made his rounds, two men rolled a metal table out of the garage.

They locked the table's wheels in place and then ducked back into the warehouse, reappearing with a series of electronic scales.

"This looks like the real thing," I said to Charlie. "I think they're actually going to weigh this garbage and sell it."

Cheski and Lamendola, wearing street clothes, came walking around the corner. "Is Frank in the lot?" Cheski asked. I motioned to the Gremlin, and we watched as Frank mimicked the routine of the other scavengers. The suited Chinese man approached Frank. My heart ticked up a notch, and I could see Cheski and Lamendola instinctively spread their legs, right hands resting on their hips.

Frank nodded to the Chinese man, exchanged what looked to be pleasant words, shook his hand, and then turned his attention to the contents of the Gremlin. He pretended to rummage through the half-empty boxes and then lifted out a string of Christmas lights. Then he made a big show of placing the copper wires he had brought on top of his stash.

He walked casually over to the men monitoring the scales as if he were a professional scavenger with a big night's score. Frank was about ten yards from the trunk when a young man shot out from an alley way, and made a mad dash for the Gremlin.

A scream, originating in my gut, gained the power of a locomotive as it hit my vocal cords. As the shriek ripped from my mouth, a cacophony of high-pitched Chinese voices, equally as frantic, flooded the parking lot. Frank spun around as the young man made a grab for the copper wire. Despite the thief's head start, Frank ran full steam ahead in hopes of catching up. Cheski and Lamendola bolted forward, guns drawn.

The owner of the deli that Charlie and I were standing in front of rushed outside and started to hit Charlie with an unidentified vegetable the size of a small baseball bat. I stared helplessly as Frank was kicked to the ground. *All this for some copper wire,* I thought.

A pop, sounding something like a pneumatic nail gun, rang out. I squeezed my eyes shut and crumbled to the sidewalk.

When I opened my eyes, the first thing I saw was the tall Chinese man with the fancy watch. He stood in the middle of the parking lot, arms extended to the sky, his suit sleeves sunk back to his bony elbows. A line of smoke trailed up from his gun. Cheski and Lamendola had taken cover behind a minivan, and Frank was sprawled out on the pavement, his legs shoved under the bumper of the Gremlin. The copper wire thief whizzed past Charlie and I. Within seconds, the thief had disappeared into the streets of New York.

I uncovered my ringing ears and allowed the sounds of the streets to filter in. Rising above the din of the waking city, I could hear Cheski speaking to the suited man: "Drop the gun."

A string of police sirens followed as I struggled free of Charlie's grasp and ran toward Frank's prone body. Cheski muttered a string of curses as I dashed past him.

I slid my hands up and down Frank's body, praying I wouldn't find an open wound. His torn shirt revealed a hairy but bullet-free chest. With his head gently resting in my hand, I felt a moist spot below the crown of Frank's skull.

"Frank," I whispered, "can you hear me?"

His eyes blinked open and then rolled back in his head.

FORTY-SEVEN

FRANK REFUSED TO GET into the ambulance. He was embarrassed, I'm sure, that he had been distracted by a low-life garbage thief. Moreover, the theft revealed Frank's ignorance about the garbage trade. Apparently, hundreds of dollars in wire is two zeroes more than the average scavenger's haul.

"I'm fine," he yelled as the EMT wrapped a gauze bandage around his head. A second EMT shone a pen light in Frank's eyes. "It was just a bad fall. I don't have a concussion," he said as he swallowed two aspirin. "Get Mr. Lu over here," he said to Cheski.

Cheski escorted Mr. Lu to the ambulance. Lu continued to bow and shake hands along the way. "What's with the hand shaking?" I mumbled. "Is he a local politician?"

"Businessman," Frank said as Lu approached.

Lu bowed to me and shook my hand. "Very sorry, I shoot the gun to stop the thief," he said, introducing himself. "Luen Lu, businessman, scrap metal."

I looked at Frank, and he nodded as if to confirm Mr. Lu's profession. "That's it?" I asked Mr. Lu. "You're just a scrap metal dealer?"

"Big business," he said. He spread his arms wide and pointed to a shiny new Lexus as proof of his success. "In US, just a scrap dealer, but in China, important man."

"You ship all of this stuff to China?"

Lu bowed again.

"He sends the e-waste to China to have it stripped by hand," Frank said. "Probably costs him pennies a day in China."

Lu nodded eagerly. "Good prices, great margin. No good in US."

I leaned into Frank and tucked a loose strand of his hair under his bandage. "Who was the guy that jumped you?"

"Punk," Lu said, smiling. "Jealous of Mr. Lu's success."

Frank pointed to my bag. "Show him your sketches."

I opened to the faceless picture of Gayle with her black, bobbed hair. Mr. Lu burst out laughing, and I realized that the entire female population of Chinatown met this description. I leafed through the pages to the sketch of the doughy man. Lu leaned into the picture. He didn't seem to recognize the man we suspected had pushed Bob to his death. Instead, Frank asked Lu about Harry Goldberg and HG storage.

"Very good deal," Lu said. "Two warehouses, big haul, make lots of money in China."

At least now we knew where the e-waste from the warehouses had gone. I thought about the hundreds of workers in China toiling away at mounds of toxic computer equipment that the EPA wouldn't touch without face masks. As much as I loved garbage, it hurt me to know that underpaid people were being overexposed to harmful materials, all for a few centimeters of copper wire. Lu didn't care, and I was sure as hell Harry Goldberg didn't give a crap who combed through the contents of his warehouse. His cousin David may have thought twice had he known, and Bob, my recycling champion, had probably been frantic that he couldn't stop the illegal transfer of toxic e-waste. Frank interrupted my thoughts and asked Lu about Bob.

Lu filled his cheeks with air and lifted his arms to his side. Bob's weight, it appeared, had made him instantly memorable. Lu started to laugh again and then circled his finger by his ear, indicating he thought Bob was crazy.

"He want those warehouses, but I promise HG to empty in twenty-four hours, and I win. Instead, the big man tell me he just want the computer hard drive. Useless," Lu roared. "Not worth me removing."

Frank tried to nod as he held his bandaged head with his hand. He was in pain. I reached out to him before he could speak. "You don't have to explain. I get it." And I did. Bob and Gayle were collecting hard drives and although their motive was still unclear, Harry Goldberg's warehouse would have been a big score for them.

FORTY-EIGHT

CHARLIE VOLUNTEERED TO DRIVE home. We forced Frank into the back seat in case he wanted to stretch out. "But don't lie down," I instructed. "You can't lie down with a concussion."

"I'm aware of basic first aid," Frank said. "What's bugging me is that we still can't figure out the purpose of the hard drives. From what I can gather, hard drives can't be repurposed. Am I right, Charlie?"

"I'm with you," Charlie said. "Now that users can save to the Cloud or an inexpensive external drive, hard drives are becoming obsolete. There's so many storage options now, I'd be very surprised if used hard drives had a secondary market."

"What about donations in foreign countries?" I asked, thinking about the Robin Hood reference. "Maybe Bob and Gayle were donating the hard drives to third-world countries?"

"No," Charlie said flatly. "If that were the case, it would only make sense to send the whole computer."

"Then why are Bob and Gayle posing as Robin Hood and Maid Marian?" I said. "It seems like they're collecting hard drives and redistributing them to needy people."

"Who needs a hard drive within two weeks?" Charlie countered. "Technology isn't a life-or-death situation."

It certainly wasn't for me. I'd be perfectly happy if I never had another awkward email exchange or a poorly connected cell phone conversation again. That wouldn't be the case today, since Charlie's phone continued to buzz.

"I forgot about the baby," I whispered to Charlie as he handed me the phone. I was a terrible friend. We had nine months to prepare for this birth, and we chose Katrina's due date to leave the house. I'd have to fire myself from my BFF position.

"Hey," she moaned. "Norma's not answering. Are you sure she stays overnight at your parent's house? Maybe she's at her own house?"

"You called my mother's house number?" I asked.

"I called Norma's cell too," Katrina huffed and puffed. "Nothing. Vicky said the contractions are too far apart for her to come over now, but I'm scared. I don't want to be alone."

"I'm so sorry, Trina. Keep breathing. We're on our way," I said and then turned to Frank. "We forgot to tell you Katrina's in labor."

Frank groaned, and Charlie tossed him what was left of the candies. I dialed my parent's house. After five rings, the call went to the answering machine. The recording, taped by my mother during a bender, instructed the caller to leave a *methage*. I made a mental note to have my mother update the recording, and then I left an urgent message telling Norma to call me. I frowned at Charlie's phone.

"Are the pigs winning?" Charlie asked.

"I'm not playing Angry Birds," I answered.

"Katrina will be fine," he said. "People have babies all the time."

"*Women* have babies all the time," I said, "and that's not the issue. Norma's not home. Where would she be at this time of the morning?"

Frank leaned forward from the back seat. "You can't locate Norma?"

I shook my head. Frank punched the roof of the car with one hand and held his head with the other.

FORTY-NINE

"VICKY SAID I COULD go on like this for a day," Katrina said. She was bent at the waist, using our kitchen table for support as she breathed through a contraction. Each time she exhaled loudly in rhythm, her weight caused the table to skid a fraction of an inch across the floor. I eyeballed the hanging lamp over the table—it was a few inches off center.

"What's better? Sitting or standing?" I cringed as I rubbed her back. I hated to admit it, but maybe Carolyn Corey had done me a favor carrying my child for nine months. In her ratty bathrobe and bare feet, Katrina looked as though she'd been thrown off a covered wagon and left to die on the open prairie.

"Neither," she said. "It's like having the flu. No single position is better than another, but when the contractions subside, I get some relief."

"What can I do?" I asked.

Katrina sunk back down into a kitchen chair and motioned to the counter. "Freeze whatever is left out and wash the surfaces down. Then, vacuum the main floor of the house. Also, there's a load of laundry in my room that needs to go down to the basement."

"You want me to clean the house?"

"I do. I'll feel better if the house is neat. Jonathan's driving down from Boston and I want everything to be right."

A clean house, I thought. *That's ironic. I'll have to remember to tell this kid it wore secondhand cloth diapers as an infant, but the house was as neat as a pin.*

I glanced at my watch. It was 7:45 a.m. None of us had slept the night before, and I had a sneaky suspicion Katrina's labor would keep us up another night. Frank had dropped Charlie and me at Harbor House and then driven over to my mother's place to check on Norma. I wondered if Norma had been "mooning" somewhere else besides Dr. Corey's house, hence her absence at five in the morning, though I had a hard time believing she worked nights. I didn't want to upset Katrina, so I started to clean the kitchen. Minutes later the phone trilled.

"Finally," I muttered, pulling the ancient phone cord toward the pantry. "Is she there?"

"CeCe," Frank started, and all I could think of was, *Not Norma. She had nothing to do with this.*

"Please don't say it." I glanced over at Katrina, who had waddled over to an open breakfront with a dust rag in her hand. *Keep cleaning,* I willed her as I stretched the phone cord to its limit.

"I'm sorry, Ce," Frank continued. "Norma's dead."

"What?" I said, but I knew when Katrina called us in Chinatown, unable to reach Norma, that something had gone terribly wrong. "How?"

"It looks like a strangulation. There are signs of a struggle," Frank answered. "I have to assume it was your father." Oh god. My father had literally tried to choke information out of Norma.

"Jesus, Frank," I said. "If this really is my father's doing, then we needed to find Gayle yesterday."

I peeked back into the kitchen. Katrina wiped and restacked a set of mixing bowls.

"What about Corey and Kelly?" I whispered.

"They're upset. No word from Gayle," Frank said. "Hold on, Cheski's trying to reach me. I'll call you in two."

I hung up the phone and stared out a tiny window in the pantry. It wasn't worth telling Katrina about Norma. Nor could I call my mother as the news would surely trigger an emotional relapse. Instead, I called Dr. Grovit at home. I imagined him sitting in the same spot in his disaster of a kitchen where we had left him with his empty glass of water and a sink full of dishes.

"Dr. Grovit here," he answered.

"Hey," I said. "Are you okay?"

"I'm very upset, but I'll survive. How are you?"

"Not great," I said, and then added. "Can you leave town for a few days?"

"Will you tell me why?"

"I can't, but I think you'll be safer if you hit the road," I said. "Has my father contacted you again?"

"Last night, by phone," Dr. Grovit said grimly. "It was unpleasant. He was completely irrational and highly agitated. I'd go so far as to say delusional, and I'm saying that as a doctor."

"How so?" I asked.

"Your father seems to think he still works at the labs, and he was worried that if your daughter's true identify were to become public, his career would be ruined. He insisted I knew where she was. Eventually, I hung up on him."

My heart sank as my fears had been realized. My father, having gotten nowhere with Dr. Grovit, had probably tried to physically wrestle information out of Norma.

"But his career has already been shot," I said. "Why would he be worried about a reputation he'd already lost?

"Because he's delusional. It doesn't need to make sense to you or me. The issue is that he believes it, and that's what makes him dangerous," Dr. Grovit said. I could hear his kitchen chair scraping along the floor as he rose. "I have a brother in Brooklyn I can stay with."

"Thank you," I said as I jotted Dr. Grovit's brother's number down. I placed my finger on the old-fashioned phone's wall mount and disconnected the call. The vintage phone was hefty, but the weight made each call feel important, and so far my conversations were anything but light. As soon as I replaced the clunky black receiver, it rang again.

"CeCe?"

"Speaking."

"This is Barbara."

"Oh my god," I gulped. "Where have you been?"

"I'm in South Dakota visiting family."

"What happened to Wyoming?"

Barbara paused. "I was in Wyoming, but how did you know?"

"Dammit, Barbara," I yelled. "It doesn't matter how I know. What's important is that stuff is blowing up here, and we really needed your help. How could you disappear with no forwarding address?" My anger surprised me, but then again another murder had just taken place, and the stakes had skyrocketed. When Barbara had left, there was only one dead body. Now there were two and a missing teenage girl.

Barbara began to weep. Through the old-fashioned receiver, her cries crackled as if she were calling from the moon. "I'm sorry," she said. "I called the food co-op yesterday, and they mentioned someone had asked for me. That's what prompted me to call. Please understand—I couldn't handle being home without Bob."

I apologized profusely and briefly, very briefly, filled Barbara in on the events of the past week. I described Gayle with both her natural blond and dyed-black hair, but Barbara couldn't think of anyone that met the description, nor was she familiar with the online social site where Bob and Gayle were communicating.

Finally, I asked what was sure to be a painful question for her. "Is there a chance Bob was into anything heavier than pot?" Before Barbara could answer, I mentioned the faint puncture marks on Bob's arm.

"On his arm?" Barbara replied, her voice softening. "That's not from drugs. Bob had dialysis last year."

"Excuse me?"

"Our family physician had been on Bob's case about his weight so Bob went on a crazy crash diet for a few months that ultimately harmed his kidneys. It took eight months of weekly dialysis for his kidneys to recover."

"I had no idea," I said. It astonished me to think how little I actually knew about Bob. How little any of us knew, for that matter. It was as though Bob had shared bits and pieces of his life with various people, and until all the parts were retrieved and combined, like one of his intricate dioramas, the truth would remain elusive. "I'd like to give Frank your number," I said, more a directive than a question. Before I hung up, Barbara agreed to keep the line free for Frank's call. I knew my next call should be to Frank, but instead, I dialed the number for Kelly Goff's blue-shuttered house. He answered on the first ring.

"Gayle?" Kelly said, his voice almost pleading.

"No, it's me, CeCe."

"I'm hysterical," Kelly said. "She hasn't made contact since yesterday. I just read that kids missing more than forty-eight hours are likely dead."

"She's not dead," I said although given what had happened to Norma, I wasn't so sure. "And stop reading crap online. I need to ask you something. How did your husband Michael pass away?"

"Kidney failure," Kelly replied.

I brushed my fingers across my mouth and blew softly into my hand just to assure myself that I could still form words. Kidney failure. Was there something in the water around the recycling center? Before I could ask for details, Kelly added, "It was a genetic anomaly."

"How did Gayle take it?

"Horribly. I shouldn't have allowed it, but she used to go to the dialysis center after school and sit with Michael while he received treatment. She's mature in so many ways, but in this case, she was too young to process the consequences of his illness. In retrospect, I should have shielded her from the medical part. It was deceiving, because until the end, Michael was quite healthy. Dialysis, when it's effective, is a modern miracle. On his nontreatment days, Michael seemed fine."

"And he received treatment once a week?" I said.

"More in the final months."

I ended the phone call and slid down to the floor. At my ground-level view, I noticed that our bottom row of pantry shelves were in dire need of vacuuming. I considered alerting Katrina to the house-keeping emergency, figuring it might keep her occupied between contractions. I poked at a Godzilla-sized dust ball with my finger and watched as it rolled aimlessly backward, gathering loose pieces of lint along the way. By the time the dust ball landed securely in a corner, it had almost doubled in size. I considered Bob's network of people, from his art to his job to his social communities online. I wondered how far his network extended and how long it took him to build his seemingly disconnected web of contacts. Bob, of course, had been contagiously friendly and like the dust ball, he had a way of attracting people. Yet, it still didn't seem to make sense. I stood up too quickly, causing a head rush that was accentuated by my lack of sleep. I grabbed for a shelf to steady myself and stepped out of the pantry to find Katrina dusting a row of cookbooks.

"How are the contractions?" I asked, ignoring the stars fading from my vision.

"I'm getting better at breathing through them," Katrina said, but her face crumbled as another stab took hold.

"I'll be within yelling distance," I said, and then headed upstairs. I found Charlie in his bedroom, head buried in a computer. A screen of HTML code let me know I had come to the right person.

"Hey," I huffed. "Is there a way to find out how quickly Bob grew his network of contacts on the Other Life social site?"

Charlie looked up. "I'm assuming you want me to perform this magical feat without logging on as Bob?"

"You know you can do it," I said, stroking Charlie's Silicon Valley–sized ego.

"Gimme a few," he said.

"Awesome." I gave Charlie a thumbs-up and ran to Frank's make-shift conference room. I spotted Bob's notepad on the conference table and flipped through the pages. Bob, my favorite Freegan, hadn't wasted an inch of paper. Each page was meticulously filled out in neat, legible handwriting. I considered Bob's age: mid-sixties. Not so old that the technological revolution has passed him by, but old enough to revert to his old habits—a pencil and paper. I didn't know what Charlie would find, but I suspected that Bob's Internet avatar was relatively new, as was his interest in hard drives.

I picked up the phone extension in that room and called Frank.

"I'm on my way over," he said, and with that I told him about my conversation with Barbara and Kelly.

"Kidney disease," Frank repeated slowly. "And Michael's complications were genetic in nature?"

"According to Kelly, yes."

We didn't speak as Frank digested the information. The silence was endless, so I walked to the window of the conference room and stared out across the bay to the Sound View labs. I had seen photos from the seventies of the first buildings erected on the site. The original buildings had long since been torn down and replaced with more modern facilities to better service the international hub of scientific advancement. The labs had been my father's baby. He had hosted the ribbon cutting for every single building on the property. I knew there was no way he would allow the product of his achievement to be torn from his life. He probably felt as strongly about the labs as I did about finding Gayle. It was too bad our motivations for finding Gayle were diametrically opposed: he wanted to kill her, and I wanted to hug her.

"You still there?" Frank said.

"I'm here."

"Do you know what's strange about being adopted?" Frank asked.

"I don't."

"Well," Frank started, "for me, it's the idea that I don't know who I am, or rather who I'm from. Genetically speaking, I guess I could establish some history through genetic testing, but it's not the same as knowing who put me here and how that makes me the person I am. Genetic testing doesn't have all the answers."

"Oh," was all I could manage. "I guess I could see that."

"I'm wondering if Gayle was also thinking about her own family history."

"But why? She's just a young girl. Teenagers are so far removed from their backstory."

"Teenagers who aren't accompanying their adopted father to kidney treatments aren't thinking about their ancestors' lives. But we know Gayle is not average, and her experiences seem to be extreme for a young person. Maybe, after spending hours at a dialysis center full of ill people, she had reason to ponder where she came from."

I thought about what Frank said as I watched a small boat bob along the bay. I remembered the time I forced Teddy and Charlie to ice skate right up to the line where the unfrozen choppy waters of the Long Island Sound met the mouth of the bay. It was a ridiculous stunt, but I wanted to know if a wave could freeze in motion, and it seemed the only way to answer my question was to skate to the edge. If there was one genetic truth in this bizarre mess, it's that a child of mine wouldn't let an important question go unanswered.

"And then," I continued Frank's thought, "her aunt, whom she trusted, unwittingly tips her off to the person who might be able to tell her about her genetic origins." Of course, I could relate to Gayle's curiosity, but I worried about her journey to this terrible precipice.

"Yes," Frank said. "Corey warned Gayle about a man named Prentice. A quick Google search on the name Prentice, would identify your father as the former founder of the labs, the same labs where her aunt had started her medical career. It was easy enough for me to uncover the link between your father and Lifely, and I'm sure a computer-literate teen could have done the same. She must have believed your father had been involved in her birth and could help her reestablish her genetic history."

Wow. How dangerously right. "But how did she find my father?"

"Just because we never looked for your father doesn't mean he couldn't be found. Let's face it, he had to have contact with someone since he still paid your mother's household bills. Whether he liked it or not, he had established a paper trail over the last year."

"And then there's Bob and Michael," I added. "So do we think Bob had befriended Michael at the dialysis center and that's how he met Gayle?"

"It seems logical."

"Frank, if we don't find Gayle soon, we'll never know," I sighed. I was exhausted, but I found the energy to tell Frank my theory about Bob's pencil and paper note-taking. "I'm finding it hard to believe Bob had been socializing online for years. This was a guy who built things with his hands, stuff he could see and touch. I think his activity was recent, and I bet the timing was tied to his visits at the dialysis center, which started and ended within the last twelve months."

We sat in silence again until Charlie burst through the door.

"Hey, Sherlock," he said as he tossed some papers my way. "Other Life actively promotes shared user code as long as it benefits members. I wrote a quick app that allows users to summarize their connections on a time line, sort of a graphic tracking of your popularity. Once I installed the app and connected to Bob and a few of his other friends, I was able to access Bob's activity, which is all within the last year. Look at this," he said, pointing to a graph. "His activity shot up in the last three months."

"Frank," I said, "did you hear that?"

"Loud and clear," Frank said through the handset. "But I have a question. Barbara said Bob had recovered from his kidney problem. Is that correct?"

"About a year ago. Barbara said something about a home dialysis machine that he then used periodically."

"I think you're right," Frank said. "And it appears Bob had recovered around the same time Gayle's father died, so the two men definitely overlapped in their treatment."

"Yup."

"Okay," Frank said. "I've got some stuff to think about. In the meantime, I need CeCe to stay with Katrina, and I'd like to borrow Charlie for a few hours. You game, Charlie?"

"Not feeling it," Charlie said as he scrunched his face up. "I've done plenty of illegal things, but I steer clear of illegal organ rings."

I balled up a piece of paper and chucked it at Charlie. "How can you write amazing computer code one minute and be a total moron the next? My daughter is not selling kidneys on the black market."

"You two got a better theory?"

I stared at Charlie for a minute and then said, "I got nothing."

"I do," Frank said, his voice tinny through the speaker. "But I really need Charlie's help. I'll be there soon."

FIFTY

FRANK LUGGED AN OLD desktop computer into Harbor House and placed it on the kitchen table. He attached the power cord and then left to retrieve three more computers from his car. By the time he was done, our kitchen looked like a New Delhi call center.

"Does anyone realize I planned on giving birth in this room," Katrina yelled, "today?"

"If Charlie is as fast as I think he is, we'll be done pretty soon," Frank said.

Katrina keeled over and screeched, "Great mother of God, this freaking hurts!" For the first time ever, I watched as fear enveloped Frank's face. This was a man I'd seen shot at, attacked, and jumped by a garbage thief, yet never once had I seen him flinch.

"It hurts that much?" Frank asked. He took a step back from Katrina as if her baby might burst forth *Alien*-style.

Katrina straightened up and in a light voice said, "Kidding, but you've only got about seven minutes before a real contraction blows through this kitchen."

Frank walked over to the computers and pressed the power buttons. A low hum followed by a crunching churn indicated the computers were almost ready for Frank's challenge.

"So what am I doing?" Charlie said in a ready-stance, hands on his hips.

"These computers were in the evidence room at the station, but the cases are long closed, and no one bothered to pick them up. I'm going to give you an hour to figure out as much as you can about the owner of each computer."

"Nice," Charlie said. He pretended to roll up his shirtsleeves, despite wearing his trademark t-shirt. "What am I looking for?"

"I don't want to lead you. Let's see what we get first," Frank said, and then he pulled me aside as Charlie sat down. "Corey thinks she may have spotted your father driving by her house. I've got two patrol cars in the neighborhood. Corey's husband took the kids to their grandmother's, and I'm leaving Lamendola at Corey's house in case Gayle or your father makes an appearance. Corey is on her way over here."

I sighed, "We can't do this to Katrina. She needs peace and quiet."

"I thought about that," Frank said, "and then I realized Corey knows how to deliver a baby."

"Good point," I conceded, wondering why in the hell Vicky the midwife hadn't arrived. I guessed that's what you got for paying a professional with homemade jelly. I looked over at Charlie, who was engrossed in four screens at once. Katrina could give birth on the floor and Charlie would never notice. "What about Kelly?"

"Gayle texted him about an hour ago. She insisted she's fine and said she'll be home soon."

"Can't you trace her cell phone?"

"She keeps turning her phone off." Frank smiled. "She's good."

"I'm glad," I said, taking credit for anything Gayle did despite having no influence on her formative years. "So what now?"

"We're waiting on Charlie," Frank said, and then turned to our resident hacker. "How goes it?"

"So far, I've got one user with a foot fetish."

"I remember hearing about that guy," Frank said. "He broke into homes and stole women's shoes."

Charlie lowered his head and went back to work while Frank hovered over him.

Katrina was puttering around the library when Corey walked in. "Hey, I let myself in," she said, and then looked at Katrina. "Oh boy, you're in labor."

"I know. My midwife was supposed to be here an hour ago."

"Let me wash my hands, and we'll see how far along you are," Corey said, moving to the kitchen.

I tailed behind and said, "Can we talk about Gayle?"

Corey soaped up to her elbows and rinsed with extraordinary care. "If your father lays a finger on Gayle," she said as a spray of bubbles from her jittery hands sprinkled the backsplash, "I'll kill him."

"Get in line," I said, handing her a fresh towel, but she shook her head.

"It's safer to air dry." We walked back to the library, Corey's hands upright.

"Where could Gayle possibly be hiding?" I said, trailing behind her. "Are you sure you and Kelly contacted all her friends?"

"With the zest of an obsessive boyfriend," she replied.

I paused, "Does Gayle have a boyfriend?"

"Not that we know of," Corey said, and then she nodded for Katrina to lie down on the library couch.

I stepped back politely until I was even with Katrina's shoulders. Despite our close friendship, a full Monty reveal seemed unnecessary.

"Where does she go when she wants to be alone?"

"After Mike died, she spent a lot of time in her room on her computer," Corey said, peering between Katrina's legs. "Do you know if it's a boy or a girl?"

"We wanted it to be a surprise." Katrina beamed. "Life moves so quickly now, there are few real surprises left to be had."

"Have you met my family?" I said, squeezing her hand. "We're like a Henry Ford assembly line of surprises."

Katrina laughed as Corey gently lowered her knees. Corey glanced at a clock on the wall and said, "It's almost noon. I'll bet this baby is born before happy hour. Try to rest."

"I'll call Jonathan and see if he's stuck in traffic," I said to Katrina before turning to Corey. "If she's hiding from my father, I'm assuming she's not stupid enough to hide in her own home, or yours for that matter."

"That's why we can't find her," Corey barked, and I could see frustration in her furrowed brow. "Where would you hide if you didn't want your father to find you?"

Hmm, I thought. That was a very good question. Of course, I never had to hide from my father because during the time we had shared a roof, he became a master at avoiding me. Any attention the esteemed Dr. William Prentice had to offer was directed solely toward my brother, Teddy. I took a good look at Corey. Her lids were heavy, and her curly hair refused to be tamed. This woman was in no mood to deliver a baby, and if I had to guess, she was also pretty sick of my family. Maybe I should remind her that her involvement in the Prentice saga had been all her doing. If she had left my egg alone, we wouldn't be here. I excused myself and walked back to the kitchen. "Find anything?"

"Lots of stuff," Frank said.

"But did you find what you were looking for?" I asked.

"He's not looking for anything in particular," Charlie said, lifting his head for the first time in an hour. "Am I right?"

"Correct," Frank replied. "I'm trying to understand what you can find out about a person if you could get access to their hard drive."

"Okay," I said, spreading my arms. "Tell me who we have."

Charlie pointed at the first computer, a Dell laptop covered in stickers of dinosaurs and soccer balls. "I already know this person has kids by looking at the exterior of the computer, but even if the computer were clean, the Documents file is filled with information about his family."

"Like what?" I asked.

"Camp forms, school forms, extracurricular activities forms, school-trip permission forms, lunch forms." Charlie took a breath and laughed. "We should tell Katrina and Jonathan to avoid a hyphenated last name, because she's going to be retyping it until her fingers are raw."

"I hate hyphenated names. So pretentious," I said. "What else?"

"Vacation itineraries with flight information seem pretty common to save," Frank said, staring over Charlie's shoulder, "and anything that will be updated the next year, like tax information." Frank took a seat as Charlie scrolled down the Documents file. "It's just so easy to hit Save that no one bothers to clean stuff out until the computer crashes, and by then it's too late."

Charlie clacked away at the key board and said with genuine glee, "Hello, data. Here is the mother lode of information."

"What's that?" Frank asked, placing his finger on the Save As box.

"It's the Temp file. Every time you open an attachment from your email, it goes to the Temp file, and the user then has the option to save the attachment. However, if you don't save the attachment, your Temp file saves it for you. Mr. Foot Fetish's Temp file is packed with ads and coupons for women's shoe sales."

We stared at the screens, a meaningless glowing wall of indecipherable file names.

"How about this?" Charlie said, moving quickly from computer to computer. "I'm going to sort the Temp files by date." As quickly as the computers refreshed, a sense of order took over the screens.

"Wow," Frank said. "You can see the tax-related files falling in March and April."

"And the school forms," I said. "Here in September and then more activity in the spring, probably before camp starts."

"Something is going on at the end of the calendar year," Charlie noted as he pointed to early November, where each computer held a noticeably larger document. He opened up the files on each of the computers. "Ah, these are Flexible Spending forms. I guess you need to be a full-time employee to receive this. Not my bag."

"I've never seen one of those forms either," I added. "Lots of pages to fill in."

"Actually," Frank said, "your insurance company gives you the specific form to claim reimbursement for health or childcare expenses. All of these people, including our shoe fanatic, must be employed and have insurance." Frank smiled. "Even the criminals in Cold Spring Harbor are upscale."

I turned to Charlie. "We should get insurance. I've been bumming free services off Dr. Grovit and the labs for far too long."

"Too bad we can't find a way to Freeganize medical services. Imagine if you could buy a packet of discounted doctor visits, and then pass the vouchers to friends if you didn't need them."

"Love it," I said.

Frank ignored our bantering and picked at the bandage on his head. He was about to address us, when instead, he called out for Corey, who was coaching Katrina through a mighty contraction.

"You have news?" she asked, jogging into the kitchen.

"No, but I have some questions," Frank said. "Your practice doesn't take insurance?"

Corey's face registered disappointment, but she answered politely as she once again cleaned her hands at the sink. "We don't, but a patient can submit independently to their insurance company after they have paid us in full."

"And patients pay up front?"

"Assuming we see the patient through to delivery, we have a three-month payment schedule."

"How much?" Frank asked.

Corey tilted her eyes to the floor, and I could see she wasn't keen to reveal her practice's fees. "Three payments of thirty-five thousand each. Payments are collected at the beginning of each trimester."

"What if a patient comes to you in the last trimester?" I couldn't help my Freeganism. I had been conditioned to search for money-saving angles regardless of the service offered.

"Then they don't have a fertility problem," Corey answered, as if I had asked the stupidest question in the world.

Charlie whistled. "That's some serious cash."

"For wealthy couples with fertility issues, money is no object."

"What about poor people with fertility issues?" I asked.

Corey shrugged. "Either they never conceive, or they miscarry due to inadequate prenatal testing."

"Have you ever been scammed," Frank asked, trying to find the right words, "financially?"

Corey crossed her arms over her chest and searched her memory. "Once a patient filled out all the paperwork using her sister's name. Apparently, her sympathetic sister had insurance, and the pair were submitting our bills through the sister's insurance company. We got paid up front, but it turns out the insurance company got screwed."

A thought popped into my head. "Is it possible Bob tried to recycle insurance coverage?"

"That occurred to me," Frank said. "But if you receive medical services under someone else's name, the policyholder will get notification from their insurance company and realize a mistake occurred. The poser would be caught immediately because the policyholder would know whether or not they had received services. Imagine if the bill for my head dressing," he said, touching his head, "was sent to someone else. That person would know they hadn't been jumped in Chinatown." Frank stood up and started to walk around the kitchen table while Corey, Charlie, and I made space for him. He weaved his way through the computer wires and then stepped over Katrina's vacuum. As he paced, he ground his teeth and rubbed his bandage until he finally came to a halt.

"Unless," he said, "the person who received the bill is already dead."

"Why does a dead person need insurance?" I asked.

"They don't," Frank said, now excited. "But someone else might, and until the deceased's insurance company has been alerted of their passing, I'm going to bet their insurance is still active."

"Wouldn't a family member call the insurance company to let them know grandpa has kicked it?" Charlie asked.

"Not immediately," Corey spoke up. "It's not like insurance companies give rebates. Plus, medical bills will keep coming for months after a death, especially for a death related to a long-term illness. From what I've seen, the family wouldn't want to terminate a plan that has been paid through to a future end date. Even if that date is in the near future." Corey turned to Frank. "When Michael was sick, at the end, his insurance company attempted to limit his visits since the treatment was no longer as effective. We fought it. But"—she paused and sat down—"not everyone has a medically trained advocate for a sister." Corey's voice thickened and despite her years of medical training, it took everything she had to maintain her professional composure. "Dialysis is literally a life-or-death treatment. If you need it, you must receive it regularly and on a regimented schedule. There's no room for an insurance snafu or a missing piece of paperwork. I had to fight for every treatment at the end."

"What happens to dialysis patients whose insurance is dropped?" I swallowed hard. "Or patients who don't have insurance?"

"They die. Quickly," Corey said. "For years, dialysis centers took patients for free, no questions asked. Then it was revealed that many of the patients were illegal immigrants unable to receive proper treatment in their home countries. The centers were going broke treating the uninsured and had to turn patients away. It's still happening, and in my brother's case, the insurance company tried to discourage final-stage treatment." Corey started to tear up and then reiterated Kelly's sentiments. "Kelly and I were foolish to allow Gayle to attend Michael's treatments. She must have witnessed heart-wrenching scenes."

"As did Bob," I said sadly, "and he was one of the lucky ones. He had insurance and unlike many patients, his kidneys recovered. It probably tore him apart to see people turned away."

Frank retrieved the photo of Bob's Last Supper diorama and held it up for everyone to view. "These people at the table," Frank said, "they must be fellow dialysis patients. I wonder if Bob and Gayle helped secure insurance for them by recycling the gap that occurs when a person dies but their insurance is still active."

"The ultimate artistic portrayal of hope," I said, staring at the diorama and the joyously exaggerated faces. Finally, the common denominator had been uncovered. The diverse group in Bob's diorama, ranging in age from eight to eighty, may have been connected medically. "By identifying people who had died and locating their personal information on their hard drives," I said. "Bob might have been able to help people who still had a chance at life."

"It's genius," Charlie said. "Bob used the recycling center e-waste as his source of hard drives."

"But what did Gayle provide?" I asked and then turned to Corey. "Could she hack a computer?"

"Total geek in that department," Corey answered as she wiped her nose. "Now that I think of it, she was the only girl in the technology club at school."

Charlie stood up to stretch. "Gayle probably also suggested Other Life as a safe way to communicate with needy patients."

"I wouldn't describe a dialysis patient as needy," Corey corrected Charlie. "Desperate is more like it. A few weeks may be too long of a window for a dialysis patient."

And there it was. The two-week time frame mentioned on the social site. "I can't believe it," I said. "These people must have been notifying Bob each time the policy he had given them ran out. With each message, he'd have a two week heads up to find the patient a new policy."

297

"But to find a new policy, he had to find a dead person," Charlie said.

"I can't imagine the pressure," I added. "I'm wondering if the recycling center wasn't producing enough e-waste and that's why the warehouse interested him." I thought about Bob, chuckling with me over the Dawn doll head I had used to bargain for a car. How could it be that at the same time he had helped me find a car, this cheerful man had literally secured a lifeline for a terminally ill patient? I turned to Charlie, "If you hadn't been with Frank at Bob's house, we would have never stumbled onto the Other Life site."

Charlie shook his head. "I'm amazed that Bob and Gayle figured out where to hide without detection. That's no small feat for a man his size."

"I don't think Bob had a choice but to hide in a world where his size could be altered," Frank added. Charlie and Frank's words stuck with me. Gayle, it appeared, seemed to be an expert at hiding. She'd hidden her friendship with Bob, her parents were unaware of her extracurricular activities, she'd devised a new hair-do, and she'd done a darn good job of burying her communications in the depths of an online fantasy world. If only I could figure out where she had chosen to hide from my father.

Frank moved rapidly around the room. He had picked so furiously at his head wrap that tiny pieces of gauze followed him like a trail of bread crumbs. "We're missing something," he said. "We haven't figured out the doughy man's motivation for killing Bob."

"Maybe he was on to Bob," I said.

"But we think he was represented at the table, and if we believe all the figures had something in common, then the doughy man had to be a dialysis patient too," Frank reasoned. He stopped pacing. His face lit up, and I knew he was peeling back the layers almost as quickly as he dismantled his bandage. "The ID tag," he said as he reached for his iPad and scrolled through his notes. "One of the local companies that uses employee ID tags is a satellite office for an insurance company."

"Do you know the company?" Corey asked.

"Sure, it's called Health Associates," Frank said. "The local office is small, but it's a national provider. HA covers the police department and municipal workers and that would include recycling center employees."

Corey frowned, and her Irish freckles disappeared into the wrinkles around her eyes. "My niece is smart and from what I'm hearing, Bob is no slouch in the brains department. But from my experience, the insurance business is incredibly complicated. I think we're giving these two too much credit."

"How so?" I asked.

"Gayle and Bob must have had someone on the inside to help them, and I'm wondering if it might be this doughy man you're referring to."

Frank nodded. "Someone who worked at an insurance company while receiving dialysis," Frank said. "But maybe, as the stress to find more unused policies mounted, the doughy man wanted out." He picked up his ringing phone and listened intently. "We've got trouble," he relayed. "A security guard at the labs thinks he saw your father on the campus."

"We have to stop him," I said, and then I shared the conversation I'd had with Dr. Grovit earlier in the morning. "My father has lost it. He thinks he still works at the labs."

"The labs are the last place I'd expect your father to show his face," Corey said.

"No kidding," I said and then added, "but my father isn't working with a full deck. If it were any of us, we wouldn't consider returning to the scene of our professional disgrace." And just like that, it came to me. "Frank, I think Gayle is hiding at the labs." Frank stared at me as if my father's mental deterioration were contagious. "Don't you see?" I stammered. "If Gayle did her research, and I'm sure she did, then she discovered the irreparable damage my father had done to his career. Like Carolyn said, the labs are the last place anyone would expect to see my father. If I wanted to hide from him, that's where I'd be."

The room fell silent, broken by a blood-curdling scream. Katrina was about to deliver.

As Frank worked out a plan, Vicky waltzed in the front door as if there were still nine months to go on this ticking time bomb of a baby. Instead of a warm welcome, she was hurried aside as Frank flew out the front door.

"I'll call Cheski and have him meet you at Health Associates," he yelled back to me. "And bring your sketch of the doughy man. By the time you get there, I'll have found a contact for you."

I grabbed my keys and headed for the Gremlin. Corey was right behind me.

"You're not staying with Katrina?" I asked Corey.

"The midwife is here. If Gayle is at the labs, then that's where I'll be. I'm going to stop and pick up Kelly first," she said as she headed for her car.

300

FIFTY-ONE

THE HEALTH ASSOCIATES REGIONAL manager, Marcia Melia, met Cheski and me at the elevator. One look at Cheski's uniform, and Melia motioned us quickly down the hall. "I think maybe we'll use the conference room," she said as she hustled us away from the open workspace, but not before a few curious heads peered over a bank of cubicles. We followed Melia, an attractive woman in her late forties in a snuggly fit pencil skirt, into a conference room with no windows. Cheski nudged me in the ribs and raised his eyebrow as Melia leaned over to swipe the electronic lock on the conference room door.

Cheski was mildly distracted by Melia's butt. I, on the other hand, was fixated on the ID hanging around her neck.

We took our seats and Cheski, using the same easygoing style he had exhibited at the food co-op, zeroed in on Melia's sweet spot.

He put his hand in the middle of his chest and said, "Double bypass, two years ago, never saw a bill."

Melia beamed. "We're very proud to provide the police department with comprehensive coverage. How can I be of help?"

"We'd like you to look at a sketch of a person of interest," he said. Melia nodded.

I opened my sketch pad to the second drawing I had done of the doughy man, the one with the thinning combover. I placed the pad on the table and spun it in Marcia Melia's direction. Her flushed chest and crimson cheeks told me she could identify the doughy man by name, but instead Melia rolled her lips and rested her hand on her chin as if she really needed to think about the man's identify. Unfortunately, the clock was ticking. Unless Gayle burst through the doors with a top hat and cane, singing "Hello My Baby," we needed an answer.

"Do you recognize this man?" Cheski asked.

Melia adopted an indifferent frown and tossed her head from side to side.

"We believe his name begins with an L," I interrupted, forcing Melia's hand. I watched as she fiddled with her name tag.

"May I ask what this is about?"

"Think of it as a customer service issue," Cheski said. Melia wouldn't give.

I had an urge to cry *uncle* or *checkmate* or some other inane competitive cliché, but I held my tongue. Instead, I shifted forward in my chair until I could see Melia's photo ID. "I'm assuming all HA employees have a photo ID?"

Cheski smiled and piggy-backed on my question. "Maybe it would be easier for us to look through your employee photos ourselves?"

Melia nodded slowly as she evaluated her limited options. "His name is Lonnie. Lonnie Drummond." She cleared her throat and addressed Cheski. "I've been working here since high school. I started as a keyboard processor, and this job is very important to me."

Cheski reached out his hand without actually touching Melia. "That's why we came directly to you." Man, he was full of it, but it seemed to be working.

Melia softened. "I've noticed some"—she paused—"discrepancies in our payments recently."

"Do you think Mr. Drummond is embezzling money?" Cheski asked.

Melia shook her head. "No, that's the problem. I've been around long enough to know when money is missing."

"Then what is it?" I asked.

"This might sound odd, but I think Lonnie's department may have…" She paused again and searched the windowless room for answers before continuing. "I can't say for sure, but I think Lonnie's department may have inadvertently paid out for services to members who had already passed away." Melia appeared confused at her own discovery. "It's ridiculous, of course. Why would a dead person require medical services? It's most likely a computer issue, but I'm not a fan of loose ends, and I brought it up with Lonnie recently. He insisted the overlap was a timing thing, but he couldn't provide proof. We had an argument about it recently." Melia lowered her head.

"Could you be more specific?" I asked and then clarified, "Do you remember the day you argued? The exact date?"

Melia answered quickly. "The Monday before last. I remember losing sleep over it on a Sunday night. I promised myself I'd ask Lonnie to run an updated report first thing Monday morning." She threw her hands up in the air. "I still haven't received the report. I had to issue Lonnie a formal warning. In twenty years, I've never had to do that. I haven't fired a single person, but I made it clear that he'd have to go if he kept up his behavior."

Now it was my turn to raise my eyebrow. Bob fell to his death on a Thursday, a few days after Marcia Melia threatened to fire Lonnie Drummond. Timing seemed to be a reoccurring theme in this case. I wondered if Lonnie was Bob's inside man, his connection to the insurance industry. I also wondered if Bob and Lonnie's last conversation had to do with Lonnie's inability to deliver given his situation at work. It sounded like Marcia was a few key strokes away from figuring out that Lonnie had processed some rogue claims.

"Ms. Melia," I said, "how is Lonnie's health?"

"He does have some health issues," Melia replied. "In fact, I reminded him of our generous health benefits when I read him the riot act. Let me tell you, he started to come around after that comment. If I remember correctly, he took a half day last week to get his head together."

I didn't need to ask. I knew Lonnie had taken a half day on a Thursday. Lonnie, a dialysis patient, couldn't afford to lose this job.

"I'd like to meet Mr. Drummond," Cheski said. Melia leaned back in her chair, her shoulders lowered as the tension released from her body. "He's off-site today."

"Doing what?" Cheski asked.

"We received an exploratory call for program services from the Sound View labs. Very short notice, but it's a huge account. Lonnie is pitching the senior administrators on a full-service plan today, including dental." She beamed. *The commission on this one deal would keep Marcia Melia in designer skirts for years*, I thought. "If Lonnie nails this account," she continued, "it will be tough for me to stay mad at him."

Cheski thanked Melia for her time and promised this would be resolved quickly. He handed her his card and asked that she call him immediately when Lonnie returned to work. The elevator opened, and as soon as the doors closed, Cheski blew a gasket.

"Everyone involved in this case is at the labs right now." He started to tick off the players starting with his thumb. "Your non-birth daughter, your crazy-ass father, and now Lonnie Drummond, otherwise known as the doughy man. All of them are at the labs while we're standing here." Cheski heaved his stocky frame through the elevator doors and jogged to the car.

I stayed in the elevator, my face in hands. Up until this point, I had never experienced a maternal moment, but all I could think about was how many ways I would punish Gayle if she came out of this alive. It was a ridiculous thought, as I had never even met Gayle. However, now, I understood how a parent could experience anger and fear for their child at the same time. What the hell was she thinking? Why hadn't she come home when she realized the situation had escalated? Was she too young to truly comprehend what had happened to Bob? Or was it even simpler than that? Was Gayle merely a scared teenager, nervous about the punishment her father might dole out? Lost computer privileges? No more trips to the mall?

"CeCe," Cheski said when I caught up with him, "this is getting weird."

"Ya think?" I said as I jogged alongside him. About halfway to our car, Cheski stopped hard and bent over.

"Your heart?"

Cheski waved me away. "I'm fine. I lied about the heart bypass to get Melia to talk. It's something else," he said as he straightened up and dialed his phone. "Frank," Cheski breathed heavily into the phone. Suddenly, I wasn't so sure Cheski's nonexistent heart condition was a ruse. "Did you speak to the security guard that spotted

CeCe's father?" Cheski asked Frank. I inched closer to hear Frank's response.

"Actually, a female assistant called it in," Frank replied, but before he could continue, Cheski cut him off and explained where Lonnie Drummond was about to spend the afternoon.

"There *is* no security guard," Cheski said. "It's a setup. I'll bet you won't find the female assistant either. Someone arranged to have all of these people on the Sound View campus at the same time."

FIFTY-TWO

As if I wasn't already scared out of my mind, Cheski's NASCAR driving pushed me over the edge. My hometown whizzed by me and within minutes, Cheski plowed straight up the labs' main drive toward the entrance. Without bothering to find a parking spot, he braked and bolted out of the car.

"Don't follow," he yelled. I sat in the car and glared at the front doors while I plotted my next move. I was about to open the car door when I stopped. For some reason, I didn't feel compelled to disobey Cheski's order. Exhaustion had caught up with me, and the muscles in my legs felt inches too long for my limbs. I stumbled out of the car and wobbled over to a park bench, where I gripped the slats for support. Next to the bench, a carved wooden sign, detailed the labs' history. Established 1980, it read. *That's a lot of years of bad*, I thought, and then I considered how much I hated, and I mean really hated, Sound View Laboratories. As Cheski had pointed out, everyone involved in the case was currently on the premises. It was an odd-ball reunion of the most controversial people in the life of CeCe Prentice. Dr. Carolyn Corey, my egg thief, was somewhere on the campus searching for the daughter I had never met. Lonnie Drummond, the key suspect in my good friend's murder, was currently pitching a multimillion dollar insurance package in a conference room. And then there was my father, fresh off his strangulation spree and lurking the halls of the Sound View labs.

I'll just sit and let this play itself out. I draw pictures, not guns. Cheski and Frank could handle the showdown. To distract myself, I moved closer to the wooden sign and read a few more lines of promotional bullshit when something caught my eye. A recently placed placard hung on the far corner of the sign.

IN MEMORY OF OUR ESTEEMED COLLEAGUE, DR. THEODORE PRENTICE.

I hung my head and watched as a stream of mucus ran from my nose to the pavement. I reached into my shorts pocket and pulled out a linen handkerchief. This one had a Q embroidered on it. I didn't know anyone with the initial Q, but I figured the original owner was probably safer having never met me. I glanced back at the sign and sneered at the pathetically sparse dedication to my brother. God, how I wished Teddy and I had been related. My whole life, it seemed, had been a useless quest to capture a sense of attachment. One that my self-centered father had been unable or unwilling to provide to me as a child. I also knew I was the only one who could make a change.

I stood up and climbed over a row of bushes. I removed Teddy's placard and tossed it into a pile of cedar mulch. My brother deserved more than a lame sign the size of a Hallmark card. He needed to be honored in a much greater way. If I could make that happen, then I'd feel connected, and there was only one way to preserve the link between my brother and me. I had to find Gayle.

I strode over to the front doors of the labs' main entrance. In my head, I strode. In reality, I shuffled as I found my sea legs. The doors seemed heavy at first, but I forced myself to focus on the scene unfolding in front of me.

Cheski and Frank were in a heated conversation with the receptionist, an old-timer I actually knew. I made my way over and leaned across the chest-level desk.

"Hi, Marjorie," I said. Marjorie had been with the labs since the beginning, and she had spent a career fawning over the labs' doctors, literally feeding my father's God complex. I was fairly certain my father's fall from grace had rattled her sense of social order.

"CeCe," she exclaimed, clearly surprised by my visit, "these men insist your father is here, but I certainly did not sign your father in. I was one of your father's greatest fans, but this is not the place for him now."

"He's here," I said. "I know that's disturbing, but you'll have to trust me."

"But I didn't call the police," Marjorie insisted. "These men said I called the police."

I believed Marjorie. She had no motivation to lie. As far as who had called the police, it didn't really matter. My father was here.

"After my brother was murdered," I said, pointing down the hall in the direction of Teddy's old office, "did the labs institute increased security precautions?"

Marjorie lifted her ID tag. Her photo, with its halo of pink hair, smiled back at me. "We have to wear these tags. It constantly snags on my sweater. I don't even like wearing the sweater, but the air conditioning in here is set in the arctic range. It must cost this place a fortune." Marjorie droned on for a few minutes before I interjected.

"Any other security protocol?" I asked. Marjorie shook her head no. "Do we agree that my father is smart enough to outsmart a plastic tag?"

Marjorie nodded affirmatively. "He would have hated these tags."

"What about Lonnie?" I turned to Frank.

"According to Marjorie, she hasn't signed anyone in by that name," he replied as he pulled the sign-in sheet toward him. Marjorie cringed. The sign-in sheet was her domain, but she seemed a bit more willing to work with Frank since my arrival. "Thank you," he said as he ran his finger down the list of names.

"Dammit," Frank hissed under his breath. His turned the paper back to Marjorie with his finger on a gap from two to three o'clock. "Marjorie," he said calmly, "it's almost 4 p.m. When did you take lunch?"

"One-ish." Marjorie replied and then added sheepishly. "I may have been a little late getting back."

"Who covered for you?" I asked.

Marjorie rolled her eyes. "Some new girl with awful black hair."

I closed my eyes. A girl with black hair. What had Gayle gotten herself into? I didn't want to open my eyes, but a booming voice, one I recognized, filled the main corridor with a string of obscenities.

"You're telling *me* to speak with the head of Human Resources? Do you have any goddamn idea who I am? Can someone please tell me why the hell I was not informed we were changing the company health plan?"

I knew my father was in the building. And now, Marjorie did too, as well as half the people on the floor. If Gayle was here, as I suspected, I hoped she was hiding in a broom closet, tucked safely away. Although I hadn't spotted my father yet, he continued to rage about being left out of a meeting.

310

A pudgy man with a combover and an enormous stack of glossy brochures trotted down the hallway toward the reception desk. "I was told a conference room would be available," he huffed in Marjorie's direction. "I've been standing in the hallway for twenty minutes listening to this lunatic," he said as he tilted his head toward the sound of my father's approaching voice. Marcia Melia had already tipped us off as to Lonnie's location, but I knew he was the doughy man from my sketches. I'd definitely gotten the hair right.

Lonnie lifted a stray piece of greasy hair and slapped it back in place. He brushed past Frank and Cheski as if he were cutting in line at the supermarket. He placed his brochures on the desk and addressed Marjorie. "Excuse me, but I'm from Health Associates and I'm supposed to be giving a presentation on a new plan for Sound View Laboratories." Lonnie was out of breath. "This man"—he turned to point to my father—"is making it very difficult for me."

I watched Dr. William Prentice, the founder of the Sound View labs, turn the corner and eye Marjorie.

"Thank God," he bellowed. "Marjorie, tell this man who I am."

My father's appearance unsettled me. Although dressed professionally, his shirt was untucked and his tie askew. Apparently, Norma hadn't gone down as easily as he expected.

Marjorie froze. She'd had enough interactions with my father to realize he wasn't himself. She didn't know he'd recently murdered his housekeeper, but she could see he'd come unhinged. Her freshly applied peach lipstick looked even more out of place as her mouth slackened. She started to back away, her balance compromised by her age. Marjorie may have been tedious, but she was no dummy and as she had said earlier, my father no longer belonged at the labs. As she continued her retreat, her swivel chair rolled backward and caused her to stumble. Her stunned reaction angered my father, who expected service with a smile. He shook his head violently. It was as if a sliver of truth had pierced his jumbled brain and upset his equilibrium.

"Marjorie," my father barked, "I'm asking you a simple question. Answer or I'm firing you." Frank stepped in, but not before Marjorie replied.

She nodded at Lonnie and said, "I'd like you to meet Dr. William Prentice." After a painful hesitation, Marjorie mumbled a fatal last remark. "The former CEO of Sound View Laboratories."

My father stared blankly at Marjorie. He blinked as if a foreign object had obscured his vision. His face was red, and I wondered about his blood pressure. He might have a stroke before this was all over. Maybe that would be a blessing.

"Former?" he said slowly. He turned to Lonnie. There was no recognition, but I was concerned when he turned toward Frank and me. His eyes glazed over and I couldn't tell if he was winding up or down. I'd never seen him act like this.

Frank's jaw moved slowly. It was a crowded room. He needed to arrest my father and Lonnie for two separate crimes. He also suspected Gayle was in the building and that Kelly and Corey were close by. At this point, anyone could see my father was a ticking time bomb and a few false moves could cause a melee.

Lonnie noticed the change in energy and for the first time, he realized that Cheski was wearing a uniform. He didn't seem pleased about an encounter with the cops. I might have felt the same had I been instrumental in executing an insurance scam. Despite trying to help the sick, Lonnie obviously knew he'd done something wrong, something illegal. He also knew his boss, Marcia Melia, was close to figuring it out and in his defense, I guess he had tried to warn Bob that the jig was up. How hard he tried to warn Bob was another matter. Had he pushed Bob to his death? Gayle knew what happened and so did Lonnie. By the look on Lonnie's face, there was likely more than one reason for him to avoid the police.

"Lonnie Drummond?" Frank asked.

The soft flesh around Lonnie's midsection started to shake and his neatly draped combover shifted forward on his shiny forehead.

"Yes?" he stammered. He grabbed for his brochures and held them protectively across his chest.

Frank flashed his badge, but before he could notify Lonnie of his rights, Lonnie dropped his rubber-banded pile of marketing materials on the floor. The hefty stack of slick, heavy-weight paper slapped the ground, and I reached to cover my ears. The sound snapped my father to attention.

Cheski walked to my father with his hand out. My father, the consummate CEO, thought Cheski was trying to shake his hand. He extended his arm to return the gesture. Cheski grabbed my father and shoved him against the receptionist desk.

Lonnie seized the opportunity. He turned and started to inch toward the front doors.

My father, in his delusional and restricted state, directed Lonnie to halt. "You'll stop right there. I won't have this behavior at my labs." Then he wrestled with Cheski. "Let me go," he said. "I've done nothing wrong."

It was the understatement of the year. "Nothing wrong?" I said. "You haven't done anything right."

Frank held his hand up to quiet me down and then pointed to Lonnie. "Mr. Drummond, I'll need you to stay there."

Frank couldn't afford an escalation. His goal was to get all parties into custody without incident. Frank moved a chair from the seating area over to my father. "Take a seat, Dr. Prentice," he said.

Cheski reluctantly released his grip, but my father, in an unanticipated move, pushed Cheski. His overblown ego had finally consumed him. Cheski, taking Frank's peace-keeping lead, offered my father his seat again. I couldn't believe Cheski's self-control. It was all I could do to keep my fists by my side.

While Frank and Cheski tried to talk my father into submission, Lonnie took advantage of the distraction and continued toward the doors. Frank and Cheski, without coordinating, both went for Lonnie. For a short, fat man, he moved swiftly.

"I said stop," my father yelled again after Lonnie. My father stood from his chair and walked into the middle of the reception area. Heads popped in and out of offices.

"All of you, back to work," he barked.

Frank and Cheski turned to my father. Lonnie took off like a slow-moving bullet. He was halfway to the doors when my father reached into his suit jacket. This time, he drew a gun and pointed it at Lonnie.

Frank and Cheski dropped to the ground.

It only took a second for my father to pull the trigger and release a bullet into Lonnie Drummond's heart.

Marjorie screeched and with the gun still smoking, my fathered turned his aim toward Marjorie.

"Marjorie," he demanded, "tell these people my correct title."

"Dad," I squeaked, "please put the gun down." My father redirected his aim at me, his eyes fluttered.

"Christ," I mumbled as I watched Lonnie take his last gasp.

"Where's the girl?" he yelled at me. "That little bitch is the reason I'm not getting the respect I deserve. I should have never tried to re-create another defective version of you."

I was about to speak when Frank answered for me. He stood up, showed his badge, and said firmly, "Dr. Prentice, put the gun down. The girl is not here."

The thought screamed in my head: *But she might be!*

"The police?" my father roared as he shifted his gun toward Frank. "Incompetent fools. You'll never find her. She's a grifter, a snake," he spat as he looked back my way.

In the split second it took my father to readjust his gaze, a hulking figure appeared from one of the offices. Kelly Goff, with his linebacker build, dove forward, grabbed my father at the waist and tackled him to the ground. Sparks exploded from the ceiling as my father's gun fired into the recessed lighting overhead. Out of the corner of my eye, I saw Marjorie give into gravity as she flipped backward over her chair. Frank and Cheski scrambled forward toward the pile of bodies.

I sunk to the ground and crawled around the receptionist's desk toward Marjorie. Flecks of glass covered her body like red sprinkles on an ice cream sundae. A doctor in a white coat stuck his head out of an office door, and I pointed to Marjorie, a stream of blood draining from her neck. The doctor tiptoed toward us, a black bag in his hand. He felt for Marjorie's pulse and gave me the thumbs up. I poked my head over Marjorie's desk. My father's hands were in cuffs, Lonnie Drummond lay lifeless in a dark pool of blood, and Kelly preened. Frank was walking to the receptionist desk. He handed me his phone.

"She's here," a woman's voice said.

"Excuse me?" I croaked.

"This is Vicky, the midwife. She wanted me to tell you she's here."

I could barely believe what I'd heard. In the midst of it all, I'd forgotten about Katrina, again.

"A girl." I wept. "Tell Katrina I'm so happy for her."

"No," the midwife corrected. "Katrina had a boy. She wants you to know that Gayle is here, at the house."

FIFTY-THREE

FRANK AND I STOOD on the Harbor House porch. I was scared and tired, and I couldn't get myself through the front door of my own house. I considered relocating permanently to the porch, maybe screen it in, add a daybed. It might work, but Frank, sensing my hesitation, placed a firm hand on my back, opened the door, and forced me across the threshold.

My eyes danced wildly around the room. The first person I saw was Vicky, Katrina's midwife, who welcomed me with a bear hug. I barely knew the woman, but her hearty embrace was much appreciated, although undeserved considering I had ditched Katrina and her on my way out earlier in the day. I introduced the midwife to Frank, and the three of us headed into the library.

Katrina, positively glowing, cradled a swaddled bundle close to her chest. A tiny hand poked through the striped blanket, and I sighed openly. Jonathan, her boyfriend and our absent housemate, sat proudly next to his new family on the couch. In a threadbare, winged-back chair sat a lovely young girl with a terrible dye job.

"How?" It was all I could think of to say to Gayle.

"Shit happens." She shrugged.

"But, how did you end up here?" Frank said. "We thought you were at the labs."

"I was, but once I realized I could get Dr. Prentice, Lonnie, and the police to the labs, I knew it wouldn't be safe for me to stay," Gayle said. "I kind of wanted to stay. See how it turned out." Her voice, full of teenage optimism, revealed her age. The lilt and rhythm matched that of a young girl, although physically, she could—and had—passed as a woman in her early twenties.

"So shit doesn't *just happen*," I corrected. "You actually arranged for all these people to be at the labs."

"It seemed—" She paused. "Efficient? You know, like, why waste time going after all these people separately?"

A teenager concerned with waste and efficiency? *Screw the blood test. This kid is mine.*

"Lonnie Drummond is dead," Frank said. "He was killed at the labs."

Gayle's face fell and she seemed to grow years younger. "He pushed Bob," she said quietly. "I saw it."

"We know," Frank said. "None of this is your fault, but it would have been nice to know what you had planned as opposed to walking in unaware."

Gayle nodded and I could see she was just a girl who had gotten in over her head.

Frank motioned to the kitchen. Gayle turned to Katrina and Jonathan and said, "Thanks for letting me sit with you. Your baby is beautiful." She rose from her chair and I was immediately taken with her height; she was easily five inches taller than me.

I watched, in awe, as she glided past me toward the kitchen. "She's so tall," I whispered to Frank.

"Your dad and your aunt will be here in a few minutes," Frank advised Gayle as we sat down at the kitchen table. "Since you're underage, I won't ask you any questions until they arrive."

Gayle nodded. We sat in silence, and I was thankful for the lack of distraction because it gave me time to stare. And stare I did. I couldn't take my eyes off this young woman, with her slender fingers and bright blue eyes. Her skinny jeans narrowed gracefully along the curve of her calf, leading my eyes down to her feet.

"Eight and a half," she said, referring to her shoe size. "You're shorter than I expected."

My god, I thought. She knew exactly who I was. "So, it was you I saw at Bob's house?" I asked.

She lowered her head. "I didn't break in. The door was open, and Bob's a friend," she said as she considered her words. "I needed something from his house."

"A home dialysis machine?" Frank asked.

"Maybe," she said. "But you're not supposed to be asking me questions."

Frank laughed and leaned into Gayle. "I don't want to get ahead of myself, but I believe we can convince Health Associates that Lonnie Drummond acted alone. If that's the case, then there is no case, since both Bob and Lonnie are dead. That is, of course, if Maid Marian retires her avatar."

A mask of worry clouded Gayle's face. "But people are dying. Bob was upset about it."

"And Lonnie?" Frank asked.

"Lonnie was worried he'd lose his job. He pushed Bob, but I think it was out of frustration. I don't think he meant to—" She started to cry.

"I promise we'll find a way to help," I said, finally reaching out for Gayle.

She took my hand easily and said, "Bob liked you." A warm feeling flooded my body, and I had an urge to sketch every emotion bottled up inside me. We released our hands as Carolyn and Kelly entered the kitchen. Gayle ran to her father, and he drew her into his arms. It was a tight embrace, but I knew, eventually, there'd be room for me.

FIFTY-FOUR

The T, on the bottom of one doll foot and chair in Bob's diorama, stood for Terri. Frank and I watched as the real Terri, a middle-school girl pumped her legs hard, her swing soaring higher with each kick. Terri's mother, a friendly woman with a gaggle of kids, was single and had been logging long hours as a home health aide when her daughter first got sick.

"I couldn't afford insurance," she said. "I was able to cover the medical bills for a few months, but eventually the money ran out. I tried the government website, but it kicked me out, and I got crazy frustrated. Terri had weeks, not months."

"Did Bob Rooney approach you?"

"Barely," she said. "He handed me a small slip of paper one day on my way out of the dialysis center." She laughed heartily. "I thought it was his phone number. Like I'd call a guy thirty years older than me."

I liked how she focused on Bob's age and not his weight. "What did the paper say?" I asked.

"I thought it was information about an online support group. Too touchy feely for me, but I was pretty low at the time. I logged on using the instructions in the note, chatted with some computer generated person and the next thing I knew, an insurance card arrived in my mailbox. Every few months, a new one arrived. I thought, what the hell? Who cares if I get caught? My daughter was dying."

Frank nodded. "And now?"

"Once Terri's situation improved, I was able to go back to work. I recently got a job at a nursing home with coverage."

Not every story ended like Terri's. In all, Bob, Gayle, and Lonnie had helped over three hundred patients extend their lives. A third were still alive by the time the investigation came to a close. Many were in the United States illegally, some were turned down by their insurance companies, and others simply didn't have insurance or couldn't afford it. Frank, for the first time in his career, lied his pants off to keep Gayle's role under wraps. In addition to the short conversation in the kitchen, he interviewed Gayle only once, about a week later.

"There were too many sick people," Gayle explained. "At first Bob thought we could help like maybe fifty people, but the requests kept coming. In the beginning, Lonnie recycled cards from HA insurance holders who had passed away." Gayle scrunched her nose up, and I could tell she was uncomfortable talking about dead people.

Frank helped her out. "I'm guessing he started to run out of dead people."

"Pretty healthy bunch, those HA card holders," she replied. "The old hard drives turned out to be a great source. That was my idea. It came to me after my Dad died and we tossed his computer." She smiled like a child earning a gold star. "But then, we started to run out of computers at the recycling center too. That's when Bob suggested the auctions."

"Were you aware of the warehouse at HG storage?" Frank asked.

Gayle nodded. "The problem was the equipment was old, maybe too old, and we would have had to sort through it and then determine if the owner had passed away. It was too much work, and I'm not *that* good with computers." Gayle took a breath and continued, "Then there was the jerk at the storage place. He wanted a lot of cash for the warehouse computers. Bob kept arguing that he could do the guy a favor. You know? Like cart it away for free? Then the guy got in trouble because the stuff was toxic. I think he thought Bob had ratted him out to the EPA."

Frank didn't take a single note. He didn't want anything on paper, and he refused to bring Gayle into the station, instead opting for the makeshift conference room at Harbor House. Cheski and Lamendola had been a hundred percent on board and resumed their station-house responsibilities as if nothing had happened. For all the public knew, Lonnie Drummond had been running an insurance scam. He had attempted to source hard drives from the recycling center, but Bob Rooney, the friendly neighborhood garbage guy, got wind of the scam and reported Lonnie to the police. Luckily, Bob and Frank's phone conversation provided the necessary evidence to establish contact between Bob and Frank only days before his murder.

"Did Bob notify anyone about the toxic e-waste?" he asked.

"No way. He didn't want any trouble from the storage dude."

"And Lonnie?"

"Lonnie fielded calls from providers."

"So he lied to doctors about who used the cards?"

"Yeah, pretty much," Gayle said. "Lonnie, my dad, and Bob met at the dialysis center where they were all receiving treatment. That's where they cooked up the plan to reuse policies that hadn't expired. I knew Bob because my dad and I used to see him at the recycling center and the dialysis place. I never actually met Lonnie. I knew he worked for an insurance company, but Bob wasn't crazy about him and he didn't want me too involved. The first time I saw Lonnie was at the recycling center when I went to meet Bob. I wasn't even sure it was Lonnie at first."

"Is that why you ran?" I asked.

Gayle started to cry. "If I had stayed, Bob might have lived."

Frank put his arm around Gayle. "You're a kid, try to remember that."

"I wanted a way to remember my dad after he died. I sort of knew what he had been doing with Bob because in the end, when he was really sick, he just started telling me all this crazy stuff. He was so mad that ordinary people were dying just because they didn't have insurance. After he died, I asked Bob if I could help. I showed him the Other Life site, and that's how we started to safely communicate with patients and with each other." Gayle looked sheepishly at us. "I liked it, you know? I felt like I had done something real."

"But then the pressure kicked in," Frank said.

Gayle nodded. "People really needed help, hundreds of them. Lonnie freaked out a few weeks ago. He was afraid to lose his job *and* his insurance and he wasn't, like, a healthy guy. Then Bob started to worry that the storage guy had gotten suspicious about our interest in the warehouse computers. It's a little weird to keep asking about a warehouse full of rotting computers."

Frank nodded and turned to me. I said, "So Lonnie wanted Bob to shut down the scam?"

"Yeah," she said. "He was afraid his boss had already figured it out, and he was afraid of the storage guy. He was afraid they were doing something criminal, and he'd end up in jail."

It was quite possible they could have all ended up in jail.

"And you saw Lonnie push Bob?" Frank asked.

Gayle nodded. "But like I said, I don't think he meant to kill Bob."

I couldn't bear the suspense any longer. "How did you find out about me?"

"That was pretty easy." She smiled. "My aunt told me to be aware of anyone named Prentice. I figured if I had to be on the lookout, I might as well know who to look for. I read everything I could find about the Prentice family."

"When do you get your homework done?" I asked.

"I'm failing," she laughed, and then her face fell. "I wished I had found you first. Instead I made the mistake of finding your father."

"Where did you find him?"

"He owns an apartment in the city. I went to your family's house. Huge, by the way. I looked through the mailbox a few times, maybe I opened some stuff. No big deal."

Frank rolled his eyes and added postal fraud to the list of his niece's offenses.

"Anyway I realized pretty quickly he would be a problem for me, because once I made contact, he tweeked out."

"Is that when you dyed your hair."

"Yup." She tossed her head a few times. "It sucks. I know."

"So how did you get to me?"

"I raided my aunt's home office and dug up everything I could find about the labs. That's how I found Liz James." Gayle rolled her eyes. "Five hundred dollars later, she gave me the information I wanted. I borrowed the money from Bob, but he made me tell him why first."

"So he knew you and I were possibly related?" I asked.

"Oh yeah. He even drove me to Liz's apartment to make sure it was legit."

"What did he say when he found out?"

"You ever see his chin when he laughed?" Gayle said, spinning her finger from her chin to her chest.

The pinball tilt, I thought. What a wonderful memory to share with Gayle.

"I'd like to share something with you," I said to Gayle.

"Shoot."

"First, there was a wonderful man named Teddy who I believe is your biological father. He passed away, but he had a twin brother." I nodded in Frank's direction and Gayle's mouth dropped.

"Okay," she said slowly as she took in her biological uncle.

"You should also know that Dr. Prentice has a wife. My mother."

"I have a grandmother?"

"Yes, and she's a trip. You'll totally love her."

"If she's that cool what did she see in Dr. Prentice?"

"Not a whole lot," I said, and then paused. "That's why he's not actually my father."

"Seriously?" Gayle seemed relieved. "I guess I'm glad about that. Will I meet your father too?"

I shrugged. "I've never met him."

Gayle laughed. "This is gonna get good."

THE END

© Tina Hoerenz

ABOUT THE AUTHOR

Deirdre Verne (Scarsdale, NY) is a college professor and active blogger. A writer whose target audience is the millennium crowd, Deirdre's interest in green living inspired her to create an off-the-grid character who Dumpster dives her way though a suspense-filled mystery series. A member of Sisters in Crime, Deirdre's short stories have appeared in all three of the New York chapter's anthologies: *Murder New York Style*, *Murder New York Style: Fresh Slices*, and *Family Matters*.